SCROLLS

OF

PROPHECY

ROBIN STRONG

SCROLLS OF PROPHECY

Copyright © 2023 by Strong Stories, LLC

Contact info: www.robinstrongbooks.com

Cover design: GetCovers
Author photo: That Maya Girl Photography

ISBN: 978-1-960597-01-4 (hardcover) 978-1-960597-00-7 (paperback) 978-0-9862317-9-7 (ebook)

Published in the United States, May 2023.

IAN'S NOTES

FRIDAY, NOVEMBER 18TH

I want a new beginning. The Garden was my chance for a better life. Then Lucy got in the way. She convinced Evie and her small band of disloyal followers to escape onto a new server. But the majority stayed with me, and I consider that a win.

Besides, there's no guarantee Lucy's plan even worked. I wouldn't be surprised if her makeshift portal sent her precious friends to their death. Frankly, I don't care. I've expelled Lucy from The Garden—and my life—for good.

Now I must decide what to do with the Simples left behind. Part of me wants to pull the plug. Sometimes you've got to end things to get a fresh start, and heaven knows I need one. Another part wonders if it might be worth keeping them around. After all, the people who stayed offer one thing Lucy never did: Unyielding love.

Maybe I can still make the world of my dreams after all.

CHAPTER 1
IN THE SHADOWS

THE SILENCE of night shattered as a heavy steel box hit the stone floor. The reverberation echoed through the chamber halls before slamming into my chest. A surge of adrenaline forced me to my feet. All my senses strained as I tried to understand what was happening, but the loud crash quickly dulled into a tinny vibration before vanishing. I stood frozen, unable to hear anything beyond my pounding heart.

Sweat trickled down the base of my neck as the musty night air pinched my nose. With racing thoughts, I scrambled for a light switch, fumbling past the pile of books on my nightstand. My clumsy fingers knocked a heavy, leather-bound volume on my toes. Jaw clenched, I tried to ignore the pain as I felt for the knob on my lamp. There was a dull click as I turned it, but the blackness remained.

My mind was a flurry of questions. *Why was the power out? What time was it? And what the hell was that noise?* I felt my way along the wall and pushed open the curtains. A sliver of moonlight peeked through the clouds, illuminating my bedroom just enough to orient myself. My breath snatched as I noticed a light flickering under the crack of my door. Dread settled into my bones as I realized what was happening.

Someone was in the Sanctum of Scrolls.

I was no stranger to the dark. Despite my lineage that destined me for the spotlight, the shadows defined my entire life—a fact that haunted me daily.

A long line of pious men tasked with sharing Great's truth paved my future path. I was the son of High Scribe Josiah Zimran, named after my great-grandfather Asaph Zimran. Dad was the leader of the Quorum of Scribes, who were commanded to record Great's words and enforce His laws. For over two thousand years, their light showed the way for all humankind, and I was on track to join their legacy.

As a child, I was told countless stories of dissenters who ventured into the blackness of sin, forever lost by their decision to turn from the light. Their stories haunted me. Terrified of falling from the truth, I vowed to keep my eyes focused on Great's word. The Holy Scrolls filled me with hope and gave me purpose. My diligence to Great's work lit a fire within. As long as I stayed near Great's warmth, I felt safe from the cold call of curiosity that sometimes crept into my heart.

But while I yearned for the light, I couldn't ignore the shadows that lined the luminous path of my future. The blackness marked clear boundaries to the thoughts Great forbade me from exploring. Even the slightest temptation filled me with dread. My suspicion of the dark made it familiar— keeping it forever in my mind. And as my twenty-first birthday approached, I found new doubts bubbling from obscurity, threatening to sniff out the flame I had labored to keep ablaze.

. . .

A single hallway separated the Chamber of Artifacts from my bedroom. As Junior Scribe, I lived in the Sanctum, tasked with guarding the Sacred Scrolls and other ancient artifacts. Ceremonial in its nature, I never imagined my role would actually force me to defend the treasures inside that magnificent edifice. Despite my tall frame and sturdy build, nobody praised my physical prowess. My father often complained I was too sensitive and needed to toughen up. Now that an intruder was creeping outside my room, I had to agree.

I tip-toed toward the large, wooden door. With my ear pressed against it, I listened for signs of impending danger. Scanning my room, I found no weapons, and my t-shirt and pajama bottoms offered zero protection. Dad was right—I wasn't weak, physically speaking, but I didn't have the mental fortitude to pick a fight. At that moment, I had no clue what to do.

My fingers wrapped around the thick metal handle, and I prayed for a miracle as I inched the door open. The hinges creaked. I winced, holding my breath as I crept out of the room. A shadow danced along the floor at the end of the hall as a faint beam of light passed through the open doorway. I closed my eyes, straining my ears for any hint of what I would find around the corner. A soft thud and a few muffled scratches gave little insight.

Nobody taught me how to act in these kinds of situations—a glaring oversight considering my duty as the protector of the Sanctum. Was I supposed to pounce or remain stealthy? Could I sound the alarm without being noticed? Every rational thought evaded me since the best part of my brain was still asleep. An unfamiliar primal instinct kicked in, and I was surprised when my body lunged forward into a sprint. My feet picked up speed as my fingers clenched into tight fists. I ran, rounding the corner, as a guttural roar howled from my belly.

"Geeeeeet outta heeeeeere!"

The jarring impulse to fight startled me with its desperate

urgency. I was moving too fast to calculate how things could turn sideways, let alone see who I was leaping toward. Rushing head first toward the enemy, my bare feet pushed off the plush rug lining the walkway as I lunged for the man.

Except I missed him entirely.

Instead, I knocked the flashlight out of his hand, sending it—and me—barreling to the floor. It rolled, spilling light along the cobbled stonework while my body slammed into a display case, toppling it over. The sound of shattering glass shredded my ears.

"Shit!"

Frantic, I found my footing and looked for the stranger in the shadows. Spinning around, I panicked as a towering figure loomed over me. I attacked, swatting what turned out to be a large tapestry hanging from the ceiling. Backing away and trying to avoid the shards of glass now scattered on the floor, I glanced back toward the stranger. But a swift kick to my legs sent me crashing to the floor before I could defend myself. My body hit the ground with a heavy thud, and the man pinned me down.

All I could see was his shape. A thick heavy coat and knitted ski mask made it impossible to know who had tackled me. Outside the spacious windows, clouds drifted away from the moon, providing just enough light to see the man's penetrating eyes zeroed in on mine.

"Shhhh." The man disguised his voice as he urged my silence. "I'm not going to hurt you."

"What do you want?" I tried hiding my terror, knowing he could probably hear my throbbing heart, giving my fear away.

The man's eyes drifted toward the hallway that led to the Holy Scrolls. It was only then I realized how short he was. Hoping my size could outpace his apparent training, I twisted to one side, breaking free from his grasp, and snatched his arms behind his back. Yanking the man to his feet, I was surprised—relieved, really—by how easily I overpowered him. I reached for the red emergency button while maintaining my grip on his arm with my other hand. Alarm bells rang throughout the Sanctum and adjacent courtyards, summoning security. Emergency lights popped on, giving an eerie but clear view of the situation.

My grip tightened around the man's wrists. "Don't even think of escaping."

He tried pulling away before sighing heavily and succumbing to my strength. As a handful of guards stormed the Chamber, I felt the tension in my chest relax.

"Restrain him." I shoved the intruder toward one officer, who handcuffed the man. With the immediate danger under control, I surveyed the scene.

The nine-hundred-year-old stonework of the Sanctum stood as a testament to New Freeda's craftsmanship—and the Scribes' lasting power. The gilded building engulfed the skyline. Its central location made it an easy target for anyone stupid enough to try and overtake it. But with its massive courtyards, fences, and perimeter guards, the Sanctum had never been under attack. Who in their right mind would defile Great's holiest edifice?

At the center of the building stood the Chamber of Artifacts, which now looked like a crime scene. The circular room connected four separate hallways, each leading to different parts of the Sanctum. Massive windows with heavy, red velvet drapes consumed the north side of the Chamber. The south end featured large glass cabinets showcasing various religious and secular artifacts.

Locked chests on the top shelves stored the most precious relics. Heavy and ornate, each trunk weighed thirty pounds when empty and could reach a hundred or more when packed. When I noticed the open slot at the far end of the shelves and its missing crate battered on the floor below, I realized the intruder wasn't just a common thief. He knew exactly where the most prized possessions were held.

I pushed the trunk aside, hopeful that I had stopped the robbery in time. A large fist-sized crater in the stone floor revealed the place of impact. Recalling the deafening crash that woke me, I could almost imagine the box smashing into the ground. My fingers traced the hole and followed the spiderweb of cracks spreading from its center.

The chest's lock was busted, and its contents spilled onto the floor, including some expensive silks and ancient tablets. I noticed a tear inside the fabric lining when I inspected the chest. Poking my finger through the hole, I felt the smooth surface of a small, metallic case concealed within. My hands tugged on the mystery package, ripping it from its hiding spot. In it, I found jewelry made from seashells, a folded piece of parchment, and a small dagger inside. It was a strange collection of items, but not because they seemed valuable or particularly interesting.

It was odd that this was the first time I had seen them.

As Junior Scribe, soon to be ordained as a member of the Quorum of Scribes, I was supposed to know everything inside those trunks. I had spent the last four years cataloging and memorizing every historical artifact—a privilege only granted to Great's chosen leaders.

I leaned in closer to the thief, pointing to the chest. "What do you want with these?"

The man turned his head, masking his eyes.

"I don't think you understand the situation," I pressed. "We need answers, and we will get them." Grabbing the top of his black ski mask, I yanked it off. Soft chestnut curls fell from a messy ponytail, framing the face of a young woman.

Mouth ajar, I froze. "What—who are you?" I threw the mask on the ground, inching closer to her face.

Her hazel eyes, steely and unmovable, drilled into mine with an unnerving confidence that overshadowed her petite frame. Her resolute assurance only made my dread more palpable. She pressed her rosy lips together with a deliberate inhale. Her voice came straightforward and unafraid.

"My name is Bianca, and I'm here to share the truth."

A DECREE FROM HIS HOLINESS

Before the light, there was only darkness. In Great's eternal mercy, He saw reason to bring forth life, creating man in His image. He shielded the pure in heart from the shadows of eternal death, but unfortunately, the devil persuaded Evie and many others to follow her into obscurity.

To further protect His children, Great ordained the first Scribes —charged with preserving His words and teaching others to harken unto them. For most of history, the people remained faithful to Great's cause and flourished under His loving eye.

Now, we stand at a crossroads. More than two thousand years have passed since the Exile of Evie, when Great cast out Lucifer for leading so many to their doom. Unfortunately, many are turning toward the darkness of the devil once again.

As your High Scribe, I send my blessing and a warning: Great is testing your faith. You must guard your heart against anyone not following the Scribes' teachings. Doubt your doubts. Reaffirm your obedience so Great may save you at the End of Days.

- Holy Scribe Josiah Zimran

CHAPTER 2
WEIGHTY RESPONSIBILITY

"HOW COULD you let this happen, Asaph?"

My father's roar rattled the pictures on the wall as I trembled in the sturdy leather chair across from his desk. It was still dark outside, but it wouldn't be long before stories of the break-in and Bianca's arrest would spread across New Freeda. No doubt rumors of her attempt to steal holy artifacts would cause alarm in town.

After locking Bianca in one of the Sanctum's basement holding cells, I changed my clothes and made my way to Dad's, hoping to tell him the news before he heard it elsewhere. Dread seeped into every crevice of my body during the quick, ten-minute walk.

It was customary for the High Scribe's family to live in the historic mansion just outside the Sanctum grounds. With perfectly manicured lawns and a sea of flowerbeds, the estate rivaled the beauty of the most famous gardens.

We moved into the house when I was six, just after Dad's ordination to the highest office. I worried I would get lost in its never-ending rooms, and I didn't understand why a family of three needed so much space. Now that it was just Mom and Dad living under its roof, I couldn't help but picture its many rooms, most untouched except by the maids who cleaned them. Still, Dad's anger always had a way of filling the space—a fact I was relearning firsthand.

"Seriously, Asaph! How is this possible?"

"Sorry," I said half-heartedly. The adrenaline from the initial crash had worn off, leaving me numb from the shock of the night's events. "I'm not sure how I could have prevented it."

I rested my elbows on my knees. Unwilling to meet Dad's gaze, my eyes locked on the hourglass on his desk. I had countless memories of staring at its falling sand throughout my childhood. Dad's office was where all the serious conversations happened. The jeweled-colored walls and rich walnut floors provided a stately backdrop for his lectures. It contrasted my cowering posture as I waited for another sermon drenched with his disappointment.

Dad hovered over me. He was still in his pajamas, but his emerald robe gave him a polished look despite the early wake-up. "Asaph, as Junior Scroll, it's your responsibility to guard the Sanctum. You know that." His leather slippers pounded the floor as he began pacing behind the desk.

I buried my face in my hands. "And I did, didn't I?"

Dad shook his head. "I suppose." His tone made it clear he still blamed me a little. He tightened the waistband of his robe and let out a heavy sigh. "Praise Great that the woman was stopped before making off with any artifacts. Who in their right mind would break into the Chamber? And why? We've never had a breach before."

I tried to steady my foot as it nervously bounced. "Exactly," I said, braving to meet his gaze. "There's no protocol. If it really is my job to protect the Sanctum, shouldn't I train with the Scribe Guards? Maybe you can give me access to a gun or something? I felt completely unprepared. What was I supposed to do? Scare her off with my growing knowledge of Ancient Fredenian?" My fingers ran through my hair. "I'm a budding historian living in a nine-hundred-year-old building with questionable security. I'm no soldier."

Dad sighed again, closing his eyes as he sunk into the chair across from me. "You're right. It's not fair to put this on you. I'm sorry."

The crackling of a cozy fire marked time as we sat in awkward silence. I tried to read Dad's mind. Ever since I was a boy, his tangled mixture of compassion and authority had tantalized me. He often told me to be stronger and more assured in my birthright as a future Quorum member. Still, Dad knew my heart. He was proud his son was the youngest Junior Scribe in history. My eagerness to please Great softened his frustrations about my other weaknesses.

Outside the window, a subtle glow crept from the horizon, preparing to welcome a new day. Mom quietly glided into the room, her lavender robe trailing behind. She handed Dad a cup of tea before facing me.

"Tea, Asaph?" She placed it in my hands before I could answer.

"Thanks, Mom." I took a sip. The warm liquid soothed my nerves almost as much as Mom's concerned gaze.

"Are you eating enough? Sleeping okay?" she asked, inspecting every inch of my face.

"I'm fine, really." My eyes locked on hers. Despite her lean, almost delicate figure, there was an intensity to Mom's kindness that gave me strength.

I spent most of my childhood by Mom's side as she visited the other Scribes' wives. The hushed stories within that network of women revealed a different side of Mom that few saw, including Dad. She had countless ideas for improving the city and was eager to serve her community. Even though she was never given a chance to do anything of lasting importance, she never stopped dreaming of a better world.

After moving into the Sanctum, I craved those behind-the-scene moments with Mom. Leaving her care at just sixteen was the hardest thing about becoming Junior Scribe. The world forbade women from public life, and Dad quickly censored Mom at home. The longer I lived alone, the more she became a stranger to me, and I hated it. Still, Mom's vision carried me throughout my studies of the Holy Scrolls, hoping I could put her ideas to work when my time to lead came.

"You know," Mom said, resting her hand on my shoulder, "a little peppermint or ginger—"

Dad cleared his throat. "That's enough, Marie."

Mom offered a sincere but restrained smile. As the wife of the High Scribe, she was used to living in the background of Dad's spotlight. Full of grace and humility, she never questioned his authority or imposed a contradictory viewpoint on his rulings.

"Make sure you get some rest, dear. You look awful." Mom said it like a compliment, making me smile. With a gentle squeeze of my shoulder, she quietly left.

Dad placed his mug on the desk. "So," he said, standing tall. "What are we going to do?"

I felt like I was walking into a trap. "Uh, about what?"

"The intruder, obviously."

I proceeded carefully. It was unlike my father to ask my opinion. "What do you think we should do?"

With a huff, Dad vacated his office. I put my cup on his desk and followed him. He moved through the hallway, past his official Scribe portrait—the one that made me feel like he was always watching me as a kid—and down the wide staircase. Weaving through his private collection of artifacts, we headed into a room in the back corner of the basement. Dad always kept the door locked, and I was eager to know what was inside it after all these years. It turns out there wasn't much to see. It was a small space without furniture or decor. There was only one small metal box mounted on the wall.

Closing the door behind us, Dad folded his arms and leaned in. "What I'm about to show you stays between you and me, understand? Nothing leaves this room—nothing."

I nodded, too afraid to speak. Despite being an inch or two taller than my father, I always felt dwarfed by his presence. His thick jowls and rounded belly gave him a weighty power he pushed around with authority. He pulled a bejeweled ring from his left pinky and placed it in the small indent of the metal box on the wall. With a twist of his wrist, the box opened to reveal a handful of switches. He pressed a blue button, and the wall behind me rumbled as it slid away, uncovering a long, dark hallway.

Dad placed his ring back on his finger and led me through the secret passage. Stonework lined the floor and arched walls. Every twenty feet, we'd pass another opening, giving way to what seemed like an endless labyrinth of underground tunnels.

I had read about hidden tunnels under the Sanctum in my research. I even found a couple of secret exits while exploring the basement during my first year living there. But I never realized how massive this underground world was.

"Tell me what you know about the End of Days," Dad said, marching onward.

I cleared my throat. "End of Days?"

The Scribedom taught every believer three fundamental stories at a young age. The first was about the creation. In his infinite wisdom, Great separated the light from the darkness, molding the world out of nothing to provide a home for his children.

The second story was about the Exile of Evie. After failing to obey Great's commands, Evie partnered with the devil and persuaded others to follow her through the Doorway of Death, taking a third of Great's children. In righteous anger, Great cast out the devil's physical body to weaken her influence over man. Not long after, Great established His holy word through the first Scribe to ensure everyone knew His commands.

The third story was about the End of Days. Unlike the first two, it wasn't a historical account. It was a prophecy. The End of Days warned of the consequences of a fallen world.

My father stopped. "Well? Surely you've studied the End of Days?" He placed his hands on his waist and waited for my answer.

Chilled by his icy glare, I pulled my jacket tighter around me. "The End of Days tells of Evie's return," I said, pushing the lump down my throat. "Should Evie come through the Doorway of Death, Great will know his children have strayed from His commands. It's a sign the dissenters have grown too strong, and the dangers of eternal death loom over all."

My heart was suddenly thumping against my ribs. Why was Dad asking about the End of Days? Was he worried it was coming? I knew the number of dissenters was growing yearly—especially in the outer cities, but New Freeda was still full of believers who followed Great's command.

As I tried consoling my inner fears, Dad stopped in front of a large wooden door. Once again, he removed his ring, using it as a key. He grabbed my arm and pulled me inside before slamming the door shut.

Dad flipped a switch. A dozen lights bounced off the walls, momentarily blinding me. Once my eyes adjusted, my mouth dropped. The history of ancient times unfolded before me in vivid color. Detailed paintings along the wall created a beautiful mural of the world's most pivotal moments.

"I don't want to alarm you." Dad pinched his chin, his eyes settling on me.

I chuckled, trying to cover the legitimate fear in my voice. "Is that why you've whisked me to this terrifying room in a creepy underground tunnel?"

On one panel, Great's finger stretched out, breathing life into the first man. On another was a scene depicting the construction of the Ancient Altar. There was the festival of partnerships, the seven-year drought, and the story of Ash's sacrifice. One after the other, images of ancient man's triumphs and struggles were beautifully illustrated along the wall.

"Here," Dad said, pointing to the last pictures of the series. A demon dressed in a red dress lured people off a cliff into a flaming pit. "Lucifer's cunning lies destroyed a third of our people, and even though Great exiled her from living among his children, her spirit still influences many."

"The dissenters," I whispered.

"Exactly. Their influence—Lucifer's influence—is growing. How else do you explain the break-in? Who else would dare desecrate Great's holy edifice and claim they know more than the Scribes?"

Dad pointed to another image, one I didn't recognize. It showed people engulfed in flames with Great flying above them, tears streaming down His eyes. My stomach turned. Piecing together everything I knew about the signs of the End of Days, I tried reassuring myself it was still years away.

"One dissenter's failed break-in of the Sanctum doesn't mean Evie has returned," I said, hoping Dad would agree. "Doesn't the prophecy begin with her?"

My father stepped closer, taking my shoulders into his hands. "There is one thing you must realize as you prepare to become a member of the Quorum, Asaph. Great's words aren't always easy to decipher. Sometimes they are literal, and sometimes they are metaphorical. The Scribes must summon Great's spirit and interpret his words according to His will."

Dad had ruffled plenty of feathers in his fourteen years as High Scribe. Unafraid to implement Great's laws, Dad never cared about the opinion of others. *Great doesn't care what's popular,* he would always say. While some criticized his ostentatious temples and elaborate celebrations, Dad always insisted Great demanded the best. *I don't question what Great asks me to do.*

Could I live up to the title? Swallowing hard, I wiped my sweat-drenched palms against my pants. My whole life, I dreamed of being ordained, and not because I cared about the prestige. I just wanted answers. I yearned to know Great's will. But how could I be sure I was interpreting His words accurately if Great didn't speak directly to me? What would happen if I got it all wrong?

"Asaph, are you listening?"

I snapped to attention. "Yes, of course. So what are you saying? Are you suggesting this break-in is a sign of the End of Days? Is that why you're showing me this?"

Dad sighed. "No, not necessarily, but we must keep our eyes open. Whether the break-in is a sign isn't the point. We know Great's words always come to pass. And I believe the End of Days will happen in your lifetime, likely in mine. You need to be prepared."

My heart raced. "So what do we do?"

"Evie will return," Dad said, standing taller, "and Lucifer's power will strengthen. Great must punish those who fall away. *That* is certain. But in Great's infinite wisdom, He has provided a path for the chosen—"

Dad stopped before finishing his thought. "I can't share everything. Not until you are an official Scribe." He rested his hand on my shoulder. "Less than three weeks, right? I hope you're ready." The steely determination in his eyes made me pause.

Would I ever feel ready?

With a heavy sigh, Dad drifted his focus to the painting of the burning crowd. "It's imperative that you prepare yourself to make some tough decisions in the future." Dad opened the door, gesturing me to head back the way we came. "Now, you've got an ordination to prepare for. Go home and study. And remember, don't speak about this to anyone."

And just like that, my father walked away in the opposite direction. I stood alone in the hallway, numb and afraid. Like crumbs falling from the master's table, I was the dog begging for more. Why was Dad telling me this? And, more importantly, what was he *not* telling me? I needed to understand. I had to know everything.

CHAPTER 3
REJECTED PROPOSAL

"Hey, man! Wake up!"

I snapped to attention, nearly falling out of my chair as a pencil flew toward me. Bracing myself against the desk, I dodged the projectile. "What the—what are you doing?"

An enormous pile of books formed a fortress around me, but I could see James's reflection in the mirror on the wall. He stood in the doorway, aiming another pencil at the back of my head.

James Sato had been my friend for as long as I can remember. His affable manners and infectious enthusiasm contrasted against my often serious outlook on life. A jokester by nature, James knew how to push my buttons and make me laugh. Despite his sometimes irreverent humor, nobody was as faithful to Great's work as James was. His commitment to the faith inspired my own devotion.

The late Mr. Sato, James's father, was Head Guard before he died. He had been responsible for protecting the High Scribe—aka, my father. Authoritative and just, Mr. Sato shaped the way Scribes disciplined dissenters. His dedication made an impression on James, who joined the Scribe Guards three years ago, not long after his father passed. It was an honor to serve as an officer and came with tremendous respect within the Scribedom. Like me, James worked hard to earn his title, but we both knew our family connections played a part in achieving the status we enjoyed.

James laughed. "Did you really fall asleep studying again?"

"Leave me alone. I was up all night."

"Sure," James said as he walked in and sat on my bed. "I heard there was a break-in. Glad you're okay. Tell me everything. What happened?"

I shrugged, unsure of what I could say.

James took my silence as a cue to keep prodding. "I heard it was a woman. Probably some filthy dissenter. Crazy times. What exactly was she trying to steal? Man, I wish I had been on duty. I would have kicked her ass."

"She'd be shaking in her boots," I laughed.

James dismissed my taunting tone. "It's kinda scary when you think about it. I always thought the Sanctum was untouchable, you know? Like, who would even want to defile something so—" With a pause, he ruminated, trying to find the right word, "—sacred."

Spinning around to meet James face to face, I sighed. The Sanctum had never been attacked so blatantly, but I hated dwelling on what happened, especially since I still felt somehow responsible. My insecurities and Dad's warning about the End of Days left me tangled with anxiety.

"Great prophesied of growing dissension," I said. "People are abandoning the Scribe's wisdom."

James huffed. "I know, and I hate it. What makes dissenters think they know better? They're so eager to change things. They should be happy with the way things are. I mean, Great has given us an amazing world. There are too many ungrateful people roaming the streets these days." James leaned back on the bed, his hands behind his head. "If it were up to me, I'd lock them all up."

"I mean, we already send most dissenters away. Is that any different?"

James smiled. "The difference would be that *I'd* get the satisfaction of seeing their sorry faces as they realized they'd spend their life rotting in prison."

I chuckled. "Oh, well, in that case—lock 'em up."

"Someday, when I'm Head Guard, I will."

The conversation was making me antsy. "What time is it?" I asked, hoping to change the subject.

"Almost four."

"In the afternoon? Crap."

"It's good you've got me to check up on you." James laughed as he threw a pillow in my direction.

I caught it before it hit my face and threw it back. "Yeah, *so* lucky." Even with the sarcasm, we both knew I meant it. Sure, James could be overly protective, which was a little annoying sometimes. After all, I was taller and bigger and always believed I could care for myself. But James had trained with the masters. He could beat me on even my best days. After what happened last night, I was glad he had my back.

I opened a book and began adding to my lengthy notes. "So, what's up? Why are you here?"

"Do I need a reason to visit my best friend?"

"No, but you usually have one," I said with a slight smirk. "Are you looking to borrow something? You were eying my gold watch the other day. Is that what you want?"

"Rude!" James threw the pillow again, whacking me. "That watch is gaudy as hell."

"Agreed. Mom gave it to me. I was hoping you wanted it." I turned to face James. "If you aren't here to take it off my hands, you can leave. My books are calling."

"How can you possibly still be studying?" James asked, reading over my shoulder. "I bet you know more about the history and doctrines than your dad." He reached over and closed the textbook. "Enough of this. We're heading out tonight. Get ready."

"Ready for what?" I flipped the pages open again, unwilling to be distracted.

James grabbed the book, shooting me a mischievous grin. "A party. I want you to meet someone."

I sighed. "Who's the bimbo this time?"

"No bimbo—she's a classy, intelligent, faithful young woman who also happens to be gorgeous. Trust me."

"I don't need your help finding someone." I stood, taking back my book.

"Are you sure, buddy? You know your twenty-first birthday is at the end of this month, right?"

"Yes, I remember my birthday, believe it or not."

"And I'm guessing you also remember that on said birthday, you will be ordained a member of the Quorum of Scribes."

I rolled my eyes, unwilling to engage.

James wrapped his arm around my shoulder, guiding me toward my closet. He started picking shirts from the rack, holding them up to me. "Part of your sacred duty is to marry a faithful woman before your ordination. Did you forget?"

I pushed his arm away and detoured toward the bathroom. Turning on the faucet, I splashed water on my face and patted myself dry with a small towel. "No, James. I remember all of it."

"Asaph! You've got less than three weeks! The last serious relationship you had was nearly two years ago. If I were you, I'd be out meeting people. Or do you want to marry a complete stranger? You know the Quorum will choose someone if you don't soon."

Marriage was the only snag to becoming the youngest Scribe in history. In the beginning, Great commanded Steve to take Evie as a partner. *Man shall not be alone.* That was one rule everyone knew. Men had a sacred responsibility to serve as masters of their households, and it was a woman's gift to accept his proposal.

These days, most couples dated, decided they loved each other, and then the man proposed, giving the illusion of control. But for the Scribes, Great's command remained literal. My mom had no say in her marriage. None of the Scribes' wives did. Of course, most women dreamed of marrying a member of the Quorum, so it usually wasn't an issue. After all, the role of Scribe Wife was a respected title. It offered a pampered lifestyle with a nearly guaranteed path into Great's good graces.

So, yes, plenty of women were eager to marry me, but I wasn't interested in them. Images of a faceless bride spun in my brain for months, rattling my nerves. I was thick in denial about my upcoming wedding, pushing the task of choosing a bride to the back of my mind whenever it tried to surface. But as James reminded me—all too often—the deadline was looming, and my head throbbed thinking about it.

"I'm aware of the ticking clock, James, and constantly bringing it up does not help the situation."

I took back the hideous paisley shirt he had picked out. Shoving a bunch of hangers to one side, I browsed through the back of my closet. My hand stopped on a faded hoodie from high school, and I froze.

Jame's voice grew quiet. "You know, it's within your rights to force her to marry you."

The blood rushed to my cheeks as I shot James an icy glare. "You promised never to mention Paige."

"You're the one who said her name! I just recognized her sweatshirt." James folded his arms. "Look, I know the breakup was bad. I know she said her heart wasn't in it, but you didn't have to give her up. It's so obvious you still love her, and I doubt that will change in the next three weeks."

James was right, and I resented him for it. Paige had been my high school girlfriend. For three years, we were inseparable, and

I always pictured my future with her. Unfortunately, she didn't love me enough to commit to eternity. And while it was within my right to press for marriage, I couldn't do it. I loved Paige too much to force her against her will—but it was more than that.

I sat down on the edge of my bed. "I want someone who *wants* to be with me." The statement now sounded ridiculous, considering I had to choose a bride in less than twenty days or be assigned a wife by a group of old men. Forcing a loveless Paige had to be infinitely better than marrying a stranger.

James sat next to me. "The girls at tonight's party would be thrilled to be with you." He winked, trying to lighten my soured mood.

"That's the problem. They're only interested because they know I will be a Scribe. None of those women care about the real me."

"Nobody can know the real you if you don't give them a chance! Besides, who wouldn't want you? Look at those amber eyes! That thick, wavy hair? That jawline? Are you kidding me? You're a catch, man!" James tapped my leg before jumping to his feet. "So, it's decided. Tonight we mix and mingle and find you a wife!"

Walking back over to my desk, I opened my book again. "I can't—studying."

"What could you possibly be studying that you haven't already learned a hundred times?"

"I'm brushing up on the signs of the End of Days."

James blew a loud raspberry. "Seriously, man. You're such a buzz kill! We learned that stuff as kids. There's not much to it unless you know something I don't."

I stiffened my spine. "That's Scribe business."

James's face dropped. He hated when I pulled the Scribe card on him. "Fine, *your Holiness*," he said mockingly. "Keep your nose in your books. Put off the very pressing problem of your upcoming nuptials—again. But I swear, one of these days, you're going to dig so deep into the history that you might end up scraping away the very foundation that upholds your faith."

I snapped to attention. "What do you mean?"

"It's like the other day—I was doing my nightly reading of the Scrolls. I kept seeing the word *of*. The more I looked at it, the more it looked like gibberish."

I rolled my eyes. "Your point being?"

"Anything can look wrong if you look too hard." James rested his hand on my shoulder, leaning in as if lecturing me like a father. "Your heart's in the right place. Just be careful not to lose yourself trying to find all the answers. Faith isn't about knowing it all."

Our eyes lingered as his words gripped my heart. I silently scoffed. James didn't get it. The whole point of becoming a Scribe *was* to lose myself. I would happily give my life to Great to receive the answers I desired. Soon the world would look to me for guidance, and I'd be damned if I couldn't provide it.

I nodded for James to leave. "Enjoy your party."

MESSAGE FROM LUCY FERNÁNDEZ

SATURDAY, NOV 12

Ian, answer your phone.

I know you're mad but now isn't the time. This is Nationals!

Where are you!?

Seriously, I need you!

SUNDAY, DEC 18

It's been a month. I gave you space, but I really think we should talk.

SUNDAY, DEC 25

Merry Christmas! Did you get the lemon bars I dropped off?

CHAPTER 4
BIANCA'S QUESTION

It all started when I dropped that damn case. Everything was going as planned. When my grip gave out, there was no way to stop the metal box from crashing onto the floor. I'm unsure what was louder, the deafening crack of its impact or my heart thudding inside my chest.

For a moment, I considered making a clean break. The lock struck the stone first, snapping it in half and giving me easy access to the contents. There were no alarms, no men flooding the scene of my crime. But the thought of escaping vanished when Mr. Junior Scribe entered the Chamber. After his dramatic entrance, everything was a blur. At first, I thought I could handle him. He was a solid guy, but he didn't seem particularly athletic. My speed and agility kept me one step ahead—for a bit. But ultimately, I couldn't overcome the size difference. As soon as his grip locked my arms behind my back, I knew I was heading to the dungeon.

In fact, I was counting on it.

The next couple of hours were all about biding my time. The basement of the Sanctum was cold and damp. My stomach gurgled, and I realized I hadn't eaten all day. Nobody offered me a meal, but as the morning made its debut, a string of visitors gave me plenty to digest.

Starting with the lowest Quorum member working up the ranks, the Scribes took their shot at interrogating me, trying to determine how much of a problem I would be. They all had their own interview methods. Some hoped to trick me into sharing details, while others offered all kinds of grace if I confessed. One guy tried to force information with not-so-thinly veiled threats.

Of all those silly men with self-important airs, it was the High Scribe—the big tuna himself—who understood the psychology behind any proper investigation. Scribe Josiah Zimran handpicked his questions, leaving long pauses and just enough hints of sympathy to tempt me to put my guard down. He placed seemingly benign statements at my feet, like land mines ready to blow up in my face. If I hadn't sworn to secrecy, he might have been the one to break me. But throughout every question and every insult, my lips remained unmoved.

Then Zimran's son showed up.

It was well into the evening when the Junior Scribe—the guy who caught me—rounded the corner of the basement stairs. He didn't look at me as he opened the door to the annex across from my cell. Inside were piles of dusty books and boxes. He leafed through pages of heavy volumes before discarding each, creating a giant pile to his side. The look on his face grew frustrated as the stack of rejects grew taller.

"Whatcha looking for?" I called out, offering something between a smile and a smirk.

His eyes caught mine—more surprised than angry. A gust of wind from a nearby window sent a whistle throughout the dank hallway. I didn't move, and neither did he. His steely demeanor told me I wouldn't get a response.

"You're different from the others," I said—calling his bluff.

He took a few careful steps closer. His brown eyes looked

almost golden the closer he got. Pensive but cautious, his shoulders relaxed.

"What others?" he finally asked.

I leaned into the metal bars that separated us. "The other Scribes. They all took a turn interrogating me, trying to determine my fate. Are you going to try? Aren't you curious to know why I did it?"

"I'm just the Junior Scribe. And frankly, I don't care why you broke in, only that you got caught," he said before looking over his shoulder, surveying the empty halls. Every move he made felt tentative—like he wasn't supposed to engage but couldn't resist. He took another step closer. "So what did the Scribes decide?"

I could feel him pulling on my line, so I began reeling him in. "What do you know about the Place of Origin? Is the Doorway of Death real?"

He stepped back, clearly disappointed that I had evaded his question.

Of course, I already knew the answers. The Place of Origin was once called Fredenia—the world's oldest city. Its villagers were the first people. They had a lot to learn about their purpose and relationship with their creator. Fredenia had been the landmark of several pivotal moments in history, shaping much of humanity's current beliefs. Inside the city stood the Ancient Altar, a once-public edifice for sacred offerings. It was now forbidden from general use. Only the Scribes could make sacrifices at the holy spot.

The city was also home to the world's most foreboding landmark: The Doorway of Death. As the portal where Evie was allegedly exiled, taking a third of Great's children with her, it stood as the ultimate warning of Great's punishment for disobeying His word. Not long after Evie's demise, a small group attempted to go through the doorway. That's when Great commanded the Scribes to barricade the entire city, forcing everyone to move north, eventually establishing New Freeda.

Yes, I was familiar with the stories surrounding the ancient city. But unlike most people, I questioned their validity.

"Why are you asking questions everyone knows the answer to?" The Junior Scribe said, clearly annoyed. "If you're so interested, go visit the Place of Origin. That's what everyone else does."

I shook my head. "That's not true. Anyone can visit the Wall of Remembrance, but that's outside the city's border. It's hardly the same as going inside, a privilege reserved for Scribes and their guards. Isn't that right?"

"As Junior Scribe, I can also go inside The Place of Origin." He stepped back, folding his arms with a satisfied smirk. "But again, you should know that. If you're trying to get information from me, you're doing a terrible job. Maybe you should attend your weekly services. Take the children's class. It will get you up to speed on all of this."

It's true. Kids as young as three began learning about Great's words and the stories of His creation. Over centuries, the Scribes had slowly taken control of all artifacts and historical records, carefully selecting what information to share with the public. They reduced the world's history to simple tales everyone was expected to know.

So everyone knew that after Evie's exile, Great created his High Commands—laws designed to prove man's faithfulness. He tasked the first Scribe with writing His holy word while continuing to enforce the rules Himself. But as the years moved forward, Great's presence became increasingly scarce. Different interpretations spread like a plague. Every variation infected the Scribe's ability to create a unified people.

Many bloody battles and two millennia later, the Quorum had successfully consolidated their power. They boldly restricted access to the records, ensuring their official version of history was the only one taught. They did a good job reigning in information. Well, mostly.

I focused on the Junior Scribe, trying to read his mind. "What's your name?"

He paused as his eyes moved toward the exit. With a heavy sigh, he finally spoke. "Asaph."

"Asaph, as Junior Scribe, how do you interpret the End of Days prophecy?"

His face went pale. I had clearly struck a nerve, so I continued to prod.

"Do you think Evie will return? And how is that possible? It's been over two thousand years since her exile—since her *death*. Are you telling me she can overcome death? That would make her as powerful as Great."

The last statement stung. I knew I had crossed a line, and my blasphemy should have been reason enough for Asaph to call the guards, but he stood his ground.

"As Junior Scribe, my role is to help protect and preserve the records." He spoke through clenched teeth. "I cannot give interpretations. Nor would I venture one. You are a dissenter, trying to bait me with questions that have no use other than to entice me to evil. Enough of this nonsense!"

Asaph turned to walk away. I called out, hoping for one last minute of his attention.

"But you'll be a Scribe soon, right? That's the word on the street." I checked my tone, ensuring I sounded sincere. "Do you agree with the long-standing tradition of withholding information from Great's children?"

"I said enough!" Asaph banged on the wall with his fist. His cheeks were red with indignation, his chest puffed with anger—but he didn't move.

I smiled, trying to ease the tension in the air. "I like you, Ace. Can I call you that?"

No response.

"Listen, Ace. I'm sorry. I'll drop it. But I have one last personal question, if you don't mind."

Asaph exhaled loudly, shaking his head in exasperation. "What?"

I leaned in, almost whispering. "What do you want?"

He pulled back defensively. "What do you mean?"

"I mean, what do you want? What do you want to do? To be? To know?" I let the words hang in the air and watched their simplicity dance toward him.

Asaph tugged at a thread dangling from his shirt's hem. His eyes pulled inward as if having a conversation with himself—an honest but invisible discussion without hesitation or guilt. It lasted only a moment before he regained his composure.

"I want to learn and understand all of Great's words. I want to work toward being the best Scribe I can be—helping my people get closer to Great, ensuring they are saved when the end comes."

Disappointment snatched my breath. "Come on, Ace. Don't lie to me."

Asaph ran up to the bars. "How dare you!"

I slipped my hands through the gap, grabbing his wrist. Asaph pulled away instinctively before slowly stepping toward me. His quiet desperation begged me to understand him in a way he didn't even understand himself.

"I know what you want," I said.

He didn't move.

I leaned in and whispered, "You want the truth."

His chest retreated as if struck by some unseen force. Tears welled in his eyes as he shook his head, trying to maintain composure.

"Yes," he finally said, his voice shaking. "And the truth comes from Great. That's why I'm dedicated to studying the Scrolls."

Asaph whipped around, making his way toward the stairs.

I called out, hoping to get one last word before he left. "Maybe what you need isn't in the Scrolls!"

IAN'S NOTES
FRIDAY, JANUARY 13TH

It's been less than two months since I committed to this whole god role. It's fascinating how a single statement can evolve culture. One of those self-proclaimed Scribes prayed to me this morning, wondering how their people could know who they should marry. With my usual flair of lightning and thunder, I descended and declared it was man's choice.

In my head, the word 'man' was a general term. I was suggesting it was the couple's decision.

Speeding ahead ten years, I was surprised by a new gender dynamic among the people. The Scribe interpreted my words to mean that only men got a say in marriage. And that simple misfire has placed women as second-class citizens in the community. As I said, fascinating! This may call for further experiments.

CHAPTER 5
ENGRAVED INVITATION

PERSPIRATION DRENCHED my forehead as I snapped out of bed.

What do you want? Bianca's question repeated in my mind. For hours, I tossed and turned, replaying our conversation. She had crossed so many lines, revealing her obvious disdain for the sacred, and I hated myself for not walking away sooner. Shame engulfed me as her prodding revealed a disturbing shadow of doubt within.

Maybe Dad was right. Perhaps Bianca's sudden appearance in the Sanctum was a sign of the End of Days. Was it possible the devil had possessed her? Was she trying to lead me astray? I dropped to my knees; hands clasped as my head hung in humility.

"Forgive me, Great. I did not mean to lose sight of your infinite wisdom. Guide me to do better. Grant me your spirit to loosen the bands of evil and be a tool in your hands for your work."

A peaceful feeling warmed my heart. I knew what I needed to do.

"You really think this is a good idea?" James fidgeted with the zipper on his tactical vest. He sighed as the world zoomed past his window.

We sat in the backseat of a black sedan while the driver sped through the roads of New Freeda. My disturbing interaction with Bianca kept me up all night, leaving me tired and frazzled. I was determined to set things right by making an offering at the Ancient Altar inside the Place of Origin.

The four-hour ride to the original city was still unfamiliar. This was only my third time making the journey. Bringing one Scribe Guard for protection was customary, a tradition that always seemed unnecessary before Bianca. Now, I was thankful for the policy and even more grateful James was my security specialist for the day.

Only Scribes, including the Junior Scribe, could ascend the stony steps of the altar and speak to Great. It was a ritual anchored by tradition and carried on by hope. After centuries of silence, each Scribe who climbed the altar's steps was eager to be the man who opened the heavens again. It had been so long since Great had shown Himself in the flesh. Many believed the right offering could summon Him back.

A Scribe's initial offer was supposed to represent a significant sacrifice. My first time visiting the altar coincided with my ordination to Junior Scribe. I remember ascending the stairs and placing my prized violin among the many gifts of ages past. A twinge of sadness struck me as I vowed to give up music to focus on Great's work. The violin had been my first love, and letting it go was painful. But after my offering, a weight lifted from my shoulders. While He did not show Himself, I knew Great was pleased, and I vowed to make His work my new passion.

Beyond one's initial offering, a Scribe could visit the altar whenever he wanted to strengthen his connection to Great. I made my second journey after my break-up with Paige. I gifted the engagement ring she refused to accept, begging Great to soften my heart and help me move on.

And now I geared up for visit number three—hoping a new offering would uproot whatever questions Bianca had planted in my brain.

"What's on your mind?" James asked. "You've been quiet."

The interruption startled me. I rubbed my eyes, trying to orient myself based on the landmarks outside the speeding car.

"Sorry, I must have zoned out. I haven't slept well lately."

James nodded. "So why the sudden urge to visit the Place of Origin? Don't get me wrong—I'm thrilled you asked me to come as your guard. It's my first time. Did you know that? I'm eager to see it. My dad always talked about his time inside." He cleared his throat. "I mean, he never told me anything specific, obviously. I know we're not supposed to talk about what we see in there."

"Relax, man." I smiled.

James sighed, smiling back. "So, what inspired the decision?"

I turned my attention outside my window. "It's personal."

"Oh," James said, suddenly deflated. "Sorry to prod."

As my best friend, I trusted James with my life. He had always been forthcoming, and now I was shutting him out. It made me feel awful, but I wasn't ready to divulge my inner demons. I was weeks away from becoming a full-fledged Scribe, and I didn't want anyone doubting my devotion, including James.

I offered a weak smile. "Sorry, it's been a weird few days."

A part of me wished I could explain what happened with Bianca and how her questions rattled me. If anyone could make me feel okay about it, James could. But I didn't want to feel okay about what happened. I wanted to fix it, and the altar was my chance.

James smiled back. "Don't sweat it, man. You've got a lot on your plate with the whole ordination and marriage thing coming up." He rested his head against the window and closed his eyes.

A nap sounded wonderful, but the sick feeling in my stomach made the possibility of following James's lead impossible. The car rolled forward, and the sound of rubber on the pavement filled the silence while my brain tried to untangle my frayed nerves. I opened my bag, double checking I had everything I needed: My journal, some pens, and the pamphlet I brought as my offering.

On the surface, the little booklet didn't seem worthy of anyone's notice, let alone my maker. I had seen the kinds of gifts past Scribes left at the altar. Dazzling jewels and gold figurines were among the many treasures given in Great's name. It seemed almost sacrilegious to place this tattered brochure near such prized possessions.

But the pamphlet represented my ultimate sacrifice.

Three months ago, I was walking along the park near the Sanctum courtyard. It was where I often went to collect my thoughts. On that particular day, a voice whispered from the bushes. I turned as a figure brushed past me, running toward the public street two blocks away. Dressed in a navy sweatshirt with the hoodie drawn, I couldn't make out who the person was, but they dropped something near my feet as they made their mad dash out of the park.

The incident was unusual, and I should have reported it immediately. Instead, I picked up the item. It was the pamphlet. Plain in its design, the title across the cover read: *My Search for Answers*. I refused to open it as it was clearly not part of the official Scribe materials, which meant it was likely dissenter misinformation. But something kept me from turning it into security. It had been tucked inside my nightstand drawer ever since, tempting me to partake of its contents.

I never read it. That fact made me feel a little less horrible, but the pamphlet's mere presence intensified the murky thoughts I often struggled to push away—the ones that dared question the truth. I hated that I had doubts, and after my encounter with Bianca, I knew those doubts could be my undoing. I was playing too close to the fire, or in this case, the shadows. If I was serious about becoming a worthy Scribe, I needed to give up anything that wasn't Great's words.

The car hit a bump in the road, jostling James awake. Outside my window, signs of the modern world became increasingly scarce. The city skyline transformed into a lush forest of trees, telling me we were getting close.

"Hey, James?" My voice was uneasy.

"Yeah?"

"I know this is your first time to the Place and Origin, but I was hoping you'd wait outside the gates. I'd like to be alone for my offering."

The disappointment in James's eyes pierced me.

"Are you serious?" he asked. When I nodded, he snapped upright. "You dragged me all this way, and I don't get to see what's inside?"

"I know. I'm sorry, but I have to do this myself. You'll get another chance, I swear."

He scoffed, biting his tongue. "Whatever you say, *your Holiness.*"

The words dripped with bitterness, breaking my heart. It was cruel to bring James along only to leave him in the car. But any other guard would refuse to stay behind, and I had to do this alone. I was determined to set myself straight. My life as a Scribe had to start with a clean slate.

James would forgive me eventually, but that didn't make me feel any less awful.

"It won't take long," I said as the driver approached the main entrance. "I'll radio you if I need help."

James nodded. He hadn't said a word since I told him I'd go inside alone. I grabbed my bag and slammed the car door.

The large city border stood nearly twenty feet off the ground and spanned the entire perimeter of the once-small village. When first built, the wall reached not even half as high, but eventually, they replaced the original brick construction with cement and doubled the wall in height and thickness.

The Scribe's entrance featured golden plated doors that looked like the entryway to heaven itself. Long slabs of marble with shimmering accents framed the opening. Lavishly ornate, the spectacle stood as a testament to the Scribes' efforts to glorify Great.

Pulling a key from around my neck, I approached the entrance. I muscled the heavy gates open just enough to squeeze through. Once inside, thick vegetation inched along a single dirt path toward the former town's center. A handful of half-standing homes and ruins popped up periodically, but otherwise, there wasn't much to see. I hiked through a dense grove of trees toward a field with tall grasses blowing in the wind. A pond rested in the middle of the open area, and near it stood the Ancient Altar.

Weathered and crumbling in places, the giant structure was still impressive in size and longevity. Layers of rock created a broad foundation that reached nearly twelve feet high. Former Scribes took great care to preserve the historical integrity of the artifact. They carefully reinforced the stony steps, making it safe to ascend to the top. On closer inspection, you could see fossilized sea shells and other small trinkets that the original builders had placed in the cracks and crevices of the boulders.

Scattered around the ground near the altar were past offerings. The wind had blown some pieces away while past worshipers shoved others aside as they placed new gifts on the tall pedestal. The altar's treasures were worth millions of dollars between the jewels, gold pieces, and other prized possessions.

Sitting on a stump near the stairs, I unzipped my bag to retrieve the pamphlet. The confidence in my gift was fading as I scanned the surrounding riches. Would I please Great with this metaphorical commitment to His word? Or would I insult Him with these worthless scraps of paper? Between the lump in my throat and my growing nerves, I found it hard to breathe.

"Get it together," I told myself. "Do what you came here to do."

I made it part-way up the stairs and stopped to view a distant shoreline that stretched for miles on the other side of the wall. The beach was off limits to man—Great's first command. But those lucky enough to walk the altar steps got a peek at the sacred waters. The scene's beauty gave me the courage to finish my offering, but a loud rustling stopped me before I reached the top.

My breath caught in my throat. "Is someone there?"

Trying to comfort myself, I blamed the wind. Still, I decided to investigate as I didn't want my special moment ruined by any distractions, including my own fears. My heart picked up speed as I carefully rushed down the stairs. As my feet landed on the grass, I scanned the trees. Everything was quiet until branches from a large bush began shaking. Reaching for my bag, I carefully placed the pamphlet inside and swung it over my shoulder.

"Just the wind," I reassured myself again, despite no other signs of a breeze. When the bush rustled again, I reluctantly moved closer and grabbed a small rock near my foot.

"Come out!" I tossed the pebble toward the bush.

"Don't! It's just me!"

Despite the familiarity of the voice, I couldn't place it. I slipped my radio out of my pocket, ready to call James. "I said, come out!" Holding my breath, I waited and watched in disbelief as a woman with soft curls and hazel eyes slowly rose from behind the bush.

Bianca smiled as she waved.

"You! How did you—where did—why are?" My brain was running faster than my mouth could keep up. I couldn't track all the reasons Bianca's presence was impossible. How did she break free from her cell? Or travel so far? Or get past the border walls? None of it made sense. "You can't be here!"

"Then why am I here?" Her lips curled with an irritating satisfaction.

"You won't be for long," I said, clenching my fist.

I sprinted toward her, and she took off. Past the underbrush and through the thick forest, Bianca dodged around tree trunks and muddy puddles. I tried to keep up, but her smaller size made maneuvering through the tight trees easier. Some loose bark snagged my shoulder, and I hit my head on a branch, but I kept my eyes focused on her path. Bianca moved with a determined focus that worried me, especially when I realized where she was going: The Doorway of Death.

My stomach churned. I swallowed the vomit that was trying to escape my throat. Bianca's presence in the Place of Origin was already a massive transgression. But nearing the portal where Evie was exiled was the ultimate sin.

And I was following her toward it.

A surging resolution pushed me to move faster. Knowing where Bianca was heading, I veered off the twisted path she had chosen—most likely to lose me—and made headway along a more open trail.

The Doorway of Death wasn't an actual doorway. The devil, known as Lucifer, used her powers to create a rift in Great's world. She showed the portal to Evie, insisting it led to a better life. It was a lie Evie and many others believed. Passing through the invisible space, all original dissenters died without a trace.

Great ordered his followers to mark the place with a black

arch. A ring of spikes created a small perimeter around the portal—a warning to stay away. Great's instructions were clear: anyone who crossed the boundary would die.

Just as Bianca was about to cross the border of spikes, I grabbed her black hoodie. Her legs slipped from under her, and she tumbled to the ground.

"Are you crazy?" My voice echoed throughout the village, frightening a flock of birds. I jerked Bianca to her feet and restrained her arms behind her back. "You can't go through there. You'll die."

"That's not true!" Bianca thrashed against me, trying to break free.

"It's called the Doorway of Death for a reason!"

Bianca lifted her foot and slammed it into mine. I recoiled in pain, releasing her. She snapped around with her face inches away from me. "It's not a doorway to death," she said. "It's a doorway to freedom. Watch." Before I could stop her, she reached for a large stone and chucked it toward the black arch.

My heart stopped as my eyes followed the rock. It soared along the sky and suddenly disappeared through the archway.

"Dammit, Bianca! What does that prove? All it does is confirm that what goes through the doorway does not come back!" I pinned her arms against her back and radioed James with my free hand. "We've got a problem. Meet me at the gate. Have handcuffs ready."

"Asaph, listen to me." Bianca dug her heels into the ground. "You don't know the complete story. You don't need to fear the Doorway."

I whipped her around, grabbing her shoulders. My face moved in closer, locking eyes with her. "No, you listen to me! You're not supposed to be here—near this door, inside this city, or in my life! I will not listen to your lies anymore. You belong in jail."

A heavy thud punctuated my words. My eyes widened as I

saw the rock Bianca had thrown next to my foot.

"What the hell?" I reached down and picked it up. Scratched along the flat surface was the word *hello*. Panic set in fast. I didn't know what exactly was happening, but it was clear: Someone was on the other side of that portal.

My hands let go of Bianca as I inspected the stone. I shoved it toward her face. "You see this? You're going to get us both killed!"

Bianca grabbed the rock from my hand. She smiled as she traced the etched letters with her fingers.

I stumbled backward, bracing myself against a large tree as I tried to calculate what everything meant. My father's warning about the End of Days echoed in my mind, my soul teetering at the edge of destruction.

And Bianca was downright giddy.

While I processed the jumble of emotion, Bianca scrambled for a small, pointy rock and quickly scratched another message on the stone: *Who are you?* She threw the rock back through the invisible portal. Her smile grew as it vanished again.

My voice strained as I yelled. "Are you actually responding? What's wrong with you? We need to get out of here. Like, now!"

"Wait for it," Bianca whispered.

Sweat dripped down my forehead as I ran my fingers through my hair. I nearly threw up but was able to swallow the bile. For whatever reason, I followed Bianca's instructions and waited.

I hated myself for it.

"Come on, come on." Bianca was practically bouncing with anticipation. Suddenly, the rock appeared out of nowhere, flying toward us. She reached up and caught it, and I jumped to my feet. Terrified at what I might see, I peered over Bianca's shoulder as she turned the stone over. I read the response, and my insides bolted. Leaning over the edge of a fallen tree trunk, I upchucked my breakfast.

Engraved on the rock was the name *Evie*.

CHAPTER 6
BIANCA'S VISITOR

As MY HAND gripped the rock, I knew history was being made.

But here's the thing about history. It's more story-telling than record-keeping. Historians pull apart details, choosing what to elevate and what to leave behind. Gaps are filled in, ensuring the through-line points to the lessons they want us to learn. After all, it's hard to journey toward an unknown future without a clear image of where you've been. A messy past feels unsafe.

So we clean up what came before, transforming life's chaos into black and white. Right vs. wrong. Hero vs. villain. Along the way, people are herded like sheep. The obedient are fenced into a sense of belonging, while the others are removed from the group. If you're not careful, you could easily find yourself on the outside.

Ask me how I know.

I didn't go seeking the title of Dissenter. There was no baptism or initiation—no urge to rebel. My fate was sealed the moment I dared question the status quo. Maybe things would have been different if I had kept my doubts to myself. Although, I'm glad I didn't. As I wavered from the path everyone wanted me to take, I learned history was full of undeserving villains. If people could get my story so wrong, who else had been mischaracterized?

Take Evie, for example. Hers was a tale of warning. History made her one of the most hated villains ever, but I wasn't convinced. After months of searching through long-forgotten records—the kind the Scribes warned against reading—I knew Evie's real tale wasn't being told. I was determined to prove it, starting with Asaph. Holding the rock in my hand with *her* name etched on its face, I thought it might be enough to persuade him to rethink history.

I was wrong.

"Drop it!" The fear in Asaph's voice was undeniable as he wiped bits of vomit from his chin.

I pulled the stone close to my body, safeguarding it with all my strength as my eyes lit up. "I can't believe it. This proves it!"

Asaph shook his head. "Proves what?" His words blasted from his lips, singed with unmistakable fear. "That Evie—the devil's most trusted friend—is knocking at the door, hoping we'll let her in and jumpstart the End of Days? I don't want that kind of proof!" Asaph tried to steady himself, summoning his most authoritative posture while his knees trembled. "Bianca, drop the rock."

I felt terrible that Asaph was so scared, but I couldn't hide my excitement. I knew the stories of Evie's exile had been altered and exaggerated over the centuries. Though it was an uncommon opinion, some believed Evie was right all along—or, at the very least, brave. According to the dissenters, Great didn't exile Evie. She escaped.

Asaph saw the look in my eyes. He knew I would not drop the stone or my mission, so he softened his countenance, trying a different method of persuasion. "Please, Bianca, don't be rash. This is bad. It's so, so bad. Let's just leave the rock and—"

Eyes wide, Asaph pressed his lips together while his chest convulsed. Unable to control himself, he leaned over and threw up for the second time.

I took advantage of the distraction and made a dash for the black archway.

"No! Stop!" Asaph yelled from behind.

It was a race to the doorway. Dried leaves crunched under my feet as I tried to beat Asaph to the arch. Still, I knew I couldn't outrun him. His hand grabbed the back of my shirt, but his grip gave way. Free for the moment, my only thought was to reach the door and see Evie. I jumped over the ring of spikes and stretched one arm through the portal just as Asaph clenched my other wrist.

"Don't do it!" Asaph begged.

He yanked hard to keep me from slipping through the portal while an invisible hand drew me toward it. Two forces pulled me in opposite directions.

"Something's got me!" I inched closer toward the doorway's horizon, but Asaph pulled harder. His size and strength ultimately won the tug of war. My body went falling towards his, pulling whatever had me on the other side through the gateway. Asaph and I toppled to the ground with tremendous force, and a full-figured woman with tight corkscrew curls burst through the portal just before I blacked out.

"Hello? Are you okay?"

My head was throbbing. I rubbed my eyes, trying to adjust to the bright sun overhead. The blinding beams outlined the shadow of someone standing over me. My brain retraced my memories, haphazardly piecing together fragments of images from before everything went dark. When my memory restarted, I scrambled to my feet, eyes locking on the woman's face as my mouth dropped.

"Evie! I—I can't believe it. It's really you!" I wrapped my arms around her body. Her muscles tensed under my embrace. She gingerly pulled away.

"Do I know you?"

Words failed to form as my mind tripped over my thoughts, so I just smiled and shook my head. "No, I guess not," I finally said. "Sorry about ambushing you. I'm just so thrilled to see you."

"How do you know who I am?"

Scanning the ground, I picked up the rock we had passed back and forth. I pointed to the name scratched on it. "This is you, right? You're Evie."

Evie relaxed a bit. A warm smile grazed her face. "Oh, yeah. That's me. But I still don't understand. Were you expecting me?" Her penetrating gaze followed mine as I memorized her face. She was radiant—soft but powerful, curious but restrained.

"Oh shit, Asaph!" I turned over my shoulder, remembering he had been part of the scuffle. He was unconscious, with a trickle of blood on his forehead. I reached into my pocket and pulled out a handkerchief that I wrapped around the open gash. Taking his wrist, I felt his pulse.

"You were both unconscious," Evie said. "Is he okay?"

"He'll have one hell of a headache, but he'll be fine."

Evie nodded. She turned toward the crumbling houses in the distance. "What happened here? Everything looks so different." Her eyes stopped on the spikes that surrounded the invisible portal. "And how did I even get here? I thought the doorway was one-way. That's what Lucy told me."

My stomach flipped at the mention of Lucy, an archaic name for the devil. A few rare records used her full name: Lucy Fernández. Over time, she became simply *Lucifer* or *the devil*. But for some, she wasn't the so-called demon everyone feared. A small minority considered Lucy the original dissenter—a pioneer of free thinking.

I took Evie's hand, guiding her to a large stone where we sat. "You remember Lucy?"

"Of course. She is my closest friend. She's the one who gave us a world free from Ian."

Every word out of Evie's mouth energized me. Ian, the original creator, also had many names over the years: *The Voice in the Sky, The Great I am, Ian the Great*—and then, just *Great*. Like so many recorded stories, the Scribes removed any names that didn't fit within their version of history.

I had so many questions, and it was clear Evie had plenty, too. All I wanted to do was to sit and share everything, but I knew it would be a lot for her to take in at once.

Evie stood and walked along the dirt pathway. Her hands grazed the overgrown bushes as her eyes searched for something. "What happened here? It looks so different."

"Different, how?" I asked, following behind her.

"Everything is gone. My house used to be where that pile of rocks is. What happened to Fredenia?" She pushed through layers of tall grass, walking toward one of the few collapsed buildings the elements hadn't destroyed. "What's left looks so neglected—so old. How could so much change in so little time?"

"How much time has passed? When were you last here?"

Evie shrugged, calculating in her head. "Six lunar cycles at most." She continued exploring the ruins of the town she used to know.

I ran ahead, stopping her before she headed toward the grove of trees that separated us from the altar. "And what have you been doing since then?"

"I'm helping my people get settled," Evie said. "It's a lot of work." She reached down and picked a flower, drinking in its fragrant scent. She let out a heavy sigh. "There aren't many of us, so I was hoping others would come through the portal. That's why I was hanging around it."

"What others?"

"The ones who stayed behind. We miss them, and I never felt right leaving them with that monster in charge. I tried to return, even though Lucy said it was impossible." Evie stopped and smiled at me. "But here I am. You pulled me through somehow. Maybe now I can get the others to join us."

I inhaled deeply, steadying myself before delivering the news I knew would shock her. "Evie, it's been over two thousand years since you left. Everyone you knew in this world is long gone."

Evie shook her head. "What? No, that can't be right." She sank, sitting on a large stone. "That makes no sense. Two thousand years? How is that even possible?"

I couldn't decide if the news upset her or if she was just unwilling to believe it. Unsure how to explain everything, I attempted to change the subject and make my case.

"Evie, I need your help." I grabbed her hand, trying but failing to remain calm as I spoke. "Nobody here has seen or heard from Ian in ages. Everyone thinks of him as some god called Great. His supposed leaders, the Scribes, have complete power over the people. Those who don't follow every tenet of the Scribedom are pushed to the outskirts of town—hungry and isolated. There is so much anxiety over following every little command. The people constantly fear eternal punishment."

My words collided with clumsy urgency, but I couldn't slow down. "Maybe if they could see you. They'd see that you're not bad, tormented, or dead. It could change the tide. You could give people the freedom you enjoy."

"They're really gone?" A tear trickled down Evie's cheek.

With a heavy sigh, I recalibrated. "They are. I'm so sorry."

I was foolish to think I could carry on after dropping such a bomb on Evie. Her mind was clearly troubled by the loss of her former community. With a pang of shame, I realized how calloused my plea sounded next to her devastating news. I scolded myself for letting my agenda overshadow her feelings.

Evie rested her head on my shoulder. I wrapped an arm around her, melting into her warmth. We sat quietly, and I hoped the silence would help Evie settle into the news. After several minutes, I opened my mouth, venturing to gently bring her up to speed, when Asaph's voice shot through the air like a cannon.

"Bianca!"

Evie and I jumped at the noise. Asaph pushed through the foliage while his fingers traced along the makeshift bandage on his head. I didn't know if I should run, fight, or just give in. Running seemed safest, but my goal wasn't to escape. I wanted Asaph to meet Evie. So, despite the risk, I stayed put.

When Asaph saw Evie sitting beside me, the blood rushed from his face. Choking on his nerves, he gulped and lifted a trembling finger. "Is that who I think it is?"

I brushed the dirt from my pants as I stood, nodding.

"Asaph, meet Evie."

IAN'S NOTES
WEDNESDAY, JANUARY 15TH

Not everyone is happy with the changes I've made inside The Garden. *Disturbed by their role in society, a small group of women took their chances and tried to go through Lucy's portal. I knew I had to stop them before people got too casual in their worship of me. With my theatrical demands from the sky, it was easy to scare them into complacency.*

Next, I commanded the Scribes to border the city. I threw in a spooky story about Evie possibly returning, letting them believe such an event would be disastrous.

Nobody seemed thrilled I was kicking them out of their home. But after jumping ahead five years into the future, I saw progress as they built a new city further north. After another twenty years, my warnings had become legends. Fear of disobeying me deepened even in my absence, making me confident they'll stay away from the portal for good.

CHAPTER 7
PROPHETIC WARNINGS

"This is unacceptable!"

I could feel the force of Dad's voice in my bones. Despite his rage, he remained dignified as he berated me—one of his more spectacular talents.

"James should have been inside with you. I'll have his badge for this!"

"It's not James's fault." My voice wasn't strong enough to stand up to Dad's power, but that didn't stop me from trying to defend my friend. "I'm the one who told him to wait in the car. If you want to blame someone, blame me."

"Oh, I do." Dad's words sliced with painful precision.

I wrung my hands, unwilling to meet his eyes. "I didn't expect anyone to follow me, let alone someone who was supposed to be locked up two hundred miles away."

"Why were you at the Place of Origin?" Dad asked, taking a seat. "What business did you have there? You're supposed to be preparing for your ordination."

I could feel his eyes drilling into mine even while I stared at the floor. "I wanted to make an offering. With my upcoming ordination, I must ensure my heart is right."

Dad sighed. He couldn't argue with my intentions. Of course, in the afternoon's chaos, I never actually made my offering. I didn't even make it to the top of the altar before getting caught in the chaos. And while that failure felt insignificant compared to the magnitude of Bianca's escape and Evie's return, it was one more mark of shame I had to bear.

"I suppose it's not your fault." Dad's face drooped with frustration as a silent accusation lingered in his eyes. He leaned against the desk, shaking his head. "I still don't understand how Bianca broke free. Clearly, she's the one who shoulders the blame for everything. Although, if you had brought James with you—" He bit his lip.

I was grateful Dad stopped himself from mentioning my mistake again. While I didn't technically break any law by going to the altar alone, I was expected to bring a guard inside for protection. Bianca might never have made it to the portal if James had been there. Perhaps Evie would still be safely out of our lives. I wanted to protest Dad's anger, but I was writhing, knowing my role in the whole mess.

Dad paced back and forth behind his desk the way he always did when he was disappointed. "The guards took both women. They're locked up, right?"

"Yes, sir. After I regained consciousness, I got Bianca and Evie to follow me to the entrance where James was waiting to help restrain them." Instinctively, I touched the bandage on my head. Dad's eyes softened when he saw me wince—reminding me he really did care. "We placed an extra guard outside their cells to ensure they don't escape again."

"It's the devil's work," Dad said as he slumped into his seat. "Dark forces are at play. Evie is back, confirming our worst fears."

"The End of Days?"

Dad nodded.

I pressed my sweaty palms into my thighs as I sat in the

corner chair. "Are you sure it's Evie? I mean, it doesn't make sense. Why would she come back? And how? It's the Doorway of *Death*, right? Great didn't just exile her; it was an execution." My brain could not piece the puzzle together. No matter how hard I tried, the image had too many gaps. I was desperate to see a glimmer of doubt from my dad. His surety that today's events fulfilled prophecy fed my fears.

"The tumble knocked me out pretty good," I said, rationalizing the story. "It could be a trick—I don't actually remember seeing Evie come through the door. Maybe it's not her."

Dad snapped to attention, shooting an icy stare that shriveled my heart. "Great warned us of Evie's return. Are you suggesting the prophecy isn't true?"

My cheeks grew hot with shame, and I stared at my lap. "Of course not."

"Her return is our final warning. It's our last chance. If we don't act now, the End of Days will take us all."

My head was spinning. "What do you plan to do?"

Dad marched toward our family portrait hanging on the wall and slid it aside. There was a shiny black safe embedded in the wall. He pulled out a thick, leather-bound book and dropped it on the desk with a loud thud. Dad flipped through the pages, thumbing toward the back, and paused as his eyes scanned a specific paragraph. He cleared his throat before peering back at me. "The Sinner's Sacrifice," he said, tapping the page. "It's time to reinstate it."

"No!"

I didn't mean to blurt out. My pulse quickened as a flurry of nerves tickled my stomach. The Sinner's Sacrifice was a ritual abandoned centuries ago. It was a barbaric tradition where a person of lesser faith was chosen each year on the anniversary of Evie's exile to be sacrificed in Great's name. "Ancient Scribes said Great no longer demanded that kind of atonement. Why would you bring it back?"

Dad leaned past his desk, hovering over me like a vulture. "Am I not the High Scribe? Who else knows Great's will if not me? If we want to save our people, we must prove our faith." He slammed the book shut, and I flinched.

Thinking about a human sacrifice gutted me, but I tried hiding the doubt swarming inside. It was one thing to disagree with my father, but he wasn't speaking as my dad. He was speaking as Great's chosen leader. Everyone was supposed to follow the High Scribe's every word—including me. But the growing dissonance between my faith and the innate belief that this proposal was wrong became too much. I was desperate for another solution.

"Isn't killing considered a greater sin than dissenting?" I said with less confidence than I had hoped. "The ritual is evil."

Dad stood silent, waiting for me to edit my remarks. I immediately recognized my insolence as shards of shame pierced my heart.

"I'm sorry," I said weakly. "I didn't mean that. Of course, you know Great's will. His ways aren't always clear. I trust Him—and you." I tried swallowing the lump in my throat, but it remained a roadblock to my words as they squeaked past my lips. "How will you determine who to sacrifice?"

Dad plopped into his seat, leaning back as he brought his hands to his mouth. "Isn't it obvious? It has to be Bianca. It is the only way to persuade people to change their ways."

I didn't understand why I felt like the world around me had shattered. It wasn't like I was a fan of Bianca. She had been a thorn in my side since we met. Between the break-in, her infuriating questioning, and the chaotic disturbance at the Ancient Altar, her actions had more than earned her a steep punishment, but this extreme consequence broke me.

"I can tell you're struggling with this revelation," Dad said.

His eyes softened as if switching roles from High Scribe to caring father.

"Well, uh—" I was afraid to speak, worried any word would betray my faith.

"I get it," Dad said, taking a cue from my silence. "It's hard to imagine such an extreme action being necessary in today's modern world. The Scribes have always taught the importance of love. One of the first things we teach our children is to love one another."

I slowly nodded.

"But one rule stands supreme. We must love Great with all our hearts and put Him first. Too many have neglected that sacred duty, so we must remind them."

I cleared my throat. "And what about Evie?" I asked quietly. "What will you do with her?"

I was still trying to wrap my head around Evie's sudden appearance. She didn't fit the image of the wicked deceiver I had been told about my whole life. Evie asked about my wound and apologized for causing any trouble. Her kind, calming presence contrasted Bianca's brash boldness. There was a spark in Evie's eyes—a hopeful and alluring curiosity.

Evie spoke little during our journey back to New Freeda. She offered a small plea to return through the portal. When I denied her request, she calmly surrendered to her fate, following Bianca's lead, which was surprisingly cooperative.

"We will also offer Evie as part of the sacrifice," Dad said matter-of-factly. "She'll be right next to Bianca."

Light-headed, I swallowed hard. "When do you plan on doing all this?"

Dad twisted the ring around his finger as a smile crept across his face. "The anniversary of Evie's exile is three days away. That's just enough time to prepare a ceremony people will never forget. It's positively prophetic, don't you think?"

I failed to find the energy to speak. With a weak nod, I tried to ignore the gnawing terror building inside of me. Dad must have recognized my resistance. He pulled me into a warm embrace, reminding me of his kindness.

"It's okay, Asaph." Dad's voice was suddenly soft. "This is all part of the plan. You'll see. Great's work will continue to roll forth. Think of all the people we'll save as they reaffirm their faith. While the sacrifice may seem extreme, the reward will be worth it."

The walk home from Dad's felt like a march toward the inner caverns of my soul. With each step, my heart heaved deeper toward the earth. The sun melted past the horizon, turning the sky a vibrant red before settling into a dark blue blanket littered with stars.

"Dear Great," I whispered, veering off my homeward path toward the courtyard garden. "I could use your guidance."

My hand brushed along the scratchy bark of a nearby tree. Peering over my shoulder to ensure nobody was around, I dropped to my knees, braving to speak freely.

"Help me understand your wisdom. Help me feel okay about this decision to reinstate the Sinner's Sacrifice. I'm struggling to understand, but I surrender to your will."

My words trailed off as my mind sharpened, ready to feel any kind of response. Holding my breath, I closed my eyes, imagining Great standing over me. My father's promise that this sacrifice was an act of compassion repeated in my head. I tried to imagine all the lost souls who would witness Evie and Bianca's death. Would it be enough to change their hearts? And even so, was it the right thing to do?

No matter how I spun the story, I felt empty. Darkness swooped in and enveloped me. Gasping for air, I opened my eyes as a floodgate of emotions made me collapse from the weight of it all. Desperate for relief, I cried—begging my heart to release its burden. My body pulsed under my sobs as tears washed over my face.

There has to be another way. There has to be another way. The thought repeated in my mind until it sparked an idea. *I* could be the other way. Great could use *me.* My tangled insides slowly unraveled as I imagined Great's love soothing my weary soul. I have never heard Great speak, but He often touched my heart. As the night breeze cooled my cheeks, His love warmed me. There was no obvious answer, but there was the hope of one.

For now, that was enough.

I slipped my hands into my jacket's pockets and slowly got up. Still lost in thought, I meandered the maze of paths that eventually led me home. Exhausted, I pulled the covers over my body and hoped a good night's sleep would lead me to a more concrete solution. But just as my eyes got heavy, Evie and Bianca's voices drifted from outside my window, dashing that hope.

"My boys are going to worry," Evie said. "I should have stayed away from the portal."

"I'm sorry, Evie. This is all my fault," Bianca responded.

Confused, I shot out of bed. Glancing out my window, I expected to see them in the courtyard, but it was empty. Then I remembered the small window near the top of each cell inside the basement dungeon. The women's voices must have traveled from the prison and bounced off the stone wall near my bedroom window. It was as if I was standing right next to them —the acoustics made their voices so clear.

A surge of anxiety instantly replaced whatever calm I might have felt in the park. With a deep breath, I leaned in to hear their conversation better.

"Tell me about your children," Bianca said. Her tone was much friendlier than when she had spoken to me.

"Cade is like a lightning bolt—fierce, loud, and sometimes dangerous." Evie laughed. "Ash is more sensitive but has a strong sense of justice. They both remind me of Steve in their own way." There was a catch in her voice. "Sorry, that's my former partner. He died after Ian's torrential outburst."

The name Ian stuck out like a forgotten memory. I couldn't place where I had heard it before—somewhere in my studies—but it didn't matter. Hearing Evie talk about her life added weight to the heavy shelf I had built inside my mind where I stored all my doubts. Too afraid to face my questions head-on, I often set them aside, hoping they would someday answer themselves or become irrelevant. But now I could hear the shelf splintering from the weight of it all, and I wasn't sure what I would do if it came crashing down.

"I'm very sorry about your loss," Bianca said somberly. "I can tell how much your family means to you."

I was reeling. How could Evie have a family? Were there really people living on the other side? Either Evie was lying, maybe delusional—or everything I had been told about her was wrong.

"My boys are my world," Evie said. "I would do anything for them."

"I'm sure they love you very much. You are a great leader for your people."

Evie laughed. "You speak like you know me."

"I do, in a way." As if she was carefully choosing her words, Bianca paused. "I've studied your life and know how much you worked to help your community. Your bravery in walking through the portal, not knowing if anyone would follow you, is inspiring. You're my hero."

A gust of wind rustled the leaves of a nearby maple. I strained my ears to hear. The silence seemed to speak to the effect of Bianca's words on Evie.

Bianca clearly had a distorted view of history, turning Evie from villain to hero, but I couldn't help but feel her sincerity as she spoke. No matter how wrong Bianca's beliefs were, at least they seemed genuine.

"I'm no hero," Evie finally said. "I abandoned so many, knowing Ian would continue to harm them. There's nothing heroic about it."

"That's not true," Bianca snapped back. "You gave those people a choice, leading by example when you took that uncertain leap. From what I've read, you were a courageous leader. I meant what I said: You're my hero.

"Because of you, I'm determined to help the people of New Freeda find the truth. When I get scared, I think of you. You give me courage."

"Thanks," Evie whispered. "Your words mean a lot. You remind me of Lucy in a way. I'm glad I'm here with you, no matter what happens."

Bianca's tone turned firm. "Evie, this is not the end. I promise I'll get you back to your people."

"And if you can't? What will they do to us?"

I knew what they were going to do, and it haunted me.

My eyes locked onto the moon outside my window as I contemplated the choice before me. It was wrong to go against the High Scribe, and I knew it. But I also knew Great was speaking to my heart, telling me to act. His spirit was showing me a different way—a better way. Maybe it was part of my test to prove my worthiness as a Scribe.

I focused on that idea rather than dwell on the looming thought that my father could be wrong. Either way, Great was using me to save Bianca and Evie, and I was determined to obey.

A DECREE FROM HIS HOLINESS

With a heavy heart, my duty as Great's chosen leader is to inform His children that Evie has returned through the Doorway of Death. This event was prophesied more than two thousand years ago, revealing the devil's success in these modern times.

As your High Scribe, I have communed with Great to know His will. It has been determined that we must re-enact the Sinner's Sacrifice. Offering the blood of the unworthy is our only hope of proving our faith, devotion, and worthiness.

The ceremony is in three days. We will broadcast the day's event from the Place of Origin. We desire all to witness our collective strength in renouncing the devil as we pray for Great's mercy. Until then, I send my blessings.

- Holy Scribe Josiah Zimran

CHAPTER 8
BIANCA'S PLAN

"Bianca? Are you still awake?" Evie's usually rich voice barely reached a whisper as it seeped through the stone wall that separated us.

"I am," I said.

It was late into the night and several hours since we had spoken about Evie's family. Earlier, we both stood at the front of our cages, unable to see more than glimpses of our fingers grasping the metal bars. Now I imagined Evie resting on a small cot in the back corner—just like me—hoping she had found some smidgen of comfort even though I had none.

I was still ruminating on Evie's words. The thought of her young boys missing their mother gutted me. After all, it was my fault Evie was here. I was so desperate to see her and prove the stories of her exile were lies that I didn't consider the consequences of pulling her through the portal. Now we were in separate cells, relying on each other's voices for company, and I began doubting everything I had planned.

"I can't sleep," Evie said. The words seemed caught in her throat, making me wonder if she had been crying. "I'm scared. What do you think they'll do to us?"

"It will be okay, I promise."

I tried to believe my own words. If things got bad, I had a last-ditch idea for getting us out, but I hoped it wouldn't come to that. I was still betting on Asaph to do the right thing and release us. Despite his justified distrust of me, I knew I could persuade his heart. There was a spark inside of him, ready to burn.

"Quiet!" a guard yelled. His echo ricocheted through the poorly lit hall. Just as the vibration of his command died down, the small bulb at the end of the tunnel—casting barely enough light to make out basic shapes—went dark. A dull thud hit the ground.

"Hey, who's there?" a second guard shouted, followed by another thud.

Muffled footsteps punctuated the otherwise eerie silence. I held my breath and moved closer to the bars.

"What's happening?" Evie whispered.

I strained my ears to assess the situation, but it was hard to hear over my nervous heartbeat. The only light now came from the dimly lit moon outside my cell's tiny window, making it even harder to know what was happening.

Pushing my head against the cage, I cranked my neck to see a shadowed body on the floor where the guard had stood. Another black shadow scurried toward me until a face popped through the bars. I jumped back, trying to make it out in the moonlight.

"Ace?"

"Shhhh…" Asaph said as he fumbled with something.

"What's going on?" Evie asked from the neighboring cell.

Clouds moved across the moon, masking what little light we had.

"Shoot. Where is it?" Jingling metal clanked from Asaph's coat pocket. "Ah, here we go." The dark outline of his arm reached toward the lock of my cell. The clouds drifted past the moon, allowing a moonbeam through again. An anxious grimace dressed Asaph's face. "More guards will be here any minute. We need to move quickly. Not a sound."

The adrenaline of the moment seeped into my muscles, energizing me despite the lack of sleep. Asaph pulled on the metal doors. A loud creak rang through the stony hallways. His hand clasped my arm, pulling me out of my cage. "Don't even think about running," he whispered.

"Who, me?" I couldn't help but push back a little, but his tightened grip quieted me.

Following Asaph to Evie's cell, I watched him wrangle with the massive keychain. His shaking hands fumbled, and the keys tumbled to the ground. Frantically, Asaph picked them up, trying to find the right one in the dark.

I glanced over at the guards on the ground. "Are they going to be okay?"

"Yeah, they'll be fine. Just sedated."

Ca-chunk.

A loud metal clang rippled down the hallway. My eyes instinctively pressed shut as a blinding light filled the basement. An angry voice quickly drowned out the buzz of overhead fluorescents.

"What the hell is going on here?"

I fought back the light as I pushed my eyes open. A young man with black hair dressed in a Scribe Guard uniform looked right past me. His deep brown eyes burrowed into Asaph.

"James? What—uh," Asaph said, clearly rattled. "It's not what it looks like."

My heart thumped harder against my ribs. Evie, stunned, retreated into the corner of her cell.

"It looks like you're breaking the prisoners out of jail," James said. "What I don't understand is *why?*"

Asaph grabbed my arm and pulled me behind him, placing himself in front of me like a shield. "Please, James. You need to trust me."

"You're not the one I'm worried about." James pointed to Evie, still locked up. "You know who that is, right? And *that* one —" he said, pointing to me, "—is the reason she's here. They both belong in jail."

"If people think the End of Days is near, what will happen? The chaos and fear will send everyone into a panic. I'm sending these women back through the portal. It's the only way to keep the peace. I've prayed about it and know this is Great's will."

It was unclear if Asaph was telling the truth or just what this James guy needed to hear to let us go. I had no intention of going through the portal, but if the story freed us, I'd go along.

The two men stared as if having an unspoken conversation. A familiarity among them seemed to go beyond their official titles. Distant sirens pierced the night air. With every second, they grew louder.

Asaph sighed. "Please, James."

"Run," the man said.

"But Evie," Asaph said, scrutinizing his keys again.

"You don't have time. Just go—*now*!"

Asaph shook his head. "James!"

"I said now! More guards are on their way. Go!"

Panic overwhelmed me at the thought of abandoning Evie. I reached for Asaph's keys. "We can't leave her!"

Asaph grabbed my arm, easily overpowering me as he dragged me toward the back exit. "It's too late," he muttered.

As we passed James, I could hear him whisper into Asaph's ear. "You know I trust you, man. But you better be sure about this. We're both risking a lot."

"I know," Asaph said with tenderness in his voice. "It's the only way. Believe me."

"I believe you believe Great," James said as he moved out of the way to let us pass.

We retreated deep into the dark hallway, which was much longer than I had expected. Asaph stopped at a small storage closet. The room had metal shelves full of cleaning supplies and other odds and ends. Asaph grasped the outside edges of the unit and pushed it to the right, revealing a small space behind it. A steel grate lined the floor inside the tiny nook. Asaph hoisted the heavy lid, holding it up while motioning me to go down the vent it had been covering.

"Are you serious?" Cobwebs stretched across the opening, leading into a black abyss. "I'm not going down there."

Asaph sighed and reached for something out of his back pocket. He clicked on a flashlight and handed it to me. The bright beam nearly blinded me. I pointed it down the small shaft. There was a small ladder that I hoped led to an actual path. "Hurry. Go!"

Reluctantly, I crouched and began my descent. We were already in the basement, so I reasoned it couldn't go much further down. Sure enough, 8 or 9 rungs later, my feet touched the ground. Taking careful steps, I extended my flashlight toward the only open space, revealing a long tunnel that stretched beyond what I could see. The sound of Asaph's feet hitting the ground made me feel a little safer. At least I wouldn't have to traverse this creepy passageway alone.

"Don't speak until I say so," Asaph whispered. "Sound can travel in odd ways in the Sanctum."

I quietly obeyed and let him take the lead. After the intrigue of a hidden alley, the walkout was pretty dull. Twenty minutes later, the stone pathway turned into a dirt road that gradually inclined toward the surface. The night sky and a cool breeze greeted us several blocks from the Sanctum in a forested patch of nature.

Asaph found a tree trunk and sat down. The weight of the situation pulled him forward as he rested his elbows on his knees. "Dammit," he muttered under his breath.

I carefully sat down next to him. "You okay, Ace?"

He straightened up, meeting my eyes. "No! Of course, I'm not okay! I've made things so much worse. Not only is Evie still locked up, but my best friend thinks I'm a traitor. How long until my father hears what I did? And *why* did I do it? Evie will still die, and odds are they'll catch us by morning."

"Whoa, slow down, buddy. Let's breathe," I said. "First of all, that James guy? He didn't seem like someone who'd rat you out. Don't assume the worst in people, especially not your friends."

I patted his leg. "Second, I'll take the blame if they catch us. I escaped once. It's not unreasonable that I could do it again. I'll tell them I forced you to come with me."

Asaph's shoulders relaxed. "Really? You'd do that."

"Eh, if we get caught, I'm screwed. No need to take you down with me."

"Thanks," he said.

"Don't thank me yet. There is still the whole *Evie is going to die* business. Can you please elaborate?"

Asaph closed his eyes, shaking his head. "How did this get so messed up?" His leg bounced as he ran his fingers through his hair.

"Ace." I snapped. "Focus. What did you mean when you said *Evie is going to die*?"

He inhaled sharply, biting his lips before releasing the air in one giant puff. "When Evie came through the Doorway of Death, it signaled the fulfillment of prophecy."

I nodded. "The End of Days—yes, I'm familiar."

"Okay, then you know pulling Evie into our world is a major deal. People will freak out."

"Maybe. Or maybe they'll realize the prophecy is ludicrous. Anyone who meets Evie will immediately see she's no threat."

Asaph scoffed. "Have you met people? Like actual people? They'll believe whatever they are told, assuming the right person is talking."

I stood, shoving my hands in my jacket pockets. "And I'm guessing your father will be talking."

"Yes. He has already planned to reinstate the Sinner's Sacrifice. He says it's Great's will, although my heart tells me Great has something else in mind. But that doesn't matter. I'm not the High Scribe. Dad is. And he's preparing to sacrifice you and Evie as a warning to everyone else."

"Yikes." I rocked back on my heels, nodding. "Another testament to Great's tender mercies, right? Destroy anything that doesn't align with the prescribed doctrine. You really believe this crap?"

"Stop it." Asaph's voice was unflinching. "Obviously, we don't see eye to eye on pretty much everything. But this *crap*—as you call it—is my whole life. Great's work gives me peace and purpose. My life has meaning because of Him."

"Sorry," I said softly.

My regret was instant. It was hard for me to give Asaph the reverence he demanded. I had seen too much trouble come from that kind of dangerous allegiance. Still, I knew debasing his faith wouldn't make him leave it. My mind wrestled with what to say, knowing it was up to me to persuade Asaph to keep helping me.

An owl's hoot floated along the breeze. As the winds died down, the silence grew awkward. I sat beside Asaph, summoning all my empathy, hoping my words would be enough.

"You have a special relationship with Great, and I appreciate your willingness to go against your father's orders to free me. That takes tremendous integrity."

"My dad is a good guy," Asaph said, sitting a little taller. "It's difficult being the one person everyone looks to for answers. He spends hours on his knees, speaking to Great and reading His words."

"Sure," I said half-heartedly.

Asaph stood and turned. His eyes drifted off to some unknown future. "But I think my father is wrong about this." He seemed almost afraid to speak the words. "I don't want death or panic to infiltrate New Freeda. Bringing back the Sinner's

Sacrifice will only create more fear. Sending you and Evie back through the portal is the best thing for everyone. I prayed and felt Great's spirit confirm it."

"Does this mean you no longer believe the portal is a literal doorway to death?"

Asaph's eyes flinched. "What? No, I didn't say that—" He rubbed his eyebrows, pushing away the growing tension in his forehead. His frustration was palpable. "I don't know, okay! Evie said she has a family there, so I guess it's safe. Or maybe not. Perhaps it's the easiest way to get rid of you guys. It's just—I think..." His words sputtered like an engine without gas.

"It's okay not to understand everything," I whispered.

Asaph slumped down next to me. "Not when people expect you to have the answers."

"You're a good guy, Ace. Saving my life? It was the right thing to do."

He looked at me, his face awash in regret. "So why did I get caught?"

I shrugged—a pathetic attempt to console him. My heart ached as I witnessed his struggle.

Asaph jumped to his feet again, pacing back and forth. His footprints created a chaotic scene in the dirt that matched his emotional state. "If Great wants this, why did I fail? Why didn't He ensure the escape of you *and* Evie?"

A dozen thoughts battled for attention. Asaph was in a delicate position, and I knew even the most rational answer could deflate his eagerness to follow me. So I went with the safest response. "Maybe there's more to Great's plan. There must be a reason."

"Maybe."

"Not maybe." I shot up and patted him on the back. "Do you trust Great?"

"Of course."

"Then trust His process. Great is using you for an even bigger purpose. I know it."

Asaph scoffed. "Okay, so what do we do next?"

I grabbed the backpack off his shoulder and unzipped it. I ruffled through the contents. There was a journal, pens, snacks, and water.

"Hey! What do you think you're doing?" Asaph grabbed the bag just as I found a small pamphlet at the bottom.

"What's this?" I ask, reading the cover. *"My Search for Answers."*

Asaph snatched it from my fingers. "That's personal. I didn't give you permission to search my stuff."

"Jeez, relax. I just wanted to see what you brought. Not much by the look of things."

"Sorry, I'm a terrible felon."

I laughed, happy to hear the hint of humor. "We'll need more help if we're going to break Evie free. We should head to Taprin."

Asaph froze. "Taprin? No way. We can't go there. It's completely off limits."

"So you've heard of it?"

"The derelict city created and infested with the most loathsome dissenters. Yes, I've heard of it."

I laughed. "Wow, tell me how you really feel."

"It's the absolute worst place," Asaph said, crossing his arms. "It's full of horrible people living the most unsavory kind of life. And it's forbidden for any believer to visit."

"Sheesh. Somebody's memorized the propaganda."

Asaph stood his ground. "I'm serious. I won't go—I'm already in enough trouble."

I placed a hand on his shoulder, locking eyes with him. "As I said, I'll take the blame for everything. But if we want to save Evie before she's sacrificed, we need help. Taprin has resources."

Running his fingers through his hair again, Asaph let out an exasperated sigh. "Fine. But the first sign of trouble, I'm out."

I chuckled. "I wouldn't expect anything less from you."

CHAPTER 9
HIDDEN FEARS

I HAD no intention of going to Taprin.

Thinking about it wasn't just uncomfortable; it was dark. Up until the moment Bianca had suggested heading to that heinous city, a comforting warmth had led me. Great guided me to help her escape. That was His plan. The assurance I was following His orders propelled me to act. Now, my gut was screaming to be careful.

Of course, I had hoped to bring both women with me, but that obviously wasn't in the cards. Still, Bianca was a problem that needed to be removed now. She could believe we were heading to Taprin if it meant getting rid of her. I was still planning on making a stop at the Doorway of Death. Bianca insisted it was a portal to freedom, and for her sake, I hoped she was right. But whether the gateway actually led to Evie's people was not my concern. Bianca's passage through the door meant peace for my people *and* freedom from a nagging dissenter.

We walked along a dirt path covered by a canopy of trees. The distant sirens at the Sanctum faded as we moved away from the town center. James's disappointed expression seared into my mind, which was already a tangled mess of fear and shame. No matter how Bianca tried to comfort me, insisting this setback was part of Great's plan, internally, I was berating myself for leaving without Evie. She was right there. I could have freed her if I had just one more minute.

"Do you know where you're going?" Bianca said as we moved further into the shadows of the forest.

I flinched as a twig snapped underfoot. My frayed nerves made every sight, sound, and smell a threat. "Away from the Sanctum."

Bianca sighed, pressing on. "Okay, so do you know how to reach Taprin?"

"Of course I do," I shot back.

It was only partially true. The city was a six-hour drive south of New Freeda. But my navigation skills were subpar. Beyond the city center, I was useless with directions since I always had access to a car and driver. My job was to know and understand the Ancient Scrolls, not memorize routes to the most wicked city in the world.

"Well, unless you plan on walking for a few weeks, I suggest we take the train." Bianca hopped on a large boulder and looked up at the stars. She shook her head and pointed. "The station is in the opposite direction."

"There will be too many people there. It doesn't seem safe."

"It's easier to hide in a crowd, trust me." A satisfied smirk spread across her face, making me think Bianca had too much experience as a fugitive. "Besides, what other option do we have?"

"Fine," I said, throwing my arms up. "Lead the way. Just be careful."

Bianca bulldozed past me, taking big strides back toward the town center. "Tell me," she said, ducking under branches and maneuvering between large boulders. "What was your plan for this genius escape of yours? The train station wasn't on your agenda. Did you really think we'd walk our way out of New Freeda?"

I did my best to keep up. Bianca's confidence as she led the way was both grating and impressive. A part of me was glad to let her take charge, even if I was annoyed with her constant line of questioning.

"I hadn't gotten that far," I admitted. "My first concern was getting away from the Sanctum. I figured Great would guide me after that."

Bianca rolled her eyes, and I tried not to be offended.

"You know," she said, "there's a saying I think would help you."

"What's that?"

"If you fail to plan, you plan to fail."

I scoffed. "I had a plan. It just ended with us escaping."

Bianca laughed. "Oh, okay. My bad."

I ran ahead and stopped her. "Hey, that's not fair. It's not like you're some mastermind. I mean, who gets jailed twice in one week?"

She pushed past me with a smile. "Maybe that's what I wanted."

Now it was my turn to roll *my* eyes. "Right," I said, my voice dripping with sarcasm. "How could I have thought otherwise?"

Bianca whipped around. "Listen, Ace. You have no idea who I am or what I'm trying to do. So don't accuse me of failing to plan because, believe it or not, I'm happy with how things are going."

"Bullshit!"

Surprised and slightly satisfied, Bianca smiled. "Wow, I didn't think the Scribes used such language."

My cheeks turned bright red. "Well, technically, I'm not a Scribe yet."

"Ah, so you've got a little time left to be rebellious." She flipped back around and continued marching forward. "Good. We're going to need some disobedience if we want to succeed."

A familiar sinking feeling twisted my gut. "No, that's not what I meant. It's just that—well, I'm not perfect, okay? Sometimes I swear or fall asleep without doing my nightly prayers."

"And sometimes you occasionally disobey the High Scribe and help a heinous sinner escape the just consequences of her sins." Bianca's interruption was meant to be lighthearted, but the bitter truth of her statement stung.

I folded my arms, tugging my jacket around my body, and forged ahead. The sound of crunching leaves underfoot punctuated the silence between us.

"Sorry, that was uncalled for," Bianca said quietly. "For what it's worth, nobody is perfect. Recognizing your flaws is a sign of good leadership. You'll make a great Scribe, I'm sure."

Her words drifted off with the night breeze. I didn't want the approval of a dissenter, so I didn't need to respond. Anger festered at the corner of my mind as I remembered this whole mess started with Bianca's break-in. I couldn't let her slip into my thoughts, no matter how reassuring her words were at the moment. She was not my friend.

As we neared the edge of the forest, I could hear noise from the train platform. It was about fifteen blocks away from the Sanctum. The distance gave me a moment of relief until I realized the station was probably the first place the Scribe Guards would check.

"How is this going to work?" I asked. "I have no cash, and other forms of payment can be traced back to me."

We stopped at the backside of the ticket office, its brick wall blocking us from the view of anyone on the platform.

"Don't worry about it. I've got it covered. Here," Bianca said as she handed me the flashlight. "Shine it this way."

She ran her fingers along the building, stopping about a third of the way across. She smiled as a brick wiggled loose. Checking over her shoulder and then focusing back on the block, she pushed one side in, forcing the other to extrude outward. A pile of cash fell out as she pulled the brick from the wall. Bianca stuffed the money in her bag before picking up what looked like a booklet of forged train tickets. "This should get us there."

I couldn't decide if I was impressed or disgusted. "Why do you have all this? Just how much trouble are you in?"

Bianca flashed a quick smile before handing me a ticket. "Enough."

We crept along the station's perimeter, staying crouched below the platform. It was early morning, so the station wasn't too busy. A couple of dozen people were waiting for the 5:00 AM train.

"The southbound train arrives in one minute," an automated voice declared over the PA system.

"That's our cue. We got to go," Bianca said, hopping onto the platform.

"Wait!" I pulled her back, catching her before she hit the ground.

"What are you doing? We need to get on the train!"

I covered her mouth and pointed toward the ticket booth with my other hand. Two officers meandered through the crowd, checking each passenger before investigating the next. "Scribe Guards. What do we do?" My voice was quiet but panicky as sweat dripped down my neck.

Bianca remained calm even as a dull rumble from the tracks grew louder. The small headlight in the distance became larger with every second. "We'll need to time this just right. Follow my lead."

The roar of the approaching train pulsated in my chest as it came to a screeching stop. "What's the plan?"

"Get ready to jump on my mark. Head for the back cart." Bianca reached down and picked up a large stone. With an impressive thrust, she flung it through the ticket booth window. The sound of shattering glass trumped the low rumble of the idling engine. "Go! Now!"

The broken window distracted the guards, allowing us to get to the train. Weaving through the crowds, we looked as casual as possible. With our heads down, we handed our tickets to the conductor and found a seat near the back. The next few minutes were tense as we watched the security team scramble outside. One guard nearly boarded but was left standing on the platform as the doors closed and the train moved forward.

When it finally seemed that we had made it without detection, I sighed and allowed my shoulders to relax. "That was close."

"They never had a chance," Bianca said. She sank into her seat, folding her arms and resting her head against the window. "Now get some rest. We've got a few hours to kill."

"Get some rest? Are you serious right now?"

Bianca kept her eyes closed. "Of course I'm serious. It's been a rough day. We need sleep."

"What's wrong with you?" I didn't mean to yell, but I couldn't help myself.

"Shhhh!" she said as her eyes popped open. "Do you want everyone to hear you?"

I lowered my voice but kept it firm. "Seriously, what's wrong with you? Why are you doing this? Do you realize what you've done? Do you understand the stress and fear you've created in my life since you came crashing into it? I'm the one who saved you from imminent death, and you're acting like you're doing me some favor by dragging me to the most wretched place in the world."

Bianca's lips pressed firmly against one another as her eyes drilled into me. "Are you done?"

A righteous indignation swelled within my belly at Bianca's lack of remorse. I hated that my good intentions made me an anxious mess while her steady confidence grew more stable with every reckless decision. I wanted her to feel the shame and weight of her actions, and instead, I was the one crippled by guilt.

We sat silent, staring at one another like some weird game of chicken. But the more I looked into Bianca's eyes, the more my anger faded. It was like she was tuning my emotions, tweaking and adjusting them until my rage turned to curiosity. I wanted to understand what she wasn't telling me. While every logical thought in my brain told me to shut Bianca out, all I wanted to do was drink her in.

Bianca sat still, waiting for my torrential thoughts to calm.

When I finally spoke, my words were gentle and earnest. "Who are you? What's the endgame here?"

"I'm just a girl, Ace. I'm not the villain everyone thinks I am. Like you, I'm just trying to make sense of this world and doing what I can to make it a little better."

"By making my life miserable?" I said with a slight chuckle.

She laughed. "That's not my intention, and I'm truly sorry for being such a pain in the ass."

"Are you? I think you enjoy breaking every rule in the book."

"Have you ever asked yourself if the rules are worth following?"

Wringing my hands together, I tried to push away the knot in my stomach. "I don't know any other way."

"Mmmm," Bianca said with a nod. "I used to be bound by rules, too. I spent every minute worrying about other people's thoughts, living up to all their impossible expectations." She caught my eye. "It's not easy."

"Tell me about it," I said.

Bianca smiled. "And maybe that's why I keep dragging you into my mess. On the outside, my actions seem dangerous and reckless. But I only break things that need fixing. People may turn me into a villain because of it, but that's the cost of change sometimes. And while it sucks letting people down, it's also incredibly freeing to live life on your terms. Deep down, I think you know it."

Shaking my head, I sighed. "I don't mean to disappoint you, but I'm not the rebel you want me to be. I'll do my best to save Evie, but I won't promise anything beyond that."

Bianca nodded, meditating on my words. "Do you trust me, Ace?"

My heart stopped at my gut reaction to say *yes*. I swallowed hard. "I trust you believe you're doing the right thing, no matter how misguided your actions are, but I refuse to go against Great's word."

"You realize that by helping me—just by listening to me—you're going against His words." Bianca didn't wait for a response. Instead, she leaned against the window again and closed her eyes.

I wanted to make sense of the emotions swirling inside of me. No matter how hard I tried, I couldn't escape Bianca's pull. It wasn't love or infatuation that grabbed my attention. Instead, it was her tenacious certainty that held me captive. She didn't presume to have all the answers, but there was an unshakable conviction that truth was available to those who dared look for it. Suddenly, I realized my greatest fear wasn't that Bianca would corrupt me.

I was terrified she was the only one who could save me.

MESSAGE FROM LUCY FERNÁNDEZ

THU, JAN 19

Was that you outside Haven Burgers? I tried to get your attention. I'm guessing you didn't hear me. Although, I'm sure you did.

SAT, JAN 28

Ian, are you going to ignore me forever?

CHAPTER 10
BIANCA AT THE DOOR

"Bianca, wake up."

My eyes popped open, surprised to see Asaph hovering over me.

"We need to leave—*now*."

I sat up, trying to rub away the grogginess. "We're at Taprin already?"

"No, we're at the Hadston stop."

"I don't understand."

Asaph pulled me to my feet, keeping his voice low. "Two Scribe Guards just boarded. They're in the front cart, heading our way. We need to go." He grabbed his bag and peered down the aisle to ensure nobody was coming.

My heart raced as I glanced out the window, still trying to orient myself.

"The Place of Origin isn't too far. We can hide there for now," Asaph said, grabbing my shoulders and leading me from behind. "It's our safest bet."

"I don't know, Ace." I leaned into him, my voice barely above a whisper. "You told James you planned to take us back through the doorway. They'll probably have guards there waiting for us. Why else would they be here?"

"As you said, James wouldn't rat me out. I trust him."

We hurried toward the back exit, carefully scanning the crowd before disappearing into it. I held my breath as we maneuvered through the rush of people trying to get onto the outgoing train. Asaph led me past the congested platform, breaking from the paved road onto a dirt alleyway between two old buildings. We weaved toward the outskirts of town, heading away from the crowded city.

The city of Hadston shared a border with the Place of Origin and was about two-thirds of the way to Taprin. The town itself was run down, dirty, and crowded. But it did have one claim to fame that put it on the map: The Wall of Remembrance.

Situated just outside the southern perimeter of the Place of Origin, the Wall of Remembrance was a sacred destination spot. Hundreds of believers came daily, offering prayer, song, and gifts.

Before the Place of Origin's border was raised and fortified, one could stand at the wall and see the Ancient Altar in the distance. But now, the barrier was too tall to see into the city.

Still, people trekked to the Wall of Remembrance, forced to use their imagination as they made their own kind of offering. It became a metaphor for their faith. The Wall was the poor man's altar—a symbolic entrance to the holy city despite being a literal barricade.

The train station was a few blocks from the sacred spot, but we could hear the worshipper's layered chanting from the platform. Prayers saturated the atmosphere, and a pulsating chorus of hymns and recitations provided an eerie soundtrack to our escape. As we headed north—away from the congregation of believers— their pleads dimmed, leaving behind the quiet solitude of nature.

Asaph said little as we trekked toward the Place of Origin's northern entrance. With focused energy, he kept a steady pace. We stayed near the trees and foliage, avoiding the open road that ran parallel to the wall without losing sight of it as we circumvented the city perimeter.

After nearly thirty minutes of silence, I looked over my shoulder, ensuring nobody else was around. "What's on your mind?"

"Nothing." Asaph sighed and then muttered, "And *everything.*"

I sped up, shortening the distance between us. "Like what?"

"Oh, I don't know. I was just thinking about the last few days —my botched offering, Evie's return, and your irritating confidence. All while simultaneously trying to forget that the End of Days is upon us."

I scoffed. "It's not the End of Days."

"And why would I believe you? You're the last person I'd trust. My life has been a chaotic mess ever since you showed up."

"Yeah, sorry about that."

Asaph stopped and turned. "We both know you're not actually sorry. Your intentional recklessness is proof enough that you're bad."

"I'm not being reckless," I protested as I placed my hand on his shoulder. He pushed it away. "And I *am* sorry—maybe not how you'd like, but I'm sorry I've made things hard for you."

Asaph slowly lifted his head, eying me with suspicion before continuing onward. "The Scribe entrance shouldn't be far."

There was something Asaph wasn't telling me. He was obviously battling with an idea in his mind, and I had a good guess what it was. We weren't going inside the Place of Origin to hide. Instead, Asaph was doing precisely what he told James he intended to: Get rid of me by sending me through the portal.

I just wasn't sure Asaph had the guts to do it.

When we reached the Scribe entrance, we carefully surveyed the surrounding area to ensure nobody was waiting to ambush us. The giant gates dwarfed our presence. Once inside, the overgrown bushes and crumbling edifices spoke to the longevity and neglect of a city that had once been the center of the world. I imagined Evie living among the people and cringed, thinking about her being locked in jail.

We stopped at a small stone wall that hadn't completely crumbled. I slid down the side with my back against it, relieved to sit for a moment. "You know, I could just hang back here if you want to do your thing at the altar."

The statement woke Asaph from his inner dialogue. "What thing?"

"Your offering—the thing you were about to do when I showed up the other day."

"Oh."

The suggestion took a moment to sink in. When it finally did, Asaph shook his head. "I'm not leaving you alone," he said. "Nice try."

I shrugged. "Have it your way. I just figured you'd be eager to commune with Great. But if you think you can do this alone, so be it."

"I know what you're doing."

"What?"

"You're playing me—hoping to exploit my faith so you can break free."

Jumping to my feet, I stepped closer to Asaph. "If I had wanted to break free, I would have done it already." I took another step, my face inches away from his. "And you have no clue what I'm doing."

He took a step back.

"But unlike you," I said, leaning in further, "I know what you're up to, Ace."

Asaph scoffed. "Oh yeah? Enlighten me."

"We're not here to hide. You're here to send me through the doorway."

His pupils rocked back and forth as if scanning my face, searching for an accurate reading of my emotions. But I stood steady even while the tension in Asaph's chest grew rigid. I couldn't tell if he was scared or defiant, but I was clearly right.

"So what are you going to do about it?" he whispered.

"Nothing." I shrugged. "If that's why we're here, let's do it."

"Wait, what? Are you serious?"

"Absolutely." I grabbed his bag from the ground, flung it over my shoulder, and marched toward the city's edge where the Doorway of Death stood.

"Bianca! Stop!" Asaph ran up, swiping the backpack from me. "What aren't you telling me? Why are you here? Why are you in my life? The break-in, bringing Evie back, Taprin—*what is your plan?*"

I whipped around. "I'm here to help people learn the truth."

Asaph sneered. "Yeah, you said that. And yet, all you've really done is interfere with *my* life."

"Yes! Because *you* are the key."

The color in his face drained. "What are you talking about? Key to what?"

"It doesn't matter now," I said, pushing past him. "You came here for a reason, so let's do it." I turned the corner, and the black arch came into view. I stopped before the ring of spikes and held my arms out to Asaph. "Go ahead."

Asaph's eyes grew large, his eyebrows lifting with confusion. "And do what?"

"Push me through the Doorway of Death. Come on now—throw me overboard! Get rid of me and get on with your life."

A powerful gust of wind jostled my hair while a flock of birds zoomed above our heads as I stood my ground. If Asaph wanted me gone, he needed to be the one to make it happen, but he didn't budge. Instead, he seemed frozen in a catatonic state driven by fear and not the determination he so desperately wanted.

I stepped closer, offering my hands one more time. "Well?"

Asaph looked down, wrapping his fingers around my wrists. His eyes darted toward the black arch and then back to me. I swear I could hear his heart thumping against his chest as his grip tightened. He pulled me in, inhaling sharply before pushing me away.

"I can't," he said.

"Why not?"

Asaph's eyes darted toward me. "Because I'm not a killer!"

"Ace! Open your eyes. You saw Evie come through the portal unharmed. You can't still think this is an actual doorway to death."

"Great prophesied of Evie's return. I don't have to understand the mechanics of it to trust His ways. I have read the Scrolls countless times, and this *thing*," he said, pointing to the invisible portal, "is a punishment, not an escape plan!"

"Well, don't I deserve to be punished? Haven't I done enough to prove my insolence for Great's commands?"

"Probably. But I won't make that call. If you want to go, do it. I will not force you!" Asaph's face twisted in frustration. He kicked a rock and paced along the dirt path. Simultaneously tormented yet relieved by his decision, he refused to meet my gaze.

With a heavy sigh, I shook my head. "There weren't any guards on the train."

Asaph shoved his hands deep into his pockets. "Nope."

"It was all just part of your plan to get me here."

"Yep." He plopped down on a fallen tree trunk.

I walked closer, trying to meet his downward gaze. Asaph's eyes caught mine as if to apologize for his outburst. He scooted to the right, making room for me on his makeshift bench.

"It means a lot that you wouldn't send me through the doorway," I said, sitting beside him.

Asaph shook his head. "Don't flatter yourself. It's not about you. I refuse to go against Great's will. Murder is kind of at the top of his lists of sins."

"Hmmm," I said, nodding my head slowly. "I see. So, where do you draw the line?"

"What line?"

"The line that separates the sins you refuse to commit from the ones you're okay doing?"

Asaph leaned back, his face pinching inward. "Excuse me?"

"I mean, you helped me escape after the High Scribe called for my death. You lied about the Guards on the train. And now you've brought a wicked dissenter into the holiest city. Aren't those things against Great's will?"

"Stop it," Asaph said, gritting his teeth. He stood, staring down at me.

The following silence seemed heavy with importance as he grabbed his bag and stormed away. I followed as he walked the dirt path that led to the Ancient Altar. He moved with purpose as if suddenly compelled by an idea. There was a shift in his mood —his defensiveness morphed into determination. Dropping his backpack on a rock, he methodically climbed the altar's stairs. Halfway up, he paused, looking out past the city walls.

Asaph gazed out to the horizon. "Only a handful of people have seen this view in the last thousand years." His sudden, gentle tone made me think he was talking to himself more than me.

I stepped closer, but Asaph raised his hand, telling me to stay down. Reluctantly, I obeyed. "What do you see?"

"It's a beach—beautiful and untouched by man. One of Great's oldest commands was to stay off its shores. We don't know why, only that He demands it."

I closed my eyes, trying to hear the waves in the distance, but it was useless. The rustling leaves and chirping birds masked any signs of the beach beyond the border walls.

There were few records of the forbidden shores, but I had

learned more than the average citizen about its place in history. I was curious how much Asaph knew. "Has anyone disobeyed that order? Has anyone ever stepped foot on the beach?"

Asaph's eyes landed on me. "One person," he said, annoyed that I would bring it up.

I tipped my head and smiled. "Evie."

He half-nodded and gazed back toward the shoreline. The view transfixed him, acting like a balm for the growing dissonance plaguing him inside.

I'm not a bad person, no matter what anyone may believe. There was no joy in watching Asaph's latent doubts bubble to the surface. I hated his pain and wished there was another way, but like I had told Asaph, he was the key. As I watched him stand silently with the torment building inside, I was more sure of it than ever. The best kind of revolution starts from within the system of oppression.

Most people just don't realize how often that oppression is self-inflicted.

"Ace? Why do you think Great forbids people from going on the beach?"

Asaph walked down the stairs and sat next to his bag. "It's not our place to understand Great's will unless He wants us to know it."

He closed his eyes, burying his face in his hands. I averted my gaze to give him a sense of privacy.

Something shiny caught my attention as I scanned the area below the altar. Dozens, maybe hundreds, of glittering objects stood tangled in the long grass, shimmering under the sunlight. My mouth was ajar, eyes wide open as I investigated all the discarded treasures—jewels, gold pieces, and other priceless things. With a quick glance to ensure Asaph wasn't looking, I bent over and filled my pockets with a handful of coins.

I cleared my throat and made my way back. "Ace? Have you seen this?" I asked, pointing to the cluttered field. "What happened here? Did someone drop their treasure chest or something?"

"Those are past offerings—a testament to the Scribes' continual sacrifice. We give Him our best so He can give us His."

"There's got to be millions of dollars worth of stuff here. Don't you think Great could use this wealth for something important?"

Asaph exhaled loudly. "We don't re-gift that which we give to Great. He gave us everything. Don't you think He deserves our best?"

"Sure, but... come on! Think how many people this could help!" I knew the Scribes lived a luxurious life while many worried about their next meal, but this kind of wealth hoarding was beyond my comprehension.

"The best way to help people is to ensure they're following Great's commands. You can't put a price on eternal life. Even a mortal lifetime of suffering is worth that most precious gift."

"But why can't we have both? Why must some suffer while you and the Scribes have it easy?"

Asaph's patience with my questions was thinning, but he didn't stop me, so I continued.

"It just doesn't make sense," I said. "Have you seen the people at the Wall of Remembrance? Have you seen the multitudes clamoring to offer their love and gifts to their creator? Do you understand *their* sacrifice? If Great is so wonderful, why can't He find a better way?"

"Enough!" Asaph stood and faced me. "I've had it with your questions, Bianca! Why do you insist on pulling at every loose thread, hellbent on unraveling my faith? Can't you leave things alone?"

The intensity in his eyes grabbed my throat, making it impossible to respond.

"I can't keep doing this," he said, shaking his head. "It's too hard. I have a responsibility to Great, to my people. You shouldn't be here, and I shouldn't be around you. You say you want to show people the truth, but all you've done is cloud my soul with confusion. I just—"

Asaph's voice cracked, his emotions cutting him off. He slumped down and buried his face in his hands. Tears fell. His chest shook with heavy sobs. I carefully crouched beside him, wrapping my arm around his shoulder. He leaned in, releasing the exhaustion and frustration from the past few days.

"Please," he whispered after a few minutes, "tell me why you are here or just leave me alone."

For a while, we sat while Asaph cried, and I bore witness. It seemed important to hold the space for him. I wanted to take his burden away. I wanted to get him past his pain, but the only way out was through.

After several minutes, I finally responded to his request. "You want me to tell you why I'm here?"

Asaph nodded. "Please."

With a heavy sigh, I grabbed Asaph's bag and took his hand, pulling him to his feet. "Well, I can't tell you. Words won't be enough." The glimmer of jewels caught my eye again, and a smile spread across my face. "But I will show you."

CHAPTER 11
EYES OPENED

As the son of a Scribe, I was born into tremendous privilege. My childhood home was spacious—filled with modern amenities and luxuries the average person would never enjoy. I was six when Dad became the High Scribe after the death of High Scribe Bastian. With his new title, the benefits only increased. We moved into the mansion where my parents still lived. The best teachers, countless hours of extracurricular instruction at the hands of masters, and expensive vacations gave me a rarified life.

I knew I had it better than most. Sometimes I even felt guilty about what I was born into. But then I'd watch my dad. As the High Scribe, his life was not his own. He spent countless hours reading ancient artifacts and spreading Great's word throughout the land. Strict and sometimes foreboding, Dad's powerful presence resulted from a life of service. Sure, there were perks to being a Scribe—advantages I was fortunate to enjoy as his offspring. But as my ordination grew near, I realized those benefits were trinkets compared to the sacrifice of giving yourself entirely to Great's work.

My life would never be my own.

It was a fact I accepted, mostly because I didn't know any other way. Nearly everyone I knew had some connection to the Scribedom. While I may have been a notch or two higher than my peers, everyone in my social circle had a good life. I was always told our privilege was a reward for our obedience. Stories of poverty or hardship were bedtime warnings of what would happen if you slipped off the path. It's easy to believe you've earned your luck when you're told prosperity is the consequence of belief.

That theory crumbled the day Bianca led me into the town of Hadston.

"Tell me again why we're doing this?" I asked as I walked behind Bianca. She had barely said two words since she dragged me away from the Place of Origin.

"You said you wanted to know what I'm doing, right?"

I tripped on a crack on the sidewalk, nearly crashing into a stranger. "Yes," I said, trying to find my feet again.

Technically, I had been to Hadston before. Its northern fields bordered the Scribe entrance into the Place of Origin, an area off-limits to the average person. So until Bianca and I arrived by train earlier that morning, I had no idea the city was so crowded —or depressing.

It didn't take long to see the economic chasm that separated me from the people of Hadston. Maybe my faith had blinded me from the reality of their world. It was easy to blame them for their ungodly circumstances from the comfort of my home. Now that their prayers and chants filled a nine-block radius, it was clear the people believed in Great. Walking the streets, a familiar air of judgment tried to pull me back into my bubble, but I knew there was no way to justify the gap between their lives and mine.

My head throbbed from the city noise as I followed Bianca past the train station. Street vendors yelled at children hoping to steal an apple or loaf of bread. Honking and vulgarities echoed from the traffic-lined streets.

Pulling the hood of my jacket over my head and tucking my arms into one another, I tried to make myself small. As Junior Scribe, I didn't do public appearances like other Scribes. The possibility of anyone recognizing me was slim, but I couldn't help but feel like a spotlight illuminated me with every step, even as I felt lost in a never-ending sea of people.

I tapped Bianca's shoulder. "Can you slow down a bit?"

"No." She glanced back with a satisfied smile. "I'm here to open your eyes."

"Open my eyes to what?" I dodged a garbage bin only to bump into the person digging through it. I apologized and lengthened my stride as I ran up next to Bianca. "My eyes are open. This town is a dump. Someone should clean it up."

Bianca stopped, and I nearly plowed into her. "Great idea. I bet nobody has thought of that. Who should we talk to about it?"

"I don't know. The city magistrate or a clean-up crew?"

"Okay. Who decides the funds that support those people? Who has the final say in all things?"

My cheeks went hot. I bit my lip and shook my head. "Ah, I see." I could feel Bianca judging me. "It's convenient to blame the Scribes for everything. They may call the shots, but plenty of people under them have delegated power. You can't expect the Scribes to do it all."

A couple of inebriated men yelled across the street. The taller of the two threw a punch, missing his target and toppling over a fruit stand.

Bianca snapped her fingers, demanding my attention. "Tell me, Ace. How are the streets where you live?"

She knew the answer. New Freeda was pristine. Clean roads, shiny buildings, and perfectly maintained parks made it as close to heaven as possible. I always heard my father speak with great pride about our city, often praising the dedicated leaders who kept it so beautiful.

But it was Dad's underhanded comments I wasn't supposed to hear that suddenly surfaced in my mind. On more than one occasion, I had overheard him negotiating funds or borrowing resources from other towns to add another temple or Scribe estate to New Freeda. Who knew how often those conversations happened when I wasn't around?

Then there was the purging of sinners. New Freeda had a zero-tolerance policy for criminals, which included dissenters. I always assumed it was more bark than bite. I imagined you'd have to do something really awful to get kicked out. Still, as I looked around, I wondered how many people in Hadston were just New Freeda's unwanted fruits.

Anytime I caught a whiff of Dad abusing his power like that, I reminded myself I didn't know the big picture. But really, I just hated thinking about it, preferring to focus on the positive. The world was complicated, and I was smart enough to know there were no easy solutions, so why bother worrying about it? But now that I was knee-deep in the messy consequences, I couldn't just ignore the glaring inequality.

I sighed, finally meeting Bianca's gaze. "What do you want me to see?"

"No, you got it right. I want you to see the mess here," Bianca said, her smile fading. "I want you to smell the stench, hear the noise, and feel the despair. It's all part of the plan." She grabbed me by the shoulders, moving me toward the city center.

A siren a few streets over rang in my ear. The smell of urine stung my nose. And ten feet in front of me, a woman offered a few dollars to a man huddled under a cardboard box just as some ruddy teenager grabbed the cash and ran off.

"I think I've seen enough," I said flatly.

"Great. Let's meet the people." Bianca grabbed my arm and marched forward. She reached into her pocket, pulled out a few gold coins, tapped the woman's shoulder, and dropped them in her hand.

The woman's eyes lit up at the gift, giving me a clear view of her face. Immediately, my stomach flipped as my heart seized. A lump in my throat caught my words before sputtering in disbelief.

"Paige?"

Paige's steel-blue eyes settled on mine, and my legs went numb. I couldn't believe she was standing in front of me. Her strawberry blonde hair was longer than when I last saw her. Pulled back into a braid, it draped over her shoulder. She was thinner, nearly drowning in the overside plum blouse she wore.

"Asaph?" Paige's voice trailed off. She pushed a strand of hair from her face, revealing a small X tattooed on her wrist. As soon as Paige saw me looking at it, she tugged on her sleeves, hiding it from view. "I didn't expect to see you here."

"Same." My mind raced through a million thoughts, riding the waves of a thousand emotions. Why was Paige in Hadston instead of New Freeda? Was she happy to see me? Should I hug her? Shake her hand? Or should I walk away and pretend nothing happened? My body was paralyzed with indecision until an intense longing washed it all away, leaving me hopelessly afraid to move—terrified of losing her again.

Bianca swooped in. "Hey, I'm Bianca."

Paige snapped out of her daze, shaking Bianca's hand. "Paige," she said with a weak smile. She held up the coins Bianca had given her. "And thank you for this."

Turning to the old man, Paige placed the coins in his hand. A warm smile spread across her face as she whispered in his ear. Paige turned back, gesturing toward a small outdoor cafe with a tin roof across the street. "Care for some tea?"

Bianca glanced back at me as we followed Paige's lead. "So, how do you two know each other?"

My eyes froze on Paige as she sat down at a small table. "Uh, Paige was my—"

"Friend," Paige interjected carefully.

"Yeah, friend." My heart shattered at the word. Whatever lingering feelings I had, it was clear Paige had severed any attachment. Then again, maybe she never really cared the way I did. After all, she was the one who didn't want to get married.

Still, Paige's eyes stayed focused on me, and despite the unromantic label she attached to our relationship, there was kindness in them. Maybe she didn't love me as I loved her. Perhaps she never did. But she didn't hate me, and for now, that was enough.

Bianca's eyes darted between Paige and me, trying to piece together our history. "Are you originally from Hadston, Paige? How did you guys meet? I didn't think Asaph had made it this far south before."

Paige's cheeks turned bright red. "No, he probably hasn't. I'm sure he's too busy preparing for his ordination." She turned toward Bianca, forcing a smile. "I'm originally from New Freeda."

The truth suddenly hit me like a boulder from above. Nobody willingly moved to Hadston. It was a place for outcasts and desperate seekers of miracles. Its reputation was only slightly better than Taprin's. What was Paige doing here? As the niece of former Scribe Joleth, educated and refined, there was no way her family would have disowned her. She must have chosen to be here, but why?

A waitress interrupted my train of thought. She dropped some tea off at our table and took our lunch orders. With a slow sip, the warm liquid soothed my throat but left my anxiety untouched. Then Bianca, in her usual recklessness, made it worse.

"Ever been to Taprin?" Bianca asked, tapping her mug and eying Paige.

I nearly choked on my drink.

Paige avoided my eyes. "I have."

"What?" The word spilled out before I could stop it. "Paige! How could you?"

"You can't believe everything you've heard about Taprin," Paige said defensively. "It's not terrible."

"And what about this dump, huh?" I gestured to the surrounding city. "Is this okay, too? Dammit, Paige."

"Ace, come on. Don't be an ass," Bianca said quietly.

"No, I want to know. Did you hate me so much that you chose this life over me?"

Paige stood, straightening her shirt. "You don't know what you're talking about. I'd choose your next words carefully. You may regret them."

I jumped to my feet, eyes zeroed in on Paige.

"Ace," Bianca said, grabbing my shoulders. "Relax, buddy."

"I just want her to answer my question."

"I don't hate you!" Paige yelled. "Jeez, Asaph. Get a clue. I didn't choose to move here. I was kicked out of New Freeda."

The chatter around the cafe died. I could feel every eyeball on us—so much for staying out of the spotlight. My voice cracked as I tried to get the words out. "What do you mean?"

Paige grabbed my arm, whisking us away from the crowd. Bianca followed behind.

"My family kicked me out," Paige whispered. "They sent me away."

"Why?" My mind was reeling, trying to understand what she was saying. Paige had always been faithful to Great's commands. Her story didn't add up.

We moved around the corner, hidden from the crowded streets. Bianca stood silent, giving us enough space to talk but still close enough to hear everything.

Biting her lip, Paige tilted her head. "Why do you think, Asaph?" With a heavy sigh, she blinked back tears. "Because I refused to marry you. I turned down the chance to be a Scribe's wife."

My heart was racing. "I don't understand," I said, leaning in closer. "How did they find out? I didn't tell anyone you refused me, I swear. I always spun the story as a mutual breakup."

"I believe you, but I'm sure the story looks different from the outside. My family was counting on me marrying you. When it didn't happen, no matter what you may have told others, they blamed me for not being worthy enough."

The pain in her eyes broke me, and I tried piecing myself together to make sense of it all. Even if her family believed it was Paige's fault, it wasn't enough to justify being kicked out of her home. There had to be more to the story. I reached for Paige's hand, grazing her fingers before pulling back. "Paige, I'm so sorry."

Paige brushed away a tear. "It's okay. Really. I know it sounds bad," she said with a slight scoff. "I know it *looks* bad, but I've learned to love my life—no matter how many times I wondered about the life I might have had with you." Her eyes settled on me, giving me hope that there was more meaning behind her words.

"So then... why didn't—" My voice caught before I could finish the question. I was too afraid I'd hate the answer. Shaking my head, I grounded myself, remembering where we were. "All I want is for you to be happy."

"Thank you. I am."

I shook my head, unwilling to believe her. "How can anyone be happy living here?"

"Maybe if you got to know it better," Bianca said, inserting herself into the conversation.

I rolled my eyes, irritated at having my reunion with Paige spoiled by Bianca's cryptic agenda. "Oh, goody. More vague ideas from this one."

"Ace, see beyond your world. You haven't been told the truth about everything. And it seems pretty obvious that you're not keen on believing me. But maybe you'll believe her." Bianca turned to face Paige. "What do you say? Will you be our guide to Taprin? There's someone who needs our help, and I have a feeling Taprin can assist."

Paige looked back at me with a concerned frown before speaking to Bianca. "Can we chat for a moment?"

The two women walked away, whispering. A sideways glance from Paige gave little insight into their discussion, but it was clear the matter was serious. Perhaps Bianca was filling her in about Evie and the End of Days prophecy. I still wasn't convinced Taprin could solve either problem, but I couldn't help but trust Bianca's confidence.

Of course, that didn't stop the dueling voices in my head from battling nonstop. One begged me to run—to stay as far away from Taprin as possible, even if it meant leaving the love of my life for a second time. The other told me to follow Paige no matter where she went. Taprin couldn't be any worse than the hell I experienced being away from her.

I stood dumbfounded, stuck in the middle of a no-win situation. The women made their way back, and I panicked, trying to make a decision. When Paige reached for my hand, her fingers squeezed mine, and I knew it was over. I was too entangled to turn back now.

Maybe Bianca was right. Perhaps this was all part of Great's plan. Or at least, that's what I told myself as I slowly nodded when Paige asked me to follow her to Taprin.

CHAPTER 12
WITHHOLDING JUDGMENT

FOR THE FIRST hour of the train ride, I quietly watched as the world outside turned from lush green to dusty brown. The dense forests and vibrant vegetation that marked the land between New Freeda and Hadston were long gone as we neared Taprin. Evergreens were replaced with skeleton-like shrubs—prickly and thirsty from a never-ending drought. Grassy hills morphed into rugged rock formations. It was as if the living world knew to keep its distance from the forbidden city.

Watching the imposing desert conquer the land, I wondered if I should have kept my distance, too.

With a heavy sigh, I tried to relax, but the growing tension in my body was stubborn. My eyes landed on Paige, who seemed hypnotized by the endless red rock outside. Nobody had spoken since we left Hadston's station, even though I was desperate to talk to Paige. With Bianca shadowing my every move, finding any privacy was difficult. So I swallowed a hundred questions fighting to escape my lips and only dared break the silence after Bianca fell asleep.

"What's it like living in Hadston?" I kept my voice low, watching Bianca out of the corner of my eye.

"It was..." Paige inhaled slowly and turned to face me. "Surprising."

"Was? You don't live there anymore?"

"No." Paige paused, biting her lip. "I live in Taprin now."

Her words choked my heart. I opened my mouth but couldn't respond. The news about Paige getting kicked out of New Freeda had stung. Thinking of her living in Taprin nearly destroyed me.

She shook her head. "I know what you're thinking, Asaph. Please, don't judge me."

My shock quickly transformed into a debilitating fear masked as anger. I couldn't believe this was the same person I had asked to marry me. Sure, Paige could be stubborn and outspoken, but she never let her independence interfere with her devotion to Great. Never in a hundred years could I have imagined Paige as anything but faithful. Great's light had always reflected from her eyes. Now I wondered who this stranger was sitting next to me.

I shook my head. "I—I just can't believe it. How did this happen? How did you let this happen?"

Paige furrowed her brow, locking her piercing gaze onto mine. "How did *I* let this happen? Are you serious right now?" She scoffed. "*I* didn't choose to leave. *They* kicked me out of my hometown—out of my family. Remember?"

Paige closed her eyes and took a deep breath while smoothing the wrinkles in her shirt.

"Sorry," I said weakly.

"No," Paige said, looking into my eyes. She rested her hand on my knee. "I'm sorry. I didn't mean to snap. Can we start over?"

I nodded carefully.

She inhaled slowly. "The day after our break-up, arrangements were made for me to move to Hadston. As you saw today, it's not the most desirable place to live, especially when you're used to the luxuries of New Freeda."

"It's still heads and shoulders above Taprin," I said, cutting in. "At least it's home to believers."

Paige rolled her eyes and inched closer to me. "Have you seen Taprin? Or are you just regurgitating what you've been told?"

"Is it a city built by dissenters?"

"It is."

"That's all I need to know." I crossed my arms, determined not to be swayed.

Paige pulled back, but her eyes stayed locked onto mine. I waited for her response, hating how much I wanted to kiss her. The longer we stared at each other, the more her face softened.

With a gentle sigh, Paige turned to face the window. "All my life in New Freeda, I felt like I was riding a carousel," she said as if sharing the story with the desert void instead of me. "I happily went round and round, doing everything I was supposed to do. Sure, sometimes it was monotonous, but I enjoyed the ride."

Paige turned to face me. "When I first arrived in Hadston, it all just stopped. The ride—my life—was a broken mess. Surrounded by a hundred useless parts, I had no clue how to fix it."

My eyes danced on her face as she carefully traced the hem of her blouse. "So, what did you do?" I asked.

"The only thing I knew to do. I prayed." Paige pushed away a tear, and my heart skipped a beat. I reached for her hand but decided against it at the last second. She cleared her throat. "I prayed as I had never prayed before."

"Prayer is a powerful tool."

She chuckled quietly. "The people of Hadston think so. No matter how desperate things get, they are always on their knees. When I first arrived, the crowds singing and pleading at the Wall of Remembrance inspired me to keep going—to hold on to hope.

"Every day, throngs of people clamored for a speck of space among the crowds, lifting their voices toward a twenty-foot barricade. No matter their circumstances, they believed Great was waiting for the right time to fix everything."

I smiled, imagining it. "It makes me like Hadston a little more."

"Hadston is full of good people," Paige said. "It helped me see my situation in a new light. I figured Great had a lesson to teach me through it all."

Her words warmed my heart, and I hoped a spark of the old Paige was still flickering inside. Maybe I could stoke the flame of her faith. "Hope keeps us going through hard times," I said. "It's a gift to be cherished."

Paige paused, sliding a strand of hair behind her ear. "Maybe," she said carefully. "But only if we don't misplace that hope."

"What do you mean?"

Paige's eyes lingered on mine for a moment before she returned her gaze outside the window and sighed. "Not long after I arrived, I met a man named Albert. He was old, frail, and somehow incredibly optimistic about his future. We became good friends, and he helped me stay strong during those first few months when my hope was faltering."

"What happened?"

"He got sick," she said with a catch in her voice. "He got sick as so many people in Hadston do. The city is dirty, the houses damp, the sewers overflowing."

"I'm sorry," I said quietly.

Paige tried to smile, but the heaviness in her eyes stopped her. "It was clear Albert needed help. A mutual friend mentioned Taprin had medicine that could save him, but Albert said he didn't need it—just more faith. He firmly believed Great would save him if he spent more time at the Wall. At first, I agreed. But after a few weeks, he kept getting worse, and I was getting desperate."

The sinking feeling in my gut slowly returned. "And that's when you visited Taprin, isn't it?"

Paige nodded. "I was terrified—not just because of its reputation, but because I worried Great would punish me even more if I went. I was trying to get on the right path, and Taprin seemed like a fatal step in that journey."

"But you went." I couldn't hide the disappointment in my voice.

"I went. Albert deserved to live." Her eyes pleaded with mine. "Wouldn't there be less suffering if more people got up from their knees and *did* something instead? Maybe faith doesn't have to be so passive."

A chill ran down my spine at her words. She didn't mean for them to be offensive, but they attacked me at my core. "So you think Taprin citizens have more power than Great?" I said, more disgusted than I intended.

"I didn't say that."

"But it's what you meant."

"Asaph, no. You're missing the point."

"So enlighten me! Did you get the medicine? Did Albert survive?"

The train came to a grinding halt. The screeching wheels against the rails snapped Bianca out of her slumber. Paige jumped to her feet, locking eyes with mine. "Yes, I got the medicine. Albert died anyway. He refused to take it."

A dozen emotions washed over me, but shame was the one pinching my chest.

Bianca cocked her head, clearly confused by the heightened tension. "Everything okay?"

Paige grabbed her bag and flung it over her shoulder. "Perfect. Let's go."

The two women reached the aisle, but I didn't budge. "I'm having second thoughts about—"

"Nuh-uh." Bianca cut me off and grabbed my arm, pulling me to my feet. "You're going. We're doing this for you, Ace." Her strength surprised me almost as much as my submission to her command. Somberly, I followed the two women off the nearly empty train, terrified by every step I took toward the platform exit.

The Scribes were responsible for the entire railroad industry. Taprin's stop at the end of the line was historically a destination spot for exiled dissenters. Trains delivered the most heinous unbelievers to the desert as a punishment for their sins.

But during the last century, as the number of the exiled continued to climb, dissenters banded together to build the makeshift city now known as Taprin. Once the Scribes learned the town was viable, they stopped sending dissenters there.

Hadston became a rehabilitation spot for sinners, or at least that was the story I'd been told. Now that I'd seen it, I wasn't sure any real healing was happening. Meanwhile, Taprin became a town to be avoided entirely. The only reason the train still made its last stop was that it was also near the landfill. Taprin is both a metaphorical and literal destination for trash.

Scorching sun rays pressed against our backs as we walked off the platform. I could see a fenced-off block toward the west with heaps of garbage poking above. My eyes ached from the heat and the unending orange tint of the late afternoon light. There was nothing but a dusty, dry mountain range to the east.

Instinctively, I grabbed a water bottle from my bag to protect myself from the dying land. "Where's the city?" I asked before taking a large swig of water. "Past the landfill?"

Paige pointed east. "This way."

My eyes bulged. "That can't be right." The two women continued onward, and I ran to catch up.

We huffed our way toward the mountain for twenty minutes, and I worried they were leading me toward a trap. "There's nothing out here. Is Taprin even real?" Before Paige could respond, we rounded a corner, and my eyes locked on a hint of green poking from the horizon.

"For a long time, nobody survived here," Paige said, grabbing her water bottle from her bag and handing it to Bianca. She wiped her sweaty forehead. "Those thrown out knew it was a death sentence. Even worse, many believed they deserved the punishment—as if it was a just consequence of disbelief." A few birds flew overhead, the first signs of animal life since we left Hadston. "People were discarded—thrown to their knees and told to pray for a speedy end."

My stomach twisted as I imagined it.

Paige smiled as Bianca passed the water back, taking a few gulps before continuing. "But finally, one brave woman named Vera refused to believe the lies. She looked up instead of down. And do you know what she saw?"

"The sky?" I said, shrugging my shoulders.

"And birds flying east, directing Vera toward that—" Paige pointed toward a lush landscape to our left, peeking behind the canyon ridge.

Transfixed by the growing burst of life, now just fifteen minutes within reach, I wondered if Paige was right. Could the others have saved themselves by daring to explore their options? That inquiry quickly turned sour as I realized the larger metaphor Paige was so obviously trying to make. I had only ever followed the path prescribed to me. Despite my many privileges, my life denied me one glaring thing: Choice.

Paige's words settled in my mind as we journeyed on. The dirt path transformed into a paved road. A glimmer of green grew until it consumed my view. Bare shrubs turned into layers of leafy vegetation, periodically spotted with vibrant red, yellow, and violet blossoms. Trees and bushes intermingled, creating a kaleidoscope of shapes. In the distance, a waterfall cascading from the mountaintop appeared like an actual fountain of life.

Our trio grew quiet as we made our last steps toward a large wooden gate tucked behind a path of trees. A stone wall framed both sides of the massive door that stood nearly fifteen feet tall. It was not as formidable as the barrier that ran along the City of Origin, but it looked well-maintained.

Paige stopped a few feet before the entrance and grabbed my hand. "Asaph, will you do me a favor as we go inside?"

My heart fluttered at her touch. I steadied my breath. "What?"

"I know you don't want to be here. You think this place is nothing but trouble—a thunderstorm you should avoid."

I swallowed hard, not sure where she was going.

"Will you please withhold judgment long enough to take the city at face value? Let your guard down, just a bit."

"That sounds like a dangerous request," I said carefully.

"No." Paige squeezed my hand. "It's a chance to see the world as it really is."

There's no adequate way to describe the conflicting emotions that flooded my body when we first stepped inside Taprin. I was prepared to see a version of Hadston—dirty and rundown. Instead, I was greeted with a scene as modern and inviting as my hometown.

The city's infrastructure alone was an impressive feat of engineering on par with the newest buildings of New Freeda. The streets were clean, and the sidewalks and lawns were perfectly maintained. A grand library stood in the center of town, intersecting shops, labs, and a state-of-the-art hospital.

As extraordinary as the skyline and landscape were, it was the people who grabbed my attention the most. In New Freeda, everyone kept to themselves. Here, there was a palpable energy that surprised me. Confident but relaxed, there was a stride in the people's steps that felt unrestricted. Their eyes lit up when they saw each other as if buoyed by the connection. My ears strained, wanting to hear their conversations, hoping for a clue to their inner lives.

But instead of being delighted by the impressive city or feeling comforted to learn it wasn't a condemned pit of despair, I was disturbed by one fact. Taprin was nothing like what I was told, and that could only mean one thing: Someone had lied.

My brain quickly tried to rationalize the discrepancy between what I saw and what I believed. Maybe Taprin used to be a rundown hellscape. No righteous believer would take a chance exploring, so how would anyone know about its modern transformation? Or perhaps the stories were designed to make the city less enticing. Evil could exist under the shiny facade. Maybe Great inspired the warning tales of a decrepit town to reflect the city's decaying belief.

The justification was there. All I had to do was twist the reality I saw with the larger truths I knew in my heart. So that's what I did. I made excuses and tried to ignore the gnawing pain in my stomach.

"Where exactly are we going?" I asked as we moved toward the city center.

"I sent a message to the town council before leaving Hadston," Paige said. "They are expecting us."

We walked past the gigantic library toward a beautiful stone building with the words *City Chambers* etched above the massive columns at its entrance. As we climbed the stairs to the front doors, a security guard raised his hand.

"They're with me," Paige said as she lifted her arm, revealing the small X tattoo on her wrist. The man nodded and let us pass. Automated glass doors quietly opened, leading us toward a vast lobby. Deep blue armchairs and sturdy side tables lined the walls. The soft echo of our footsteps on the marbled floors bounced toward the two-story high ceiling.

"Let Paige do the talking," Bianca whispered as we made our way to one of the back rooms.

"Why?" I winced as my words echoed through the hallway. I lowered my voice to a whisper. "Don't you trust me?"

Bianca stopped. Paige and I followed her example. "It's not that," Bianca said, eyeing Paige.

"It's just that—" Paige paused, choosing her words carefully. "Technically, I wasn't supposed to let you into the city."

My heart rate spiked. "What? So why the hell did you bring me?"

"To save Evie," Bianca said firmly.

"It will be fine." Paige grabbed my hand. Her reassuring tone did little to calm the butterflies in my stomach. "I'll explain everything to the council, I promise. But until I do, please stay silent."

I breathed in slowly. With a slight nod, I squeezed Paige's hand. Her eyes settled on mine, giving me the courage to move on. She led us into the room where a committee sat behind an elevated table near the opposite wall. Their faces lit up at the sight of Paige before moving their attention to Bianca, who offered a weak smile. When their eyes met mine, their expressions fell flat.

"Security," said the woman sitting in the center of the group. "Restrain that man." Two guards stepped forward, each grabbing an arm and tightening their grip around me.

The woman's eyes narrowed as she leaned forward. "Paige Stevens, there better be one hell of a reason for bringing a Junior Scribe into our city."

MESSAGE FROM LUCY FERNÁNDEZ

THU, FEB 2

Remember when we watched Lego Movie 2, and you wouldn't stop singing that annoying song from the movie for DAYS? Anyway, hope you're ok.

SAT, FEB 11

Saw you at Food City this afternoon. Wasn't sure you'd want me to say hi. So I didn't. But I'm doing it now. Hi, Ian. Call me?

WED, FEB 15

Ian, can we please talk? I know we can work through this.

CHAPTER 13
BIANCA'S SECRET

"I CAN EXPLAIN," Paige said, scrambling toward the council's table.

I wanted to jump in. After all, I was the one who asked Paige to bring Asaph to Taprin. She warned me this could happen. Now she was left defending my decision. But I held my tongue and let Paige talk until I knew what the council was thinking.

"The town laws are explicit," said a balding man at the end of the table.

Paige took a deep breath. I admired her ability to stay calm in tense situations. Asaph, on the other hand, looked ready to pass out.

"Council Members, I apologize," Paige said. "I should have talked to you before bringing Asaph inside Taprin. If you let me clarify the situation, I think you'll see a good reason for his presence." She looked at Asaph with a kind smile, trying to steady him. "Asaph is not dangerous, and he will not share what he sees here with anyone outside Taprin. I trust him."

A broad-shouldered man jumped to his feet. His deep-set eyes and furrowed brow sent a chill down my spine. "How can you say he's not a danger? The Scribes have the blood of thousands on their hands."

"If I may," I said, surprised by my interruption. "I'm the reason Asaph is here. This is not Paige's fault."

"And who are you?" The man's icy stare locked on me with an intensity that made me recoil.

"My name is Bianca," I said, shaking off the intimidation. I was determined to hold my ground.

"That's enough, Gerald." The woman in the center motioned for the man to sit down. She tapped her pen against the table, cocking her head to one side as she looked me up and down.

"Bianca, welcome to Taprin. I'm Nora Chan." She pointed down the line as she made introductions. "This is Gina Polk and Tad Wilkson." Nora tapped the shoulder of the woman to her right. "This is Sandra Fennick. You've already had the pleasure of hearing from Gerald Brown, and next to him is Timothy Lancaster," she said, finishing with the bald man at the end.

"Nice to meet you," I said carefully.

"We represent the people of Taprin. So-called dissenters built our community. Believers from cities like New Freeda, Middleton, and Eastview expelled our ancestors like trash, leaving them to die. Taprin became their second life." Nora's eyes zeroed in on Asaph, who glanced away. She turned her attention back to me with a calculated smile.

"Natural-born citizens now make up most of our population," Nora said. "Only a select few like Paige are allowed in our city as our resources are limited. It means the number of citizens with a tragic backstory is smaller each generation. People like me get to enjoy the fruits of our pioneer ancestors.

"In fact, my great-great-grandmother, Vera Chan, discovered this hidden, fertile land. Determined to make a new life, she made a makeshift shelter close to where this building now stands. Every day she'd travel and wait for the evening train's new batch of dissenters, encouraging them to join her in creating the city of Taprin."

"I have nothing but the deepest respect for this city and its history," I said. "The fortitude and strength of the founders inspire me. I have no intention of threatening your way of life."

"And yet, you brought the Junior Scribe here." Nora motioned toward Asaph. "His father and all the other Scribes are a constant threat to us."

"That's not true!" Asaph yelled.

I shot him a quick look of warning, begging him to close his mouth. The heat rose in his cheeks, but he quickly realized his mistake and bit his lip.

Nora stood. A determined resolve washed over her as she eyed Asaph. "Are you saying the Scribes have *not* exiled and executed dissenters for thousands of years?"

"No—well, yes, I guess—but only those who go against Great's will. Eternal laws demand justice. Shouldn't there be consequences for those who break His sacred commands?"

"Asaph, not now," Paige said under her breath.

"No, it's alright, Paige. I'd like to hear more from this wise and holy leader." Nora walked around the table, making her way in front of Asaph. She leaned in, arms folded. "Tell me, Junior Scribe Zimran, what sacred commands have *you* broken by stepping inside Taprin."

Asaph's cheeks went flush. "That's not—it's not—don't twist this around! I've done nothing wrong." Panic and confusion twisted his face as he wrestled with the reality of Nora's accusation. No matter how hard Asaph tried to turn the facts around, he kept arriving at the same dead end: His very presence in the city was a sin.

"Paige," Nora said carefully, "Why don't you remind everyone here what great transgression got *you* kicked out of New Freeda."

Paige swallowed hard, closing her eyes. Caught in the middle of her past and current life, she looked gutted. With tenderness, she met Asaph's gaze. "They kicked me out because I didn't marry Asaph."

I had suspected there was more to Paige and Asaph's relationship than they had let on. Paige's pain was evident, yet she carried on with a quiet determination I admired.

"Yes, a great evil, indeed." Nora's sarcasm struck Asaph with masterful precision. "As you can see, *your Holiness*, the Scribes are a genuine threat to us. We've stayed safe by keeping our distance—and our secrets. It's easy to keep people out of a supposedly dilapidated town. Now that you've seen our great city, who will stop you from telling the Scribes about our prosperity? Who will stop them from taking everything we have, insisting it's Great's will?"

Asaph didn't move.

A clock behind the other council members ticked loudly in the otherwise silent room. With bated breath, I tried reading Asaph's face—curious to know whether this was changing his mind or encouraging him to double down on his beliefs.

"If I may," Paige said, "There is urgent news that Asaph has shared with me that I believe the council will want to hear."

"Go on," Nora said, returning to her seat.

Paige cleared her throat. "Evie has returned through the Doorway of Death."

With frozen breath, I waited for the council's response. My heart sank when none of them seemed particularly surprised.

"What's worse," I said, interrupting to garner more urgency, "the Scribes have captured Evie. She's locked in a cell, removed from her family, and sentenced to be executed in two days."

"I see," Nora said calmly. "And how does this affect us?"

"How can you be so foolish?" Asaph yelled. "Evie's return signals the End of Days! Do you think Great will punish his true believers but spare your town?"

A few of the council members chuckled.

"No offense, son, but the people of Taprin don't believe the Scribe's propaganda," Gerald said.

"Exactly," Timothy agreed. "We know believers live and die by the Sacred Scrolls, but we prefer evidence. Our scholars know there's more to the Doorway of Death than what the Scribes share."

"But the Scribes have reinstated the Sinner's Sacrifice," I said, trying to get them to see the legitimate threat that loomed over everyone, believer or not. "Scribe Zimran is determined to put an end to the dissenters. Who do you think they'll come for next?"

Timothy ran his hand over his smooth head. "Reinstating such a barbaric ritual is concerning, although I'm still not convinced it's our battle to fight. The simple solution is proving the woman locked up isn't Evie." He turned toward Asaph. "Don't your people believe Great killed her two millennia ago? How could she possibly come back? It makes no sense."

Asaph held his ground. "Because Great prophesied it. He can do anything to help further his work—including bringing someone back from the dead. Evie's return is a sign of the world's dwindling belief." He scoffed. "Hearing you speak so casually about such sacred things proves it."

The council members exchanged glances. Nora folded her arms. "We rely on science and logic, and it's unlikely Evie would still be alive. The woman locked up is most likely an imposter with scriptural knowledge—someone who knows how to weave a good story and send an entire world into hysteria."

"No, it has to be Evie," Asaph said, his words more confident than his tone. "Great foretold of her return."

Asaph was floundering, clinging to his beliefs, while a simple alternative threatened to send him crashing down. I wasn't so easily persuaded. Nobody had worked harder to shatter Asaph's worldview than I had, but I was determined to get the council to believe him on this particular point.

"It *is* Evie," I blurted out. My voice was loud and firm,

surprising everyone in the room. Suddenly, all eyes were back on me.

"What makes you say that?" Gina asked. Her quiet sincerity starkly contrasted the rest of the council's intensity.

My heart beat faster as I searched for an answer to convince the room without giving myself away. I'd eventually have to tell my story—my whole story, but as the time approached, I began doubting everything I had set in motion.

"Well," I stammered, trying to find the right words. Asaph drilled his gaze toward me, unsure I was still on his side. I found it ironic that it was up to me to make this legend credible since I had spent so much time trying to disprove everything else. But Taprin didn't work from stories. They demanded evidence and logic. And that was hard since the truth was more bizarre than the myths created to explain it.

My pulse accelerated, and I was surprised by my growing nerves, given everything I knew. Since the day I met Asaph, I have been clear about my mission. People needed to learn the truth about the world. I also knew how heartbreaking the truth could be. The unintended consequences of reshaping someone's beliefs could be brutal.

"I *know* it's her," I finally said. With a large exhale, I paced along the marble floor like a lawyer pleading their case. "Like Asaph, I've read the Sacred Scrolls. And like your scholars, I have researched thousands of artifacts deemed unworthy by the Scribes—including rare records most people don't even know exist. Trust me, the woman locked up in New Freeda is Evie. I was the one who pulled her through. She matches the descriptions from the earliest documents. Who else could it be?"

"How did you pull her through?" Gerald asked. "You're not a Scribe. You aren't allowed in the Place of Origin."

My mind raced through the timeline, trying to figure out how far back I needed to go to make sense of everything. It quickly became clear: I had to start at the beginning.

"Do any of you know why the portal—the Doorway of Death—exists in the first place?"

"The devil used her powers to create a rift in Great's world," Asaph said, almost verbatim to the official story from the Sacred Scrolls. "She showed the portal to Evie, insisting it was a pathway to a better life. Instead, it was a trap that killed a third of Great's children."

I switched my attention from Asaph to Nora. "Is that what the council believes?"

"Not exactly," Nora said. "Ancient documents outlawed by the Scribes tell a different story—one where a woman named Lucy invited people to travel through the invisible doorway to enter a new world where they could rule themselves free from the tyranny of the creator known as Ian."

My eyes lit up after hearing the alternative version.

"Of course," Nora continued, "both stories feel far-fetched and are likely folktales created to explain phenomena not yet understood. Still, there seems to be enough evidence to suggest a large group of people disappeared. Of course, nobody can say for certain what happened to them."

"Very true," I said with a widening smile. "But it sounds like both sides agree that there is some sort of rift. Whether it's a doorway to death or a portal leading to freedom isn't what matters right now."

"Do you have a point?" Gerald said, clearly losing his patience.

"Yes." I continued pacing in front of the council's table. "You want to know how I got inside The Place of Origin. It's because I found another rift. There's another portal that allowed me to get from New Freeda to the Ancient Altar quickly and unharmed. Since I've experienced it, it's easy to believe the original portal is safe, too."

"And where exactly is this portal?" Nora asked, clearly unconvinced.

I glanced at Asaph, ensuring he was paying attention. "I found it tucked in the corner of my jail cell."

The room was quiet as the council traded questioning glances. Asaph stood, mouth ajar with disbelief. Sandra leaned over and whispered in Nora's ear.

With a nod, Nora settled her eyes back on me. "That's quite a story," she said. "And we'd be willing to believe it if we knew you, Bianca. But you're not one of us. For all we know, *you* could be the one designing this entire plot, planting the fake Evie to stir up division. Without any proof, why should we trust you?"

Closing my eyes, I took in a slow breath. My mind bounced around, making it hard to calm my frantic nerves. Venturing a gaze at Asaph, my stomach sunk, knowing how much I had disrupted his life in the last three days. He didn't deserve the chaos I brought, and now I was about to knock him over with my truth.

"Maybe you shouldn't trust me," I said. Planting my feet, I stood solemn as my eyes scanned the council. "I don't consider myself a dissenter anymore than I do a believer. I'm just a girl determined to tell the truth about this world. Unfortunately, in trying, I've told countless lies about myself. So maybe you shouldn't believe me."

Asaph's amber eyes drilled into mine.

"What do you mean?" Paige asked, her voice twinged with a hint of fear.

My throat tightened, and I pushed back the emotion rising inside. Time seemed to slow as every person waited for my response. Exhaling slowly, I closed my eyes.

"I know, without a doubt, that the woman locked away is Evie. I know because I have known Evie since the beginning— because I am that so-called devil who encouraged her through the portal. I am Lucy Fernández."

CHAPTER 14
THROUGH THE CRACKS

I AM THAT SO-CALLED DEVIL.

Bianca's words spun in my head, dizzying my world until I couldn't see straight. When her entire body distorted like a glitch and suddenly vanished, I figured my mind was playing tricks on me. I shook my head and closed my eyes. When I opened them, Bianca was gone. In her place stood a petite young woman in jeans and a faded green t-shirt with sleek, dark hair pulled back into a ponytail.

The entire room shrieked. "Security! Grab her!" Nora's command rose above the commotion. The two men restraining me jumped for the young woman.

Fear saturated my heart as I tried to make sense of this revelation. Bianca was Lucy? *That* Lucy? It had to be a mistake—a ruse of some kind. I couldn't wrap my mind around the idea and found myself looking for clues that would make this revelation okay. For the past three days, I had slowly handed bits of my trust over to Bianca, and I couldn't bare to think about the moral consequences of doing it so blindly. Had I been dealing with the literal devil this whole time? Was it possible?

The thought sickened me.

"You don't need to be afraid! I'm here to help!" Lucy yelled as the council members swarmed around to ensure she didn't escape.

"Asaph, come," Paige whispered. She grabbed my hand and pulled me away from the chaos.

I gladly obeyed, falling into a full sprint as we bolted out of the room. Keeping close to the hall wall, we rushed toward a back exit. We heard a loud *click* when the door closed behind us, managing to escape just before the building went into lockdown.

Paige moved along the open path, hurrying but not running. We tried acting as normal as possible until we rounded a corner. Hidden by the side of the enormous library, we ran toward a small alleyway.

"Here," Paige said. She unzipped her bag and pulled out a pair of sunglasses and a cap. "Put these on and give me your wrist."

"What just happened in there? Was that really Lucy? Where did Bianca go? Can we just leave her there?" My words spilled out of my mouth like marbles, rolling clumsily onto the floor. Everything was happening so fast, and I was sure I would only make things worse if I didn't get grounded.

Paige grabbed my shoulders, locking her eyes on mine. "Asaph, breathe. I know this is shocking, but we must stay focused. I don't know if Bianca is Lucy or if that whole thing is some kind of trick. All I know is the council will likely lock you up forever, and Bianca's story gave us the diversion we needed to escape. We need to get you out of Taprin—now."

I nodded my head, holding fast to Paige's unflinching gaze. If she was scared or nervous, she didn't show it. I was unsure how she could stay so calm in such uncertainty, but I tried to steady myself with her unshakable resolve.

"Now, give me your wrist," Paige said, pulling a pen from her bag.

"Why?" I asked, slipping on the shades she had handed me.

Clicking the pen's top, she quickly grabbed my arm and drew a small X that looked identical to the one tattooed on her wrist. "We're going to my house," she said, throwing the pen in her bag. Paige poked her head around the corner to survey the street. "I've got a car, but we need to lie low and act normal until we get there, okay?"

"Are you suggesting I don't usually act normal?" I laughed weakly, wanting to release some of the tension I felt.

Paige smiled, shaking her head. She grabbed my hand. I tried not to read too much into it. The situation was tense, and we both were in survival mode, but that didn't stop my stomach from fluttering every time Paige touched me. As she led me down the street, she quietly muttered, "Stay near me."

It was late in the evening, and the streets were fairly quiet. We made our way east from the town center toward a small residential area. Unlike New Freeda, with its mansions and sprawling estates, Taprin homes were modest. Native plants filled the spaces between houses, attracting bees and butterflies. Open backyards made the entire street feel like a communal playground. You could see the love and care that went into planning the neighborhood.

Paige turned, heading for a walkway to a cozy single-story cottage. With no locks on the door, she twisted the knob and led me inside. "I'm going to grab a few things from my room," she said, opening a closet near the entrance. Paige pulled out a duffel bag and threw it at me. "Take this and grab some food in the kitchen: Water, crackers, jerky—anything non-perishable."

My frayed nerves were ready to burst, but Paige worked quickly and calmly. I couldn't help but admire her confidence—a born leader. She was risking everything to keep me from being locked up, and I wasn't sure how I could ever repay her. The least I could do was quickly follow her orders.

After filling the bag with food, I headed down the hallway to find Paige taking clothes from a dresser near her bed. The room smelled like a memory. Hints of lavender and rose water kissed my nostrils, taking me back to the night we first kissed.

My hand settled on a picture frame on her nightstand. It was a snapshot of us at the New Freeda carnival. I spent every penny I had to win her a ridiculously large stuffed bear. In the photo, she raised the prize high like the catch of the day. The grins on our faces were nearly identical. We were happy.

"I can't believe you still have this," I said, showing her the picture.

Paige paused, smiled softly, and then turned back toward the dresser. "Of course I still have it." She stood silent as if stuck in thought. Gripping a couple of shirts with her fingers, she used her free hand to brush something from her cheek.

"You okay?" I placed my hand on her shoulder. She reached up and squeezed my fingers.

"Yeah, I'm fine." With a loud thud, she slammed the drawer before stuffing the remaining clothes into her bag. Her eyes, moist and red, met mine. "I have one more thing to do. Can you wait in the kitchen?"

Paige pointed me toward the front of the house and then snuck into a second bedroom, closing the door as quietly as she had opened it.

Muffled voices crept through the thin walls. It was clear Paige was talking to someone. I tried to convince myself it was only a roommate, but my heart sank thinking about Paige with someone else. When she entered the kitchen, she pushed away another tear and motioned for me to follow.

We tossed our bags in the back of a silver hatchback parked in a small attached garage. Backing out slowly, we ensured the streets were empty before driving away.

Our racing hearts left little energy for chit-chat—let alone serious questions, of which I had a million. But one thing was certain. As Paige drove along the outskirts of town, it was clear she was joining me on my journey back to New Freeda. I would not be returning home alone.

That fact filled me with hope.

For two hours, we drove in silence. The sun gradually descended behind the horizon, adding a vibrant splash of orange to the sky before disappearing completely. I must have opened my mouth a dozen times, trying to put words to my competing thoughts. But I remained mute. It was as if my heart refused to let the reality of our situation break this chance to be near Paige.

"It's going to be a long night," Paige said, braving to speak first. "I'm taking the back roads, so we've got at least another seven hours before we reach New Freeda, and that's assuming we don't make any stops."

"Would you like me to take a turn driving?" I asked. "You must be tired."

"I'm fine. You're the one who hasn't slept these past few nights."

"How did you know?"

Paige smiled. "Bianca gave me a quick rundown of your escape from New Freeda. It's hard picturing you running from the Scribe Guards."

My pulse skyrocketed. I hated that Paige knew about my unsavory choices while under Bianca's influence. "You must hate me."

"Hate you? Definitely not," Paige said.

"I had no idea who Bianca really was. I can't believe I let her drag you into this mess."

Paige nodded as if carefully digesting my words. She opened her mouth, but now it was her turn to remain quiet.

I took her silence as my cue to continue untangling my thoughts, hoping I could make sense of everything. "Do you really think Bianca is Lucy? I mean, she magically transformed into a whole other person, so I guess she must be, right? But she said she was here to help! I mean—" I scoffed. Just thinking about it ignited my anger. "After admitting to all her lies, did Lucy really expect anyone to believe her?"

"So you don't think she wanted to help?"

"I don't know what I think."

Paige tapped her fingers on the steering wheel.

"I know you have thoughts," I said. "Tell me."

With a heavy sigh, Paige unloaded. "I think it was Lucy. And yeah, she lied about a lot of stuff, but—come on, if you knew who she was, do you think you would have listened? All she lied about was her name. Everything else she just let us assume."

"Are you actually defending her?" I asked, surprised. "She admitted to being the devil."

"She admitted to being Lucy—a person who history has painted as a devil. She admitted to saving Evie those two thousand years ago—"

"—killing Evie, you mean."

Paige rolled her eyes, breaking my heart just a little. "I don't think she killed Evie. I mean, come on! You've got Evie locked in your prison. She's alive."

With a deep breath, Paige summoned a calmer self. She glanced over at me. "Listen, Asaph. You must admit that Bianca —er, Lucy—wasn't the only one who lied. You've seen Taprin. You know what it is. For years, the Scribes lied about it. What makes you think they wouldn't lie about everything else?"

My eyes locked on Paige. "Actually, it sounds like Taprin created that lie. They don't want to share what they have, so they perpetuate the myth that it's a dangerous place! You heard the council. You know their laws. As one of their citizens, you're perpetuating the deception. So unless you have another example of slander, stop accusing the Scribes of wrongdoing."

The expression on Paige's face made me regret the words

instantly. She pulled hard on the steering wheel, veering the car to the right as she slammed the brakes. The wheels bounced along the rocky terrain on the side of the road. I braced myself against the dashboard as the vehicle came to a grinding halt.

My heart chastised me for being so careless as Paige exited the car, slamming the door with a loud thud. I quickly evacuated my seat, running to catch up as she marched along the stretch of empty highway.

"I'm sorry, Paige. I didn't mean—"

Paige held up a finger. Her intense gaze made me choke on my words. Walking over to a boulder, she sank. Tears ran down her cheek while a resolved determination marked her face. Tiptoeing along the tall grass, I carefully sat beside her, and she turned to face me.

"You know what I love about you, A?"

My body froze. Paige hadn't called me that in years. In public, around family and friends, I was always Asaph. But when it was just the two of us—when we talked about our future together—Paige would call me A. That single letter carried all the hope I had tried to repress since reconnecting. With one tiny spoken syllable, it was clear my heart was still irreparably tied to hers.

"What's that?" I asked, dizzy with anticipation.

"I love your integrity." Paige rested her hand on my knee. "You're the most honest man I know, making me feel safe in a tumultuous world."

My eyes bounced, trying to memorize every detail of the moment. "It's a trait I learned from you. You've always been honest." I paused, lowering my voice. "Even when the truth nearly destroyed me."

Images of my proposal popped into my head, followed by the gut-wrenching scene of Paige's refusal.

Paige nodded, recognizing the lingering pain of our break-up.

"These days, I don't know who I can trust," I said, taking her hand. "But I know you'll always tell me the truth."

Paige sighed, pulling away. "Except, I lied to you."

Every cell in my body froze. "What? When?"

"When I said I didn't want to marry you." Paige bit her lip as tears welled in her eyes.

My heart beat faster. A rush of emotion washed over me. "What do you mean? You said you didn't love me enough to get married. Are you saying—"

"I'm saying I lied." Paige pushed back a tear.

"Lied how? I don't understand. Did you love me or... what?"

"You were the love of my life. There's only one thing I wanted more than to be with you forever."

I leaned in, eyes wide, desperate for Paige to continue. "What?"

"I wanted to be me. Fully, freely—me."

"But... I don't understand," I said, feeling my pulse in my throat. "I never wanted you to be anything else."

"Yes, but Great's commands are explicit about the role of a Scribe's wife. I had dreams and feared they'd shatter if I tied myself to you. It was a recipe for resentment and..."

Grabbing Paige's hands, I squeezed them tight, desperate for her to believe me. "I never would have taken those dreams from you."

"Not even if Great commanded it? Do you remember how quickly you gave up music?"

"That's not the same thing."

Paige half-smiled, tilting her head as she reached out and pushed my hair off my forehead. "Do you remember how quickly you gave up on me?"

"I—" My mouth froze. "No, I—that's not what happened. I just wanted to respect your decision."

"And I love you for it," Paige said tenderly. "It never would have worked. Your integrity keeps you chained to your beliefs, and I had too many questions and doubts. Ultimately, I knew I'd destroy your happiness if I tried holding on to mine."

The fractured pieces of my heart burst against my chest. I was desperate to fix this mess, to prove we could make it work. Still, I knew Paige was right. As long as I believed in the Scribedom, I could never be with someone who wasn't committed. But in the shadows of that realization was a growing doubt that threatened my once unbreakable faith.

We sat quietly, allowing the growing hum of crickets to fill the void. Pulled between my love for Paige and my belief in Great, I felt hopeless. For a fraction of a second, I imagined myself breaking free from the role of Scribe. Images of growing old with Paige filled me with overwhelming happiness that ultimately terrified me. As much as I wanted Paige, I feared the consequences of straying from Great's word. Even more, I worried I was already too far gone.

"Do you really think the Scribes have lied?" The words slipped from my lips. Instantly I wanted to take them back, realizing I wasn't prepared for the answer.

Paige gently traced the small X on her wrist. "I know they've lied, A."

"About Taprin, you've said that. But you have to admit—it's not really a lie if they believe it's a horrible city."

"It's not just Taprin," Paige said, looking up. "Did you ever wonder what happened to me after we broke up?"

"Honestly, I didn't want to think about it. It was too painful."

Paige squeezed my hand and swallowed hard. "After our relationship ended, my father packed my things the next day. He told me I was heading to Hadston. When I protested, he said it was out of his hands. He told me to go to bed because my train left early."

"I still don't get it. He just kicked you to the curb? You did nothing wrong!" With a furrowed brow and clenched jaw, my rage was rising. "Paige, I'm so sorry. That must have been awful."

"There's more," she said, taking a huge breath. "I overheard my parents arguing later that night. My dad told my mom it was the Scribes' decision to send me away. They convinced my father I was tainted—I had ruined the family with my perverted ways."

My insides twisted, and I shook my head in disbelief. How did I not know Paige had been kicked out? How selfish and self-absorbed was I to not even notice the love of my life no longer lived in my hometown? But the most painful realization was knowing my father probably directed the decision. That fact nearly crushed me.

"Mom fought back," Paige continued. "My parents yelled for more than an hour. Meanwhile, I sat in the hallway, listening to one parent fight for my life while the other was willing to toss it aside. In choosing not to marry you, I thought I was giving myself freedom. Instead, my world was crumbling before my eyes."

I choked back the rising disgust in my throat. "Paige, that's—unthinkable. I..." My mind was failing to grasp it. Why did Dad order it? I told him the break-up was mutual, and he seemed to believe me. There had to be another explanation. There was no way Great would do something so awful, and my father always did Great's will, right?

Right?

"When I got up the next morning," Paige said, "I wanted to say goodbye to my mom. Dad said she was too sick to get out of bed. I told him I'd go to her, but he refused."

With each new piece of information, I found no genuine words of comfort. All I could do was keep telling her how sorry I was.

"Did your mom ever write?" I finally asked.

Paige stood up, brushing the dust from the back of her pants. "Nope. And do you want to know why?"

I nodded, even though I really didn't.

"Because they sent my mom away, too. Her reluctance to

accept the brutal orders to banish her own daughter got her relocated to another part of Hadston. Even though she still believed in Great and his work, they labeled her a dissenter and threw her out."

Nothing made sense. My world was upside down, and I struggled to stay upright. "I can't even fathom what you've been through," I said weakly.

"It's not just me, A. I've met countless others who have been kicked out for not toeing the line. The suffering in Hadston isn't just from poverty. The people are despondent, trying to reconcile their hearts with the punishment given them."

"Why don't they go to Taprin like you? It's way better." The words left a bitter taste in my mouth. I couldn't believe I was defending the city.

"Taprin is too small to help everyone. It's hard to balance the needs of others with your own people. They want to provide sanctuary to the suffering but have to maintain a distance from those who would destroy the city. Taprin doesn't always know who to trust, so becoming a citizen isn't easy. I was fortunate in that regard."

"Is that what the X tattoo is for?" I asked, looking at the smudged replica on my wrist. "To know who belongs?"

Paige nodded. She licked her thumb and gently rubbed the ink off my arm.

My mind wrestled, trying to justify everything Paige had confessed. "There must be an explanation," I said, more to myself than her. "It must be part of Great's plan. We don't always know how things will turn out."

"You're right. Sometimes wonderful things can grow from the rubble." With a deep exhale, Paige grabbed my hand, pulling me to my feet. "I don't attribute it to Great or the Scribes, but in a twisted miracle, my story has a happy ending—or at least it did."

"Tell me."

Paige smiled. "A few months after moving to Taprin, I began

visiting Hadston several times a week to help the needy. As I made my way through the city, I eventually bumped into my mom. That's how I learned what happened to her. She lives with me now."

"So she's okay?" A flicker of relief tried to brave the storm brewing inside me.

"Physically, she's great. Taprin has the best healthcare and resources in the world. But emotionally? No, she's not okay."

"I'm so sorry," I said for the millionth time.

Paige nodded. "Yeah. It's been rough." She pushed another tear from her eyes. "Here's the thing the Scribes don't tell you about dissenters. Nobody willingly shatters their worldview. Nobody wants to rip up the foundation of their identity. You don't go looking for a devil whose purpose is to destroy you."

A twinge of guilt pricked me as I thought about all the horrible things I had said about dissenters. "No, I guess not."

"But—" Paige said, letting the word linger. "As painful and heart-wrenching as it is to lose your faith and watch your beliefs crumble, I'd do it all over again."

"Really?" I couldn't hide the disbelief in my voice. A part of me kept waiting for her to tell me she had made a mistake in choosing not to marry me. While I hated that Paige had suffered so much, I secretly hoped her struggle would send her back to me. "You'd do it all again?"

Paige smiled. "Absolutely."

"Why?"

With a determined exhale, Paige looked up at the stars. "Because as awful as it was, the journey gave me something my former life never did."

"What?"

"Freedom," she said, her eyes sparkling in the moonlight. "I'm no longer bound by someone else's rules. I get to make my own life, and I wouldn't have it any other way."

CHAPTER 15
COMING HOME

THE REST of the journey to New Freeda was quiet. Paige insisted I get some sleep, so I pretended to nap, but I couldn't get our conversation out of my head.

How could Paige's father send her away like that? Even worse, how could *my* dad demand it? I knew Dad could sometimes be cold, but I always believed Great's love guided his decisions.

Equally confusing was Paige's declaration that she was happy with how things ended. The thought that her life as a dissenter pleased her more than a life with me stung a little, but Paige's happiness made me happy. I was comforted knowing Great had given her the freedom she wanted. Even if she didn't credit Him for the outcome, I could see His hand in it.

No matter how awful things seemed, Great was directing us all.

That single thought was enough to calm my fears temporarily. Doubts about my father and the Scribedom took a backseat to the bigger picture of Great's love, finally giving me enough relief to fall asleep.

. . .

Paige nudged me awake once we made it to New Freeda. The early morning sun kissed the earth, giving the world a soft glow. After parking the car behind a building near the edge of town, Paige looked at me.

"What now?" she asked. "My goal was to get you home. I've done that. So what are you going to do for Evie?"

"Right, Evie." In the chaos of everything, I somehow forgot Evie's execution was scheduled for the next day. I thought back to my original plan—to send her through the portal. Knowing the truth about Bianca, I wondered if Evie was working with the devil. Was there some sinister plot behind Evie's sudden appearance that I was missing? I had already been played the fool once. I wasn't willing to do it again.

Paige stared at me, eyebrows raised. "Well? You can't let the Scribes kill her. You know that, right?"

"Yeah, right. Of course." I tripped over my words, trying to sound confident while my heart played tug of war with my mind.

Pushing aside Evie's tangled connection to Lucy, I remembered the warmth I felt when Great inspired me to send her home. It still seemed like the best option. And while my confidence in the Scribes' infallibility was faltering, my faith in Great was solid. He told me to choose the more compassionate path, and I was determined to obey.

"I think I can get my father to let her go," I finally said.

"Really?" Paige was unconvinced. She shook her head. "After hearing my story, you think your dad will just send her back? Asaph, have you learned nothing? The Scribes do what's best for *them*. Period." Her frustration was thick, weighing down my hopes for a peaceful solution.

"It's worth a shot," I said weakly. "Besides, I don't have another plan. I tried breaking her free and failed miserably. I guarantee there will be more guards than before. If you have a better idea, I'm all ears."

Paige sighed. "I wish I knew Lucy's thoughts when she said

Taprin could help. I still don't know why she was so set on taking you there."

I scoffed. "She was obviously trying to get me to sin. She's not who she said she was, remember?"

"Maybe," Paige said. "Although I still think she was trying to help. And even if she was luring you toward the dissenter city for some evil purpose, that doesn't change the fact that the people of Taprin are good. I hope you know that."

It felt like I was standing trial. Paige looked at me, waiting for my response to determine whether I was worthy of her help.

"Sure," I said half-heartedly. "If you say they are good people, I believe you. Still, they didn't seem particularly eager to offer assistance." I paused, realizing I was moments away from saying something offensive. I quickly corrected myself. "Not that I blame them."

"Unfortunately, I think we're on our own for this. I don't know if the council will ever trust you, and since I helped break you free, I'm probably black-listed, too." Paige sighed. "If you think you can convince your dad, I guess it's worth a shot. As you said, there aren't many other options."

"Then it's settled. I'll talk to my dad." I reached for the door handle but stopped when I realized Paige wasn't moving. "You coming?"

Paige shook her head. "I'm going to stay here. I'm not exactly a welcome guest anymore. It's a thirty-minute walk to the Sanctum—you okay to go alone?"

"Sure," I said. My disappointment was obvious.

"You've got this, A. It's going to be okay."

"Thanks." I leaned in, trying to memorize Paige's face. The fear of losing her again chained me to my seat.

Paige rested her hand on my cheek. "This isn't goodbye," she whispered.

Her lips pressed against mine, and I swear I saw fireworks. I held her tightly, glued to the moment. It felt impossible to leave, and it took all my energy to pull away. With a slight nod, I grabbed my bag, squeezed Paige's hand, and made the long walk back to my father's house.

My mother's eyes widened as she opened the door. "Praise Great!"

Her arms wrapped around me, hugging me tightly for a solid minute. "I was so worried. *We* were so worried." She leaned back and scanned my face. "Josiah! Quick! Asaph is back. He's safe!" Pulling me in again, I could feel Mom's torso shake as tears fell.

Dad bounded down the stairs. A smile spread across his face, but he quickly turned serious.

"Asaph, my boy. I'm glad you're okay." He squeezed my shoulders, offering a rigid side hug. Dad rarely showed affection through physical touch, so the awkward effort to connect was surprisingly comforting.

"Where have you been?" Mom asked. "What happened? Are you okay? Do you need food? A shower?" The rapid-fire questioning mirrored the urgency in her voice. Mom's hand pushed back my hair as she inspected my eyes. "You look awful, honey."

"I'm fine, Mom. At least, I will be."

My heart suddenly jolted as the memories of the past few days surfaced—the image of James's disappointed shock stood at the forefront. I had gone against my father's wishes, broken the law, and freed a fugitive. My parents would want answers, especially Dad.

There was no easy way to explain my sudden disappearance to them, and the thought of telling the truth made me queasy. Initially, Bianca said she would take the blame, but now that I knew who she really was, I wasn't so sure. It was hard enough trusting Bianca to do the right thing. Now that I knew she was

Lucy, offering the same grace to the actual devil seemed impossible.

"Marie, that's enough," Dad said, waving Mom away. "I'd like to talk to the boy alone."

His indomitable tone filled me with anxiety. Mom lowered her head, remembering her place. She kissed my cheek and silently went upstairs. As Dad led me to his office, my mind tried to settle on a story.

"Sit down, son." My father motioned to the leather chair across from his desk.

Every hard conversation with Dad happened in that seat, but none seemed this heavy. I tried to calm my nerves, hoping he couldn't hear my heart thumping against my chest. As he took his place across from me, Dad interlaced his fingers and leaned forward.

"I was shocked," Dad said, jumping right in, "when I got the news that Bianca had escaped again, I didn't believe it. We had done a thorough sweep of the cells, added guards, and reinforced the lock. There was no way she could have broke free on her own."

Dad paused, waiting to see my response. A drop of sweat ran along the backside of my neck, but I remained unmoved.

"Then I got the real bombshell." Dad stood and paced along the backside of the room—a clear sign of his frustration. "I was told *you* ran off with the prisoner."

I swallowed the lump in my throat. The urge to defend my actions was massive, but I waited to speak. I kept my lips shut until I understood what Dad was thinking.

"James Sato insisted you were being held as a hostage. He said the woman threatened your life."

Finally, I felt a hint of relief. I slowly sighed, trying not to give myself away. In my head, I was hugging James—grateful he had covered for me. But it still wasn't clear whether Dad bought

James's story, and with that thought, the tension in my body quickly returned.

"A few things don't make sense, so I'm hoping you'll enlighten me," Dad said, pacing again. "First, what were you doing in the basement at that hour? Second, how did Bianca break free? And finally, how did she drag you into this mess?"

With a thick plop, Dad dropped into his chair and, with a tilt of his head, lifted his fingers to his chin. He was done with his monologue as he waited for my response.

"I am partially to blame," I said, hoping to use whatever threads of truth I had to create a tapestry Dad would buy. "Bianca's story wasn't adding up, so I went to get more information." Courage slowly seeped into my cells as I borrowed the logic from the Taprin City Council. "I worried Bianca had orchestrated the whole con. She could have easily planted that other woman near the portal while I was unconscious. It's possible it's not even Evie locked down there."

"One thing at a time, Asaph. You went down to Bianca's cell, but that doesn't explain how she got free."

"Right, sorry." I cleared my throat. "I went to talk to her. It was dark, and it all happened so fast. I remember her hand reaching through the bars. My keys were in my pocket…"

"Are you suggesting she grabbed your keys?" Dad scoffed. "What about the guards? What about you?" His voice grew louder with every syllable. "You are almost twice her size, Asaph! She had no weapon. Am I supposed to believe she grabbed your key, took out the guards, and somehow used their weapons on you?"

I could tell he started this imagined scenario believing it was impossible, but by the end had almost convinced himself it was true.

Dropping my head, I let the silence speak for me.

Dad sighed. "Okay, I guess that explains the escape. But

where have you been the past two days? We've had guards searching all over New Freeda."

"The prisoner insisted on taking me to Taprin. I assume it was her home—or maybe just a place to hide."

"And did you go?" Dad asked, leaning forward.

My heart froze. So far, I had used crumbs of truth to lead my dad toward assumptions that built a convincing story. Now I had to decide whether I was willing to lie outright.

"Well?" Dad prodded.

You're the most honest man I know. The echo of Paige's words from last night rang in my head. With a heavy sigh, I confessed.

"I was in Taprin for about an hour," I said. "But I left as soon as I found a chance to break free."

"Well, praise Great for that." Dad cast his eyes upward before settling back on me. "That must have been awful, and I apologize for doubting your loyalty. I'm very relieved to have you home."

"It's been a weird, scary few days, but I'm glad to be back."

Dad nodded, and I could see his concern for me in his eyes.

I couldn't believe it. Was that it? I felt like I had run through the enemy's frontline waving a red flag yet somehow came out unscathed.

"Now, about Evie—" Dad leaned back, plopping his legs on his desk. "Do you really think she is an imposter? Is Bianca pulling the rug over our heads?"

For the first time since coming home, I felt a surge of confidence as I answered. "Bianca is capable of incredible deception."

Dad pounded his fist on the desk. "Agreed. Don't worry. We'll find her, and when we do, she'll meet the same fate as Evie."

"Which is?" I said, trying to steady my voice.

"I already told you. We're all set to go for Evie's execution tomorrow. Once Bianca is recaptured, she'll be sitting next to Evie at the Ancient Altar. We will show the world we will not cower at dissenters' trickery. People must know the consequence of sin." Dad's resolve was unshakeable.

Heartbroken, I realized I had failed Evie. Again. My mind raced, desperate to find a solution. "Dad, there's something—"

But before I could finish my sentence, a loud bang on the front door interrupted me. Dad rushed to the entry while I quietly followed. Goosebumps ran up my arm the moment I saw one of the Scribe Guards gripping Paige by the arm.

"Excuse the intrusion, your Holiness. We found her sneaking around the Sanctum."

My thoughts stumbled as I tried to escape this fresh problem. Unsure how Dad would react to Paige's sudden and unlikely reappearance, it was time for a bold lie. I wasn't about to risk her safety.

"Paige! Did you get lost?" My words surprised me as much as they did my father. "It's alright, Dad. I invited her. Please," I said, addressing the guard, "let her go."

The guard looked at Dad, who nodded. "Sorry, ma'am," he said as he released her.

Paige gave a subtle curtsey to the guard and an even larger one to my father. "Scribe Zimran. It's good to see you." Her words were timid as she shot me a sideways glance.

"Paige Stevens, what an unexpected delight." Dad smiled through gritted teeth. He turned to face me. "How on earth did you two reconnect?"

"It's a funny story, actually. Shall I tell it over tea?" I reached for Paige's hand, pulling her inside. "Thank you," I said to the guard. "That should be all."

The guard tipped his head and left.

Leading Paige into the front room, I sat beside her on the couch across from Dad, who continued to eye us suspiciously. I rang for tea and took a deep breath, ready to spin a tale.

"After escaping Taprin, I took the train back but stopped at Hadston first."

"Why on earth would you stop at that dump?" Dad said before catching himself. "It has its charms, of course. I just meant that it's not a place a Junior Scribe usually visits."

Paige cleared her throat. She kept her smile despite the rage simmering in her eyes.

"It was the fastest way to the Place of Origin," I said. "I didn't finish my offering the other day because of the whole Bianca fiasco. I felt I needed Great's guidance and watchful eye more than ever. As you can imagine, even an hour in Taprin can sink the spirit." My eyes shifted toward Paige, silently confirming that I had not ruined the city's secret.

"A worthy task," Dad said. "What does this have to do with Paige?"

"Well, I got off the train but didn't know where I was going. Somehow, I ended up at the Wall of Remembrance, and that's when I saw Paige. She told me she had moved to Hadston, hoping to strengthen her faith with daily trips to the Wall. Isn't that remarkable? Did you know she had left New Freeda?"

I held my breath as I watched Dad sip his tea.

"No, I didn't," he said, with no hint of remorse.

After everything I had heard from Lucy, seen in Taprin, and learned from Paige—nothing seemed to break the foundation that upheld my father as Great's one true mouthpiece, like catching him in his own lie. For years, I swatted away his icy judgments and misgivings because I knew, despite his many flaws, his relationship with Great muted them all.

Dad sat there, offering a fake smile to the woman I loved more than life itself. He lied about his role in sending her away and the heavy shelf in my mind—the one burdened with years of doubts—snapped in half. My vision of the Scribedom collapsed into a pile of rubbish.

It was painfully clear that the man sitting across from me was anything but holy.

I pressed my lips, fighting back the urge to explode with a

myriad of accusations. Instead, I carefully checked my emotions —a trait I learned from my father—and continued with the story.

"Yeah, Paige had been in Hadston since we broke up. Crazy, right? Anyway, we grabbed lunch and reminisced. While we ate, I felt Great's presence tell me this was the woman I was supposed to marry."

Dad choked on his tea. His cup rattled as he put it down. "What?" Dad wiped his mouth and paused as if calculating his next move.

"So you've finally settled on a wife? I was beginning to think I'd have to choose for you. Well, congrats."

Turning to Paige, Dad drilled his gaze into her. "I hope you realize what an honor this is. I pray to Great you'll respect the role of Scribe Wife." Silent threats danced in between the lines of his words.

"Of course," Paige said flatly. She bowed her head slightly as she lifted her teacup to her mouth. The corner of her lips formed a faint smile while her eyes met mine.

"Then it's settled!" Dad jumped to his feet. "Tonight, I'm throwing a celebratory dinner with the Scribes and their wives before tomorrow's big event. You two must come, and we'll make your engagement official."

"I'm sorry—what are you celebrating?" Paige asked.

My hand reached for hers, hoping to brace her from the answer I knew was coming.

"The Sinner's Sacrifice! Mark my words," Dad said, beaming with pride. "History will remember the day."

MESSAGE FROM LUCY FERNÁNDEZ

FRI, FEB 17

I know it's late, but I saw your bedroom light and figured you were still awake. Call me?

SUN, FEB 19

Ian, stop being an ass. Pick up your phone.

CHAPTER 16
LUCY'S DILEMMA

THEY SAY the truth will set you free. Sometimes, it just breaks you.

I still remember the look on Evie's face when I explained her world was a computer program built by a teenager. I unveiled her eyes, only for them to burn at the raging sun. Back then, I didn't stop to consider the ramifications of destroying someone's worldview. It didn't matter how good my intentions were or how much Evie needed to know the facts. It was as if I had tossed her into open waters, expecting her to know how to swim. Maybe if I had trickled the information, drop by drop, the news wouldn't have submerged her.

We learn from mistakes, right?

Then again, no matter how much you try to avoid it, sometimes life hands you a firehose and tells you to drink. Whether it's learning your world is a simulation, or the person you've been helping is the devil, the truth can feel like a gaping wound. Just ask Evie or Asaph... or me.

I hadn't spoken to any of the Gibsons since Ian kicked me out of *The Garden* in November. He made it clear he wanted me out of his life. Still, we had a history. After losing Ian's friendship once, I didn't want to do it again. Plus, I believed I was the only one who could talk him down from his god-like antics. I still thought he could make things right.

Occasionally, I'd text him or leave a word with his mom. I went to his house during winter break with some of his favorite lemon bars. But no matter what I tried, he avoided me. Messages went unanswered. His door was closed.

So when Mrs. Gibson showed up one chilly February morning, it was odd. Her red eyes and sunken posture told me something was wrong. But there was no way to prepare for what came next. A flash flood was waiting to wipe me out.

"Ian is dead."

The words vaulted from Mrs. Gibson's mouth with explosive power, cutting me like shards of glass. The sting was instantaneous, nearly knocking me over. But the meaning washed over me, refusing to settle into my brain.

"What? What do you mean? No—that..." I choked back the disbelief. "What happened?"

"Car accident," was all Mrs. Gibson could mutter.

She wrapped her arms around me, falling more than embracing me. Her chest shook as she sobbed into my shoulder. It was clear she was still untethered from the news herself. I squeezed her, letting my tears fall as we clung to one another, hoping we wouldn't drown in this unknown sea.

A month later, I was still struggling to accept the truth. It was easier to think Ian was just avoiding me. The rift between us became a breeding ground for plausible deniability. In my mind, he was still around, just keeping his distance. Unfortunately, the facade holding the truth back was fragile. One thought could break the dam, drenching me in the ugly reality of his death all over again.

Since my real world was too heavy to handle, I focused on Evie and her people. Before the accident, I would check their progress once or twice a week. Once Ian was gone, it felt like I spent all my free time monitoring Evie's world. Their virtual existence was my life raft. Strangely, it kept me close to Ian, harboring my love and anger for him. After all, the Simples were his creation—so was their destruction.

Evie's people didn't take their freedom for granted. Bleak memories of Ian's corrosive power were fresh in their minds, and they were determined to find a better way. They set up democratic laws and worked hard as a community to build a world they could cherish.

It wasn't easy. There was more work than there were hands, but Evie was relentless in her labors, putting in twice as many hours as the rest. I could tell she felt responsible for her people's success. After all, she was the one who rallied them to join her in this brave new world.

I watched it all from above, desperate to help yet committed to staying away as promised. But everything changed when Mr. Gibson showed up in late March with a box full of Ian's stuff.

"We know how much you two worked together on that virtual program of his," Ian's dad said somberly. "He would want you to have it. I'm sure of it."

Stunned, *The Garden* was suddenly in my possession, and I was unsure what to do. For a week, the box sat in the corner of my room. Despite what Mr. Gibson said, I knew Ian wouldn't want me inside his world. It was *his* haven, and he had revoked my invitation.

But a growing concern for Evie made me wonder if Ian's program could be their solution. With Ian removed from the equation, maybe Evie's people could return home and be strengthened by the others.

It was an idea I let simmer, knowing I would have to investigate Ian's world to see if it was viable. Eventually— reluctantly—I connected his hard drive to my computer. I didn't know what I would find. With his coding ability, time dial, and ego, Ian could have drastically altered or even destroyed his world in the three months since he kicked me out. Going in was the only safe bet. After creating a new avatar for myself—Bianca —I grabbed a headset and logged into the program.

What I saw shocked me. Nothing was the same. I had left Ian's world when it was nothing more than a small village in tatters. He had killed over half of the original 231 Simples, and only sixty or seventy people stayed behind when Evie's small group left. So I was prepared to see mild progress and potentially even more destruction, but instead, I found a modern world brimming with life.

Vast cities with intricate skylines sprawled beyond the horizon while cars, trains, and radios littered the land. It took me several days to map everything out and weeks to understand how much time had passed.

After a lot of reconnaissance, I discovered it had been over two thousand years since Evie's group left. It explained the drastic technological jump, which was only a few decades behind ours.

Ancient scrolls described visits from Ian, the handful of miracles he performed, and his countless self-indulging commandments. It made me think he enjoyed his influence over the people who had built a religion in his name. They were a zealous people, and Ian was an active god.

Until he wasn't.

Ian's sudden disappearance confused me. Pages and pages of records proved he often spoke with his people in the early days, and then suddenly—nothing. From what I could tell, he hadn't spoken directly to his people for thousands of years. Even with Ian's death, the gap didn't add up.

Unsure what to make of it all, I thought I had hit a dead end. But as I was organizing the extra headsets Mr. Gibson had brought, I found a notebook tucked under the box flap. A flood of memories hit me as I thumbed through pages of Ian's writings. Reliving our time together through his notes revealed so much about his motivations. But it was the entries written *after* Nationals—after Ian kicked me out—that finally helped me make sense of the world's stunning evolution.

Friday, November 18th:
...I'm still debating what to do with those left behind...

Tuesday, December 6th:
...Prayer seemed to be a simple first test. Would these people give up part of their precious time to commune with me? I already gave the command. We'll see what happens after I fast-forward a year...

Friday, January 13th:
...another ten years into the future, I was surprised to see a new gender dynamic among the people. The Scribe interpreted my words to mean only men got a say in marriage...

His journal recorded a twisted game of *What If?* Ian would go down among the people, calling for the sacred record keepers. Each time, he'd share one rule—just one command for them to live by. Then he'd jump ahead two, five, or maybe ten years to see the result.

Familiar feelings of outrage seeped into my pores as I read about Ian's casual indifference to the people he had created. I could hear his words from before: *They're not real, Luce.* I hated that I didn't do more to change his mind when I had the chance. My stomach churned as I imagined the millions of innocent lives ruined by Ian's experimentation. But despite the off-putting nature of it all, I kept reading.

Ian demanded gifts and utter devotion. He insisted on daily prayers and loved to instill fear within his people by threatening devastating consequences for any contrary actions. His chosen

Scribes kept the people in line by twisting his manipulative warnings into so-called expressions of love.

All of it left me very conflicted. Even while I mourned Ian's death, I had difficulty letting go of the anger I felt from his actions. Ian was no hero. Still, I couldn't help but wonder what hidden pain had turned him into the villain I found inside that notebook.

And how much of that pain was because of me?

As I flipped to the next page, my heart burst as I read the date: *February 23rd*—the day of the accident. With a strange mixture of sadness that he was gone and relief that he could no longer interfere in these people's lives, I read Ian's last entry:

I never imagined I would enjoy shaping the beliefs of others this much. But is there any lasting power to my words? These small jumps in time don't necessarily speak to the longevity of my people's devotion. So today, I tried something different.

After summoning the Scribes, I told them I was displeased with anyone who doubted my word. As a warning, I commanded the people to perform a yearly offering. The people had to choose one individual with an impure heart to sacrifice upon the great altar.

The Scribes seemed disturbed by the command but desperate to show their devotion. I'm sure they'll follow through for a while, but what if I jump ahead one hundred years? Or a thousand? Will my children stay faithful if I remain silent for two thousand years?

I want to know, so that's what I've done. The timer is already in motion. I'll check back tomorrow.

Except for Ian, there was no tomorrow.

It was the final piece of the puzzle. Ian never got to see the results of his cruel experiment, but his words had the lasting impact he desired. His influence had permeated life more than I could imagine while his people clung to his ego, tossing logic and compassion aside. They offered their unyielding devotion and dedicated their lives—their very identities—to his cause.

Ian had ascended beyond his wildest dreams. He was the mighty Great.

But who was going to tell his people their god was dead?

MESSAGE TO IAN GIBSON

I know it's late, but I saw your bedroom light and figured you were still awake. Call me?

Ian, stop being an ass. Pick up your phone.

I'm sorry. I didn't love you as you wanted me to, but I did love you in my own way. Always will.

CHAPTER 17
OLD FRIENDS

"I HEARD YOU WERE BACK," James said as he stood in my bedroom doorway.

I jumped to my feet. Reaching for his hand, I pulled James in for a quick hug. "Come in, man! It's good to see you!"

"Same," James said. "I wasn't sure what to expect after our last meeting."

The subtle seriousness in James's usually cheerful voice gave me pause. He had covered for me after my botched break-out attempt, but I was unsure how he felt about it. Did he still trust me? Was he disappointed? Relieved? Suspicious? I tried to steady my nerves, reminding myself that James had always been on my side. Now that the immediate threat had passed, I was eager to explain everything.

Paige walked out of the bathroom, stopping when her eyes landed on James. Her face went flush as she forced a smile. "Hey, James. Long time no see."

"Paige?" James froze. A sudden tension filled the room. "Wow—I, uh... I didn't expect to see you."

James had been friends with Paige since preschool. By the time I met them in seventh grade, they were inseparable. Even when Paige and I started dating a few years later, the bond between her and James seemed unbreakable. Their relationship never bothered me. It was clear theirs was a platonic love. But watching this suddenly strained interaction left me curious. Did our breakup force James to choose a side? Did he view Paige as a dissenter? Was Paige afraid he was judging her?

Shaking off the initial restraint, James opened his arms wide with over-correcting enthusiasm. "Get over here, lady! Don't leave your oldest friend hanging."

Before Paige could move, James swooshed in for a giant hug. Rigid and uncomfortable, she tried to keep her smile from faltering.

"So what does this mean?" James turned to me after releasing Paige. "Are you two—"

"Engaged," I said carefully, trying to read Paige's flat expression. "We reconnected in Hadston, and it just seemed divinely designed."

Paige smiled, and I found myself desperate to know her thoughts.

We had just returned from my parent's house, with only enough time to freshen up. Paige and I hadn't discussed the details of our coverup. She had to be anxious about the engagement story I spun for my father, and I was eager to let her know it wasn't real. I didn't intend to make her go through with the marriage... unless.

My heart skipped a beat just thinking about the possibility of us together again. I pushed the thought away, reminding myself it was merely a front for her protection.

But as eager as I was to talk privately with Paige, James's sudden appearance forced me to deal with him first. His expression was just as difficult to read as Paige's, although he made more of an attempt to act natural. He pulled a chair next to me and lowered his voice as he eyed Paige.

"I wasn't sure I'd see you again after our last meetup," James said carefully. "You know, after—"

"It's okay," I said. "Paige knows everything."

"Of course she does." James nodded. "I really am glad you're okay, but I have a million questions. What the hell happened down there? I mean, don't tell me if you can't—I covered for you when your dad questioned me—but I'd love to know why you broke Bianca free."

I sighed, relaxing my shoulders a bit. James wouldn't rat me out, and I was grateful for his confidence. "You saved my butt, buddy. I can't thank you enough. I'll tell you everything."

And I did—well, *almost* everything. I started with the prompting I got from Great, urging me to send Evie and Bianca through the portal, and moved on to our trip to the Place of Origin.

"So, did you send Bianca through the Doorway of Death?" James asked.

"No," I said, still conflicted by my decision, especially now that I knew who Bianca really was. "I couldn't do it. What if it killed her?"

James leaned back, folding his arms. "But isn't that what Great wanted? I don't understand."

His seed of doubt made all my insecurities come flooding back. James was right, Great told me what to do, and I changed the plan at the last minute. Had I failed His test? Great would have known if Bianca was the devil. He must have wanted her exiled. My stomach plummeted, and I felt a little nauseous at the thought. Great trusted me with an important task, and I failed Him.

"So where is she? What happened to Bianca?" James asked. "And when did you and Paige reconnect?"

I fumbled through the story of our journey to Hadston, running into Paige and following Bianca's urging to get help from Taprin.

"Taprin?" James's eyes grew wide. "Don't tell me you went there!"

I nodded, suddenly awash with guilt. This wasn't the reaction I had hoped for, although I'm not sure why I expected anything else. James was devoted to Great's commands—just like I thought I was until these past few days. As I recounted the journey, all the pieces that justified my decisions fell through the cracks, leaving me doubting everything I had done. Worse, I no longer felt safe giving James all the details, so I wrapped up the story as I had with my father.

"I wasn't there long," I said defensively. "We left as soon as we had a chance."

The details about Bianca's true identity, Taprin's secret, the fake engagement, and our hopes for breaking Evie free remained unspoken. Still, James knew more than Dad. He knew I had intentionally set Bianca free and failed to send her back. Worse, this version of the story had so many holes I worried James would realize I wasn't telling him everything.

I glanced at Paige, who had remained quiet the entire time— a decision I wish I had made. She squeezed my hand, offering me a semblance of reassurance. What was done was done. I couldn't take back my words. All I could do was hope James would see the intentions that guided my actions.

"I know I put you in an awkward situation that night," I said somberly. "But my heart has always been in the right place."

A bell tower chimed in the distance.

"Shoot," James said. "Is it really eleven? I gotta run. I'm supposed to meet the squad at noon. Gotta get ready."

"Where are you going?" I asked, uneasy about leaving the conversation in such a fragile state.

"Official Guard business. It's confidential." A smirk slid from the corner of James's mouth, his satisfaction unquestionable.

After months of me refusing to divulge aspects of my Junior Scribe duties, James seemed pleased to have his own covert mission.

"Once you're a full Scribe, you'll know all my secrets. Gotta enjoy what little privacy I have while I still can," he said with a laugh.

I chuckled, trying to mask my growing discomfort. "Fair enough." I followed him toward the main entrance. "It was good catching up. Thanks again for everything."

"I've got your back, man. Always." James opened the door to leave but spun around. "Before I forget—it's been bugging me since this whole Bianca mess started. What was she trying to steal in the first place? The report said she busted open a chest, but there's no record of what she was trying to take."

I paused, surprised I hadn't given it much thought. That night felt like a lifetime ago. I rubbed my chin as my mind tried to replay the scene.

"Good question," I said. "There wasn't anything special inside the box, just some random items. But I'll look into it if you want. I'm a little curious myself now that you mention it."

"Don't worry about it," James said a little too quickly. "I'm sure the Scribe Guards are doing a more thorough investigation. Just enjoy your time with this one," he said, nudging Paige on the shoulder. "With a wedding *and* an ordination coming up, you've got enough on your plate."

With a quick hug for Paige and a nod for me, James left.

The moment the door closed, Paige turned to me. "Where's the chest?"

"What? What chest?" I asked, surprised by her sudden urgency.

"The chest! The one Bianca, er Lucy, tried to steal."

"You heard James. The Guards will look into it. From what I can remember, it was just trinkets. Some silk scarves and necklaces."

Paige brushed past me, grabbing my hand as she pulled me into the Chamber of Artifacts. I hadn't been inside since the night Lucy breached the room. Except for some yellow tape wrapped around the glass case I broke and the huge dent in the floor, there was little evidence of the messy altercation.

"Which one was it?" Paige asked, pointing to the wall of trunks.

Something had sparked Paige's curiosity, so I played along. I grabbed the stepladder and fetched the box. It looked like someone had tried to fix the smashed corner, although close up, you could tell it had been damaged. The lock, however, was brand new. Digging through my pocket, I pulled out my keys. Thankfully, my master still worked.

"See? There's not much here," I said as we scanned the contents. My fingers grazed the tear in the chest's lining, and I suddenly remembered the small metal box I had found inside the secret compartment.

I jumped to my feet. "I think I know what she wanted."

Paige followed me as I ran to my room and headed for my closet. I reached under a pile of sweaters and pulled out the mystery container, showing it to her. "This box was stuffed inside the liner of the trunk."

"Why is it in your room?"

"I wanted to inspect the items. I had never seen them before, which I thought was strange."

Paige smiled, "So you just took them? Are you allowed to do that?"

I could feel my cheeks blush. "Technically, it's my job to protect and record everything inside the Sanctum. I was worried the Scribe Guards would catalog the box as evidence before I could analyze its contents. I always planned on putting everything back."

"Open it," Paige said, leaning in for a closer look.

"There's not much here, just some seashells and a small knife." I fumbled with the latch and jimmied the box open. "But this," I said as I pulled out the folded piece of parchment. "I wanted a closer look at this. Of course, that was before everything happened, and I forgot."

"What is it?"

I shrugged and carefully unfolded it. Hand-drawn lines filled the large paper. "It looks like a map."

Paige gently took the page from me, scrutinizing it. "A map of what? Why would Lucy want this?"

Trying to decipher the labels, I recognized the markings. "It's written in Ancient Fredenian." My eyes grew wide as I suddenly started piecing landmarks together. "It's the Place of Origin. Look! Here's the altar, the forbidden beach, and the Doorway of—"

I paused, zeroing in on the label above where the portal stood. "Weird. It's labeled *Invisible Doorway*. How old is this thing?"

"Maybe it's true," Paige said with a smile. "It never was a doorway to death."

I flipped the parchment over. "Wait, there's a note on the back."

Paige leaned in. "What does it say?"

I worked the translation in my mind, hoping I was getting it all right. My stomach flipped when I finally realized what I was holding. "It's a note from Evie. I think she made the map. Listen to this:

"The Voice in the Sky told me not to go through the Invisible Doorway. He says the beach is unsafe and forbidden. Lucy encouraged me to listen to the Voice, insisting it was for my safety. But we haven't heard from the Voice or Lucy in many cycles. The rain has stopped, and food is hard to find.

"This is the second map I've created after Lucy encouraged me to hold on to the first one. She said it might help our people. I hope she is right. Tomorrow we are going through

the Doorway to find food. I know it's against the Voice's command, but I can't let my people starve.

"Why does doing the wrong thing sometimes feel right?"

"Wow," Paige said. "Evie sounds like an incredible leader."

"This doesn't make sense. Besides, look." I pointed to the blank corner of the document. "There's no Scribe marking. This is not part of the official historical archives. It's probably a fake. Maybe Lucy wasn't stealing anything, just planting a dummy to get us riled up."

Paige scanned the document. "It's also possible it *was* hiding in the lining all along, which means the Scribes wouldn't have known about it or stamped it. Or maybe, you're right, and Lucy did plant it. But that doesn't necessarily mean it's a fake."

I folded the parchment and placed it back inside the metal box. "We have no evidence to suggest it's real. I'm beginning to wonder—" Dizzy with questions, I refused to consider Paige's theory. "No, Lucy planted it. It's a fake meant to deceive us. She didn't break into the Chambers to steal from the Scribes. She came to insert a fake narrative."

"Stop it, Asaph!" Paige snatched the metal case from my hands. "You will bend over backward to make the world fit your narrative. Why can't you accept something at face value? The only thing Lucy is planting is seeds."

"Yeah, seeds of doubt!"

"No!" Paige inched her face closer to mine and stared with intense confidence. "Seeds of truth."

"You don't know that!" I could feel my desperation turning into anger, and I tried to calm myself. "Let's just drop it."

Paige pulled back, sighing heavily. "You're right. We don't know and never will if we don't look into it. A, if this document is real—wouldn't you want to know?"

I trembled as desperation seeped into my bones. All I wanted was understanding, but I was too afraid to explore the shadows. Searching the dark corners of history seemed dangerous.

Paige reached for my hand, interlacing her fingers with mine. "The Scribes told us about Evie disobeying Great in those early days. This map," she said, tapping the box, "proves that Great issued the command. It verifies that Evie was the one to break that first rule."

"Exactly," I said, unsure where Paige was heading.

"But it does something even more important."

"What?"

"It shows Evie's character. And after what I've been through —hell, after what you've done these past few days—can't you see how easy it is for someone's actions to be misinterpreted? It's easy to make someone a villain when you silence their voice."

"I guess," I said weakly.

"Then maybe we need to stop questioning the supposed sins of every fallen believer. Instead, it's time to question whoever is silencing their voices." Paige slid the metal box back under my pile of sweaters.

"Ask yourself, A—why would Great create a beautiful beach only to forbid his children from soaking in the salty air?"

I shook my head, hoping for an answer. Instead, Paige asked another question.

"Why would Great close the only door that could save his people?"

"I don't know," I whispered.

"Good. Let's start there."

Furrowing my brows, I pulled back. "Start where?"

A smile lifted Paige's eyes. "With the unknown."

MESSAGE TO SCRIBE LLOYD

CONFIDENTIAL

I'm afraid tomorrow's event could turn ugly if we do not capture Bianca. We must enhance our security without alerting the public to any potential threats. Triple the number of Scribe Guards and remind them to follow my orders at all costs.

High Scribe Zimran

CHAPTER 18
LUCY UNDERSTANDS FEAR

IAN HAD a vision for a better world. He created *The Garden* as a virtual paradise to help him escape the harsh realities of life. To this day, I feel lucky he offered me the chance to experience his creation. The moment my feet touched the warm sand on that pristine beach, I was hooked. I bought into Ian's dream—excited to watch a community grow from the ambitious goal of creating a heaven on earth.

Unfortunately, it didn't take long for his Eden to fall.

It wasn't Ian's power that transformed him into a raging god; it wasn't the Simple's awe that converted them into groveling sheep. Fear changed them both. Fear suffocated love and smothered progress. It stifled creativity and outlawed curiosity.

By the time Asaph was born, centuries had passed inside Ian's world, and each new generation had inherited their parents' terror of offending their maker. Traditions pressed forward even though the creator of those beliefs was dead. Ian was gone, but the damage had already been done. Despair had taken root, shaping the world in countless ways.

So, of course, I couldn't tell Asaph who I really was. Even with his good heart, fear saturated his life. He believed his own thoughts were threats to his existence. There was no way Asaph would have given me two seconds of attention if he knew my name or my role in his history. I had to lie, or I would never have gotten my foot in the door. Ian had made me the same devil Asaph was determined to cast out.

I hoped the people of Taprin would have been different. No longer bridled to any dogma, I assumed they'd keep their minds open enough to listen to my request for help. But it was clear they lived in their own kind of fear. It's hard not to create an enemy when you divide the world into *us* vs. *them*.

It was a colossal risk to reveal my true identity the way I did. I knew the City Council would capture me immediately after I shifted to my standard avatar. In fact, I was counting on it. Still, I wasn't sure Asaph was ready to see my true self. But what choice did I have? When I realized Taprin was just as afraid of Asaph as he was of them, telling my secret was the fastest way to save him.

"Who are you *really*?" Nora Chan asked for the hundredth time.

It had been nearly twenty-four hours since Taprin Security threw me into a locked room. The windowless space wasn't even a proper jail cell. There was no bed or toilet—just a wooden chair and four cinderblock walls. Fluorescent lights left the room feeling cold and sterile. My wrists throbbed from the metal cuffs they used to bind my arms behind my back.

A few other Taprin council members had tried their best to extract information at the beginning of my detainment. But no matter how often I told them the truth, they called me a liar. Finally, after hours of interrogation, they gave up.

"Maybe some time alone will bring you to your senses," Nora said, leaving me to stew.

Had they not abandoned me, I would have minded my dire situation more. After all, playing a virtual version of myself required more effort than simply monitoring the scene from my laptop.

Once I knew the council was leaving for the night, I slipped off the VR headset and threw a couple of chips in my mouth. In cozy, flannel pajamas and with a cup of coffee by my side, it was easy to let things unfold from the comfort of my bedroom. Anytime I saw someone coming down the hall, all I had to do was plug back in like a video game.

Of course, it wasn't a game, and I felt the heavy responsibility weighing on my shoulders to fix Ian's mess.

As Nora returned for the third time to interrogate me, I was desperate for her to believe my story. Once again, she demanded the truth, which I happily obliged. Unfortunately, she wasn't buying the facts I offered, so the questions kept coming. It was time to try a different approach.

"Do we have to do this again, Nora?" I said, rolling my eyes.

"We'll keep doing this until you tell us what we want to know. Or don't—it's up to you. But there will be no food or water until you do."

Actually, I was thirsty. I popped off the headset and grabbed water from my desk. Glancing at my monitor, I giggled as Nora freaked out after my avatar suddenly disappeared. I slipped the VR goggles back on, cringing at the site of the bleak room when I returned.

"What the hell just happened? Where did you go?" Nora couldn't hide the shock in her voice. She tapped the watch around her wrist before speaking into it. "Please send in two more security guards."

My eyes stayed steady on Nora. A pleasant smile spread across my face. "I told you who I am, Nora. Why won't you believe me?"

"You say you're Lucy—the same woman who encouraged Evie to go through the portal two thousand years ago. I'm sure you understand why I'm having difficulty believing your story."

"You're a woman of science, right?" I leaned back, holding my gaze on her. "How do you explain the way I changed bodies yesterday? Or the way I disappeared just now?"

Nora shook her head as if tossing away the memory of either incident. "Parlor tricks won't fool me."

"I understand it's hard to believe. It goes against what you know about your world and its laws. People can't change bodies in a split-second or vanish on a whim." I smiled, trying to let my sincerity carry my words. "But there are logical explanations for what I did. It's not magic or trickery. I promise—it's science. It all goes back to what I've been explaining: Your world is not what you think it is."

"It's a simulation," Nora said sarcastically. Two guards entered the room, and relief swept over her face.

"Your world is part of a computer program brimming with artificial life," I said.

Nora scoffed. "Artificial? So nothing about me and my life is real?" She took a deep breath and pounded her chest. "It sure feels real to me."

"I didn't say you weren't real. I'm just saying there is another world outside this one where I live. Ian—or Great, as many call him—built this world, and I helped him run it."

"Prove it," Nora said. She folded her arms tightly, trying to contain the fear I saw creeping up her spine.

"How?"

"If your statement is true, it would suggest Great's early miracles weren't myths, and his actions were real. If you have those powers, prove it to me now."

"I just disappeared and reappeared. You remember that, right? It was thirty seconds ago."

Nora shook her head. "I'm going to need a bigger miracle, I'm afraid."

"It doesn't work like that."

"Why not?"

"I am not Ian. He coded the world, and if I tried to manipulate it, I could inadvertently wipe you all out." I raised my voice to drive home the point. "And even if I could, I won't interfere like that. I've already shown you I can alter and wield my physical body. Isn't that proof enough?"

"No," Nora said. "It's not. Why don't you get Ian and tell him we need a miracle."

"I can't do that."

"Why not?"

I closed my eyes. Swallowing the lump in my throat, I could barely say the words out loud. "Ian is dead."

"Ian the Great is dead?" Nora laughed. "Never in a million years did I think I'd meet someone so delusional! Oh no! The devil is trying to convince me Great is dead."

The two guards snickered, adding to the mocking tone in Nora's voice.

"It's just too much. If I were a believer, I'd be shaking in my boots." Nora gripped the armrest of my chair as she leaned in toward my face. "But I'm not. I've seen enough lives destroyed by believing such hocus pocus. I'm not sure what you thought you'd accomplish by coming to Taprin, but I'm here to tell you: We don't deal with nut jobs—especially when they claim to be the devil."

A third officer entered the room. Rushing toward Nora, he leaned in and whispered something. Nora's eyes widened and then shot in my direction. "It seems the Scribe Guards are standing outside our gates, demanding we hand you—well, Bianca—over to them."

I shrugged. "So do it. I'll even change back to Bianca to make it easy for everyone."

"They'll likely kill you," Nora said.

"I'm not worried."

Nora smiled, shaking her head. "You're not a very good liar."

I returned the smile. "It turns out I'm quite the deceiver. I don't necessarily enjoy it, but sometimes it's the only way to sneak in the truth."

Nora crept forward, her eyes softening. "Look," she said quietly, undercutting the stern tone from before. "I don't want to hand you over. As much as I distrust you, I trust the Scribes even less. But I can't refuse them. They'll break into our town, and who knows what kind of mess we'll be dealing with if they do."

"I understand. It's okay."

Nora sighed, carrying a hint of tenderness as she spoke. "I wished you had told me the truth. I might have been able to save you."

"And I wish you would have believed me," I whispered. "But don't worry—I can save myself."

I pulled the VR goggles off as my eyes darted toward the computer screen. Again, Nora and the guards floundered as my avatar disappeared.

"Find her!" Nora yelled as the guards ran from the room.

With a small laugh, I clicked my mouse, switching the view on my laptop to Taprin's entrance. Sure enough, two dozen Scribe Guards stood outside the city gate, two by two and fully armed. Taprin security officers were running toward the doors on the other side of the thick wall. The officer at the head of the pack talked into his radio, and I knew that was my cue.

Updating my location with a few taps of the keyboard, I put the headset back on. I opened my eyes just inside the city gates. The Taprin officers stopped the moment they saw my avatar appear. Lifting my arms, I allowed them to handcuff me. The same officer spoke into his radio. "Ma'am, we've found her. She's at the gate. We're handing her over."

"Before you send me back, can I say something to Nora?" My enthusiasm seemed to confuse the officer. He turned his back, mumbling something into the walkie-talkie. A moment later, he handed me the device.

"You've got ten seconds," Nora said through the radio.

"I want to thank you for all the attention you've given me these past twenty-four hours. It was just the distraction necessary for my friends to escape." Nora's silence made me smile.

"Are you ready?" The officer asked, taking back his device.

"Yes," I said, puffing my chest up. "—Wait!" Slipping the headset off, I reached over and updated my avatar's code, switching it from Lucy back to Bianca. I put the goggles back on. "Phew! That was close."

The officer's pale face told me the transformation had worked.

"Can you imagine how confused the Guards would have been if you handed over a stranger?" I chuckled. "That would have been awkward."

With a sneer, the officer opened the gate wide enough to push me through. I said my goodbyes to Taprin as the Scribe Guards threw me in the back of their armored van.

"Vile city," another Scribe Guard muttered under his breath just before slamming the doors shut.

"Not vile," I whispered. "Just afraid."

CHAPTER 19
PROMISES MADE

SOOTHING melodies from a string quartet bounced off the marble walls of the banquet hall. I took Paige's hand, leading her toward my parents, who were chatting with Scribe Walters and his wife on the other side of the ballroom.

The soft glow of candles in the middle of two long dining tables magnified the crystal chandelier's warm light overhead. Carefully folded napkins, priceless porcelain dinnerware, and stemware ready for the most expensive sparkling wine marked the settings for tonight's guests. Enormous bouquets added floral notes that danced through the air, completing the scene's beauty.

"Look at this place!" Paige said under her breath as we glided along the dance floor. "How much money did they spend on this one party?"

I had been to plenty of Scribe events, taking little note of the extravagance. With Paige suddenly by my side and the images of Hadston's poverty forged forever in my mind, a wave of shame drenched my heart. "Probably too much," was all I could mutter.

"Asaph!" Dad called as his eyes met mine. "Come say hello to Scribe Walters."

I waved, letting him know we were heading their way.

Paige leaned in. "Please don't leave my side tonight," she whispered. "I can't handle these people on my own. Promise me."

Squeezing her hand, I smiled—trying to apologize and comfort her with a single gesture. I mouthed, "I promise," just as we met my parents and the Walters.

"Scribe and Mrs. Walters," I said, slightly bowing my head. "It is good to see you. How are you doing tonight?"

Scribe Walters slapped my back. Exuberant and flashy, he spoke as if addressing the entire room. "No complaints here, son! It's an exciting moment in history. Seems only appropriate the Quorum should gather to celebrate."

"I'm sorry," Paige said, daring to interrupt. "What is there to celebrate?" Her tone made the question seem innocent enough, despite being well aware of the purpose behind tonight's events. Dad's jowls sank with disapproval.

"We're celebrating the opening of a new era," Walters said, raising his arms for emphasis. "Tomorrow's demonstration will reignite the faith of this generation!"

"Exactly," my father said, interjecting his authority. "The Scribes have long debated the best methods for combating the growing dissenters. Evie's execution is a divinely guided solution."

Paige knew every word she spoke was risky but pressed further anyway. "How exactly?"

Dad's voice grew firm as his patience waned thin. "By demonstrating the consequences of sin. People today are too relaxed in their faith. They have forgotten Great will not be mocked with casual devotion. Hopefully, tomorrow will remind everyone of their duty."

"Of course," Paige said, reading Dad's rising anger. She smiled through gritted teeth. "Thank you for explaining it so thoroughly. I'm sorry if I offended you."

"It's Great you should worry about offending," Dad said.

"Don't you look radiant tonight!" Mom swooped in to dissolve the growing tension. She reached for Paige's hand and twirled her around, showing off her golden gown.

Mom was merely trying to change the subject, but she was right—Paige was stunning. The dress was one of Mom's old favorites and had since come back into style. I smiled as I admired the silk fabric draped around Paige's figure.

"Come with me, darling," Mom said, pulling Paige away from the group. "You must tell me how you braid your hair like that."

Mom winked while Paige shot me a concerned look. I considered interfering as I had promised not to leave Paige's side, but I figured she was probably safer with Mom.

"Darla, why don't you go see how Scribe Godfrey's wife is doing," Scribe Walters said, gesturing to the buffet table. Mrs. Walters curtseyed, silently taking her cue to leave.

"Asaph, you need to watch that girl," Dad said once the men were alone. "She has a habit of speaking out of turn."

A lifetime of trying to please my dad battled my growing loyalty toward Paige, especially now that I knew the part he played in her exile.

"She was just curious about tomorrow's event," I said calmly. "I'm sure she meant nothing by her question."

Scribe Walters laughed heartily, placing his hand on Dad's shoulder. "It took some time for Darla to keep her thoughts to herself. I wouldn't worry too much about it." He turned to me, still smiling. "So she's the one, huh? You're finally ready for your ordination. The Quorum wondered if we'd have to choose a wife for you."

I smiled, trying to remain polite. "No need for that. I feel lucky to reconnect with Paige."

It tore me apart each time I talked about my upcoming marriage, knowing it was all a lie. I would give anything to marry Paige—anything except her happiness. Whatever hope I had for an actual rekindling shattered earlier this afternoon when Paige thanked me for insisting I wouldn't make her go through with the wedding.

Once the truth came out, the Quorum would undoubtedly step in to clean my mess. I couldn't be sure if their solution would be to find me a new wife or reject my ordination to the Scribedom outright. There was a time when both possibilities haunted me. After seeing the Scribes for what they really were, I almost welcomed it.

Dad waved as Scribe Lloyd walked toward our group. "Ah, Scribe Lloyd, glad you could make it."

"Did we have a choice?" Scribe Walters said with a laugh.

Scribe Lloyd did not crack a smile. Tall and slender, he stood as if someone had pulled his nerves taut. His serious demeanor made him a perfect fit for his role leading Scribe Security.

"Any word on the extraction?" Dad asked. "I expected a report back by now."

"Just got word. That's why I am late." Scribe Lloyd adjusted his wire-frame glasses. "The Guards are returning to New Freeda with the prisoner. They won't reach the city until midnight, but we will be all set for tomorrow's event."

"What extraction?" I asked, afraid I already knew the answer.

Dad cocked his head. "I told you this morning—Bianca couldn't hide from us any more than she can from Great. She is back in our possession. As planned, she will be part of tomorrow's event."

I swallowed hard, trying to steady myself. "Congrats on a successful mission," I said, barely squeaking out the words to Scribe Lloyd.

"Thank you," Scribe Lloyd said, eyeing me. His voice was even more restrained than usual. "Fortunately for Taprin, their pitiful officers didn't resist handing her over. Our guards were ready to break down walls if necessary. Handing the prisoner over freely is maybe the first decent decision the wretched city has made. There's not much good I can say for that awful town, but at least they understand their impossible chances against our forces."

"I'm sure the two dozen highly trained guards we sent scared them into complacency," Dad said, proud of himself. "It's too bad. I would have liked to burn that place to the ground."

Scribe Walters laughed at the idea. "That would be a sight to see! Not a bad idea to save for later should this whole Sinner's Sacrifice not scare people enough into obedience."

My head felt fuzzy while my stomach continued to churn. I needed to get away from Dad and the others, worried that if I stuck around longer, I wouldn't be able to keep my composure.

"I'm going to find Paige," I said weakly. "I promised her a dance before dinner."

Dad's eyes narrowed as he grabbed my arm. "Be sure to talk to her while you're at it," he said. "I don't want any surprises at dinner."

I nodded and left. Steadying myself against the back wall, I scanned the room for Paige. A glimmer of her dress caught my eye. Surrounded by several Scribe wives, the soured expression on Paige's face told me to hurry as I rushed to pry her away from the other women.

With a hushed tone, I led her to the middle of the room. "I'm sorry I abandoned you." I wrapped my other arm around her waist and pulled her in for a dance.

"You promised, A. Do you understand what I've been through?" Her eyes penetrated mine, and I instantly felt cut in half. My pulse skyrocketed as I searched for a better apology.

The corner of Paige's mouth turned upward, growing from a smirk into a full smile. With a small laugh, she eased my worries.

"Honestly, I was grateful your mom whooshed me away. It was better than sticking around your father. But, wow—those women are chatty! Who knew open-toed shoes could inspire such a debate?"

With a sigh of relief, I chuckled. "It had to be better than what I just heard."

"Oh? Do tell."

I pulled Paige in closer, whispering as we swayed to the music. "The Scribe Guards have Bianca."

Paige pulled back, searching my eyes. "Do you think that's where James went earlier? It has to be, right?"

"Yeah, I guess."

It never occurred to me that James was there, although I'm unsure why. He was a Scribe Guard with orders to follow, but until now, I never considered the kind of secret missions he was involved with.

"There's something I need to tell you," Paige said, lowering her voice. She glanced over her shoulder to ensure nobody was near.

My heart beat faster, and my mind immediately hoped for some sort of romantic confession. "What is it?"

"You won't like it, but you should know."

I laughed nervously as my heart sank. "You're scaring me, Paige. Just tell me."

She sighed. "James was the Scribe Guard who escorted me out of New Freeda."

"What?" I didn't mean to speak so loudly. My cheeks went red, and I lowered my voice. "James took you to Hadston?"

Paige closed her eyes and nodded. A single tear welled up in the corner of her eye. I gently pushed it away with my thumb.

"So James knew this whole time?"

My body was on fire as my mind replayed the countless conversations James and I had over the years. After the breakup, he was the one I confided in when the heartbreak was too intense. James had seen me cry, told me it would be okay, and helped me move on. Not only that, James had been Paige's closest friend since childhood. How were there no signs of his betrayal?

Never once did he give me any clue that Paige was even gone, let alone that he was the one who took her away. Or maybe I was just too wrapped in my own pain to notice.

Then the real tidal wave hit.

"Do you think—" I stopped myself, unwilling to say the words out loud. "Do you think James told the Scribes the truth? Does my dad know I'm the one who broke Bianca free?"

"I don't know," Paige whispered. "I've been wondering all day. James said he covered for you, and your dad confirmed it, right?"

I nodded. The world was spinning. My eyes raced around the room, scanning one face after the other. I didn't know who to trust or what to believe. Only after settling on Paige again could I think straight. Beyond Great, she was the only person I felt safe sharing my secrets.

Pulling Paige in closer, I whispered in her ear. "I'm sorry I've entangled you in all this."

"It's okay, A, but I'm scared."

My eyes searched her face, wanting nothing more than to comfort her. "Maybe you should leave."

"No, I can't abandon you. Not now."

I shook my head. "You're not. You have buoyed me up more than you can imagine. But I can't guarantee your safety here, and I'd never forgive myself if anything happened to you. I'll tell everyone you were feeling sick. Just slide out the back."

"Where will I go?" The desperation in her voice nearly broke me.

"To Taprin? Is that still safe for you?"

Shaking her head, Paige wiped away another tear. "Probably not."

Guilt nearly knocked me over. Paige was kicked out of New Freeda because of me, and now I had ruined her second home. I had no clue what to do.

"I've got friends in Hadston. They'll help," Paige said. She couldn't mask the disappointment in her eyes. Picturing her back in that decrepit city crushed my spirits, but at least she would be safe.

I squeezed her shoulders, not wanting to look away from her. "Will I see you again?"

"Time will tell." A small smile forced its way onto her face. "Just promise me—no matter what happens—you won't give up on Evie."

My heart nearly burst. After everything, Paige was still worried about Evie. Was there anyone as good as the woman staring back at me? Paige, the supposed dissenter, had more compassion and integrity than all the Scribes combined.

"I promise," I said.

"I'm going to hold you to it this time," she said with a small smile. She leaned forward and kissed my cheek before turning and walking away.

My eyes stayed with her until she rounded the corner. I straightened my tuxedo jacket with a heavy sigh, trying to regain my composure. Dad stared at me from across the room. Righteous indignation filled his chest, and I knew he had questions I wasn't ready to answer.

After checking the stalls to ensure I was alone, I locked the bathroom door. My reflection bounced back from the mirror. All dressed up, I felt like an absolute mess on the inside.

The news about James rattled me like nothing before. A dark cloud of confusion swirled inside my brain, and I wondered how I would get through tonight's dinner. At least Paige was safe; that alone comforted me.

Desperate to find solace, I kneeled and began praying with all the energy of my heart.

"Dear Great," I said, afraid to speak but eager to have my

words heard. "I need your help. I'm so confused right now—torn between what I'm supposed to do and what my heart is telling me."

Combing my thoughts, I deepened my breath, trying to connect with Great's spirit.

"I don't believe you want Evie to die. You are a God of love and creation, not destruction and pain. In your infinite wisdom, you must know a better way.

"My whole life, I was told to follow the Scribes. As your chosen people, you commanded them to lead us with your words. But I fear the Scribes have turned their hearts toward their riches and power instead of your compassion. Their words speak of you, but their actions do not.

"I'm not sure I can be a Scribe. Are they your chosen leaders? Can we bring honor back into the Scribedom?"

Tears welled in my eyes as my desperation increased. "I am determined to follow your commands. Please give me strength. Let me be a tool to make things right."

Goosebumps ran up my arms as a warmth filled my belly. A flood of emotions pinched my face as I blinked back tears. I never felt such a sudden, overwhelming confirmation of Great's presence. Both startling and soothing, I turned my head skyward, acknowledging the answer.

I was the one to set the Scribedom straight. It was clear Great wanted me to speak to my father. The Mighty One had touched my heart, and I was confident He could do the same for Dad. Evie did not have to die. As I focused on Great's work, He would provide a way.

I gently splashed water on my face as I leaned over the bathroom sink. Dinner was just minutes away. Dad would announce my engagement, and immediately after, I would speak to him about releasing Evie. That was the plan.

But when does life go as planned?

. . .

The chatter from the banquet hall was dying down. I sat at the far end of the Scribe's table, across from Dad, who stood at the head. The other Scribes sat in order of seniority. The women were at a table on the other side of the room. There was one empty chair where Paige was supposed to be. My heart took courage as I thought about my promise to her. I was hopeful Dad would cancel the execution, especially once I told him it was Great's will.

"I'd like to thank you all for coming out tonight," Dad said as he stood and smoothed his tuxedo jacket. His black suit made him even more foreboding than usual. Poised and confident, his voice had no trouble reaching everyone in the room. "Tomorrow marks the dawn of a new day as we pledge our devotion to Great's words."

The Scribes nodded, a few muttering, "Praise Great," as they did.

Dad continued. "It is our gift as Scribes to read and understand the Sacred Scrolls. The last time Great revealed himself in the flesh was to give the command of the Sinner's Sacrifice. This powerful ritual has been neglected for too long—pushed aside by those who say it is barbaric. But what is more brutal than losing your eternal life to sin?"

The room erupted with applause. The Scribes exchanged nods as they eagerly cheered for my father.

Glancing over my shoulder toward the women's table, I wondered how the wives viewed the reintroduction of this ritual. A few smiled energetically along with their husbands, while others seemed less enthused even with their plastered grins across their faces. Mom was the only one not smiling.

Dad's voice grew stronger, soaking in the energy of the other Scribes.

"Great prophesied of Evie's return more than two thousand years ago. Her presence reminds us of what we know to be true: Too many people have forgotten their creator. But tomorrow, they will never forget!" He raised his glass, and the other scribes followed suit.

"Come on, Asaph. Join in!" Scribe Walters whispered across the table, urging me to toast with the others. I numbly lifted my glass and choked down the bitter juice.

"Now, there is one other matter of business before we serve our meals." Dad looked across the table, meeting my eyes. I realized I had never told him why Paige left. My mind practiced a few versions of the story, hoping I could quickly explain to the group that she was sick and had gone home.

"All eyes on you!" Scribe Walters whispered, winking in my direction.

I blushed, knowing how much I wished Dad's next announcement could be true. For years, I envisioned the moment he would share the news of my engagement with Paige. Now that it was seconds away, it crushed me, knowing it was all a facade.

"As you all know, my son Asaph—our current Junior Scribe —is scheduled to be ordained into the Scribedom at the end of this month."

I held my breath and focused on my plate, waiting for this part to end. I hated having so many eyes on me.

Dad's voice grew icy. "Unfortunately, that won't be happening."

My heart fluttered as my eyes popped back on Dad. What was going on? Scanning the room, everyone looked as confused as I felt—everyone, except Scribe Lloyd. His weasel-like eyes drilled into mine as a satisfied smirk grew.

"I am heartbroken to announce that Asaph will be stripped of his current title. His recent interactions with the dissenter known as Bianca—including helping her escape and escorting her to Taprin—have disqualified him from Great's work."

The room roared. Sweat pooled at the back of my neck as my eyes bounced from face to face. Only when they landed on my mother's shocked expression did the gravity of the situation pull me under.

"Furthermore," Dad continued as he snapped a finger at Scribe Lloyd, "by Great's prompting, Asaph will join Evie and Bianca at tomorrow's event."

Mom's shriek pierced my ears above the rest of the commotion. She attempted to run toward me but was quickly stopped by security.

Dad choked on his words, playing the part of a grieving father. "Like Steve, who was commanded to sacrifice his son, I have been told to offer Asaph's life to prove my faith. Whether Great will save him as He did Ash is yet to be seen. But one thing is clear. I will not let sin defile the Scribes' good name again."

Dad nodded to Scribe Lloyd, who opened a side door. Two Guards came bounding in. Stunned at the sudden turn of events, I numbly submitted as they cuffed my hands and whisked me off to jail.

CHAPTER 20
SAY SOMETHING

I WAS FALLING with no ground in sight.

My mind struggled to grab onto something—anything to keep me from plunging further, but I knew there was nothing left to grasp. The world had shattered before my eyes, taking my foundation with it. My father had sentenced me to death, leaving me spiraling inside the void of my mind—the pain so thick, it swallowed me whole.

A Scribe Guard threw me into the cell. The thud of my body against the stone wall didn't slow my descent. As the metal clang of the jail doors reverberated throughout my bones, I wondered if the echo would last forever. Cold, damp, and all alone—I couldn't believe I was trapped within the confines of the Sanctum. It had been my home for almost five years, and now it was my prison.

"Get some rest. Big day tomorrow." The Scribe Guard snarled as he secured the lock. He laughed, spinning the key around his finger before heading upstairs. "Keep your eye on that one," he said to the two attending officers down the hall.

Trying to make sense of my situation, I laid the facts at my feet. Replaying every conversation, I frantically clawed for a way out of this mess. There had to be a loophole or clue telling me what to do. But no matter how hard I tried to see a guiding light, I was left flailing in the dark.

Shame swelled like a wave, washing over me before receding, leaving me shivering in fear. After days of justifying every broken rule or little white lie, I finally faced the reality of my decisions. I should never have listened to Bianca. I should have walked away. Long before I knew she was Lucy, it was clear she was trouble. Maybe Dad was right—I deserved my punishment.

For an hour, I sat propped against the wall, numb with guilt. I tried rekindling the inspiration I felt when I prayed to Great earlier. That was real, right? I felt His warmth. He guided me through every step. Swallowing hard, I suddenly wondered if someone else was leading me along. This whole mess started when I met Lucy. Great's warnings about her deceptive ways now laughed in my face. I should have known better.

I wanted to scream, to beg for answers. But each time I dared open my mouth, I stopped myself. Two Scribe Guards fixed their gazes on me as they stood in the hallway, keeping watch. Their soured expressions reminded me just how far I had fallen. I was no longer a Junior Scribe. I was just Asaph—a nobody.

Worse, I was a dissenter.

An alarm suddenly rang throughout the entire Sanctum. The two men jumped to their feet, giving each other unknowing looks. Rushed footsteps grew louder until another guard rounded the staircase, yelling to his fellow officers.

"There's an emergency. All hands on deck," the guard said.

"But we're supposed to stay and watch," one of the original officers replied.

"All. Hands. On. Deck. That's an order!"

The two guards followed the man upstairs. While curious about the commotion, my foul mood quickly told me not to care. I was relieved to be alone.

I looked through the small window in the corner of my cell.

A long cloud drifted overhead, veiling the moon with its dusty tail. Stars pricked the dark sky, daring to shine amidst the blackness, and a familiar thought rose to my mind: *Say a prayer.*

Now, I've prayed thousands of times—and not just for morning and nightly worship. I've dropped to my knees whenever I needed guidance. Over the years, I've built a relationship with Great worthy of a Scribe. There were countless memories of his warmth filling my heart after sincere communion. With every word, I dreamed of being the one to break Great's silence. I didn't just want His comfort. More than ever, I was desperate to hear His voice.

"Say something," I whispered as I stared through the small window of my cell, begging the skies to talk back. Holding my breath, I closed my eyes, waiting for the sweet sound of a reply.

The emptiness in the air mocked me.

I beat my hand against the cold wall. "Say something!"

Tears streamed down my cheeks as everything weighed heavily on my shoulders. Collapsing to my knees, I interlaced my fingers and bowed my head on top of them. But there were no words. I couldn't even mutter Great's name. I was forsaken and unwilling to grovel for His attention.

Minutes passed. My back ached as I remained crouched on the ground. "I would have done anything for you," I finally said. It was an indictment, not a prayer. My voice, cracking under the flow of emotions, purged my thoughts. "I would have been whatever you wanted me to be, gone where you wanted me to go. I gave up *everything* to please you, and what have you given in return?"

Jumping to my feet, I yelled to the heavens. My fingers clenched into fists, trying to keep my insides from exploding. "You told me to take these risks. It can't end like this. Do you hear me? It can't!"

Reigning in my rage, I held my tongue and strained my ears. I was desperate for a response. But then the truth knocked me over, and I scoffed. Since when did Great speak His mind? For thousands of years, His children had waited for His voice to return. Instead, we were told to rely on easily manipulated and misconstrued feelings.

I would have taken any sign of Great's presence. But in the darkness, I felt no warmth, inspiration, or even the slightest indication He was listening. This pain was mine alone to bear.

Stubborn and desperate for guidance, I kept trying. "Just talk, please! Let me know you hear me! Tell me you love me! Give me peace, understanding, or *something* to help me believe you are real!"

I have never demanded anything from Great. The idea of it seemed blasphemous, but I couldn't bear the silence. Great had filled my life with meaning and purpose, yet I was seconds away from giving up on Him entirely.

Finally, my legs broke their resolve. My body crumbled into a ball on the floor as every inch shook from an emotional eruption. Waves of pain carried my tears, making me wonder if I would drown in them. After the tsunami washed over, I begged one last time, my voice barely reaching my ears. "Just say something. Please."

"I hear you."

Scrambling to my feet, I looked over my shoulder, trying to locate the voice. I wiped away the tears from my face. My cell was empty. "Who said that?"

"I did," the voice said again. "Evie."

Embarrassment washed over me as I realized Evie had been in the neighboring cell the whole time. Pushing aside my tears and clearing my throat, I tried to regain my composure.

"Sorry about my outburst," I said sheepishly. My head gently dropped against the bars as my hands grasped the cold metal. "How are you doing?"

"I've been better," Evie said before adding a small laugh. "But it sounds like I'm still doing better than you."

A small chuckle escaped my lips, surprising me with the sweet relief of humor. "Yeah, it's been a rough day."

"I'm happy to listen if you want to talk about it."

I sat near the edge of the cell, my toes poking through the bars. Out of the corner of my eye, I caught a glimpse of Evie's fingers resting on her knees that stuck out from her cage. Even though I couldn't see her face, I found comfort in knowing she was sitting beside me, separated only by the stone wall between us. "You sure you're up for the task?"

"Tell me everything," she said.

So I did—and not just the events leading up to my incarceration. The thread connecting the last three days unraveled my life's history. I carefully plucked every fear and doubt from the dark corner of my mind and laid it at Evie's feet while sobbing, laughing, and cherishing every affirmation or caring "mmm-hmm" she interjected along the way.

When I was done, no brilliant answers danced before me. There was no epiphany or jolt of inspiration. Yet as I asked my questions, indulged my concerns, and admitted my confusion to Evie—I felt lighter. I was still in the same mess I was two hours ago, but her witness to my pain helped lift the weight I had to bear, giving me hope I could climb my way out from the void and find solid ground again.

"Sorry, that was a lot," I said when I realized the moon had shifted to the other side of the sky. "Thank you for listening."

Evie sighed, taking it all in. "It sounds like you're desperate for answers." There was a pause, followed by a soft chuckle. "You sound a lot like me."

Now it was my turn to laugh. "If you had said that a few days ago, I would have been deeply offended. It turns out you're not what I expected. History got your story wrong," I said with a sigh. "*I* got your story wrong, and I'm sorry. You're a good person."

"I'm a person," Evie said lightly. "I've got flaws just like everyone else."

"Sure, but your heart is in the right place. And that's what scares me."

She giggled. "It scares you?"

"What I mean is—if I can judge you so poorly, what else have I got wrong." I shook my head. My mind reeled just thinking about it.

"It's hard to let go of the world we've built in our minds," Evie said somberly. "I still remember the shock I felt the day I learned the truth."

My senses perked up. "What truth?"

"The truth about Ian and this world—" Evie exhaled loudly. "It was rough. I didn't take it very well."

"You've used that name before. Why is it so familiar? Who is Ian?"

"For a long time, we called him the Voice in the Sky. He was the one who created the world."

A fuzzy memory of seeing the name *Ian the Great* on one of the original scrolls popped into my head. Ian *was* Great. My pulse picked up its pace as I was both eager and terrified for Evie to continue. "So, what did you learn?"

Evie slid her hand up the bar, pulling herself to her feet. "I still don't know if I fully understand. Lucy said our world is a simulation—a replica of the world she and Ian come from."

"Wait, *what?*" The absurdity of the words signaled my defenses to stay alert. But unlike all the other times Lucy tried to tell me *the truth*, I told myself to stand down. Evie had listened to me so intently. It was my turn to return the favor. After all, listening wasn't a commitment to belief.

"So you're saying there is another world where Ian and Lucy live?" I paused, thinking it over. "I mean, I guess that makes sense. It would be weird if they were floating around the sky."

Evie laughed. "I guess you're right. I never thought about it much. That's not the part that crushed me."

"What did?"

"As I said, there's another world where Lucy and Ian live. Using the tools of that world, they created this one. I always pictured the Voice in the Sky as some wise, all-knowing god, but then Lucy tells me they are both teenagers and our world grew from some school project."

I laughed, hoping Evie was joking. The entire story was ridiculous. But shock soon replaced my laughter as I realized her unbelievable story answered many questions. The discrepancies between Great's love and anger made more sense if He were some moody teenager.

"Evie," I said, hoping for clarity, "tell me what happened when you went through the portal." I held my breath, trying to withhold judgment.

"Well, Lucy was worried Ian was getting carried away with his newfound power. He started demanding gifts and our unyielding devotion. In fact, it was after he commanded my partner to sacrifice our son that Lucy told me the truth about the simulation and her role in everything."

My mouth dropped. "Wait, are you talking about the story of Ash? He was *your* son?" The account of Steve sacrificing Ash at the altar was among believers' most shared stories. It was the ultimate tale of obedience and mercy. "Why isn't your name mentioned in that story? The Scrolls only talk of Steve and Ash."

"Probably because Ian was furious when I hid Ash to keep Steve from taking him."

The details Evie shared added a new perspective I had never considered. I couldn't imagine how scared she must have been— to say nothing of Ash's fear. Now that I was sentenced to be sacrificed by my father, the whole story felt more like a nightmare than an inspiring tale of faith.

I tried to convince myself there was an ounce of virtue

behind it all. "But in the end, Great stopped Steve from killing Ash, right? He passed the test. Great saved Ash."

Evie scoffed. "I'm not sure I would phrase it that way. Ian was the one who commanded the murder in the first place. He only stopped the sacrifice at the last second because Lucy intervened."

A small part of me was desperate to discredit everything Evie was saying. I didn't want to paint over the black-and-white world of my mind. The other part was ready to burn the whole thing down. Pushing my fears aside, I kept my questions coming.

"So, back to the portal. What happened?"

"Lucy was desperate to get my people away from Ian's power," Evie said. "There was a glitch in his original program that created an invisible doorway. I found it early on, giving me access to the rest of the world, including the forbidden beach."

It was crazy hearing Evie tell these stories. Her alternative point of view seemed credible. She filled in holes that I had long tried to ignore—giving the motivation behind these historical events that I never fully understood.

"Well," Evie said, "Lucy turned that glitch into a portal to a new world—one free from the influence of Ian and Lucy."

The hairs on my arms stood tall. I couldn't believe what I was hearing. Except I did. That was the crazy part. I believed it all. "So it wasn't a doorway to death?"

"No," Evie said. "Lucy gave us our freedom. But only a few people believed her. Ian had convinced too many they would die if they didn't stay with him."

A rapid fire of every interaction with Lucy rippled through my brain, using this new information to see her differently. I couldn't believe she had worked so hard to save Evie and the others.

But even more, I couldn't believe how unfazed I was, imagining this world as a simulation. That kind of information could easily knock you off your feet, but for some reason, it grounded me. Knowing Lucy fought to keep us alive made me think there was value to all of it. We were worthy of the freedom Lucy offered.

I let Evie's words settle, feeling a transformation inside my mind. "Wow," I said quietly. "Lucy really did all that?"

"I did," came a voice.

I turned my head to see Lucy standing at the end of the hall.

"Lucy!" Evie exclaimed, "I knew you'd come back!"

Lucy smiled as she walked toward Evie's cell. She grasped her hand through the bars. "And I knew you'd help Asaph learn the truth."

CHAPTER 21
LUCY'S PLAN

I SAW the irony of the situation. With Ian gone, I was the closest thing Asaph had to a god. After all, I was involved in the early planning of the Simples. I walked among Evie and her people, influencing them along the way. Whether I wanted to admit it or not, I was a part of Asaph's history as much as I was a character in his current story.

As I sat at my desk, watching Asaph accused, jailed, and then pleading from his cell—a part of me wanted to intervene. He was desperate for answers, and I had them all in my back pocket. I could snap my fingers and make things right. But beyond my distaste for lightning shows and self-serving miracles, something else held me back from jumping in and saving Asaph in his struggles.

In his mind, I was still the devil.

Still, my heart broke watching him wrestle with his faith, pleading in the darkness of that dingy cell. I took no pleasure in his fallen state, especially since I knew I was the carrot that tempted him down the rabbit hole. But like Alice, who found herself in that upside-down Wonderland, Asaph needed to journey through the twists and turns to find his way home.

It was all part of the plan.

Right on cue, Asaph's desperation led him to Evie, and nobody was better suited to guide him through the torrential storm of a world collapsing. Her experience and compassion were enough to pull Asaph out of the darkness, giving me hope he would finally see me for who I really was. As he and Evie finished their conversation, it was time to put that theory to the test. Pulling the VR headset on, I once again found myself in the Sanctum's basement.

I stood quietly at the end of the hallway as Evie told Asaph about the portal between his world and Evie's. As she concluded her story, I waited for Asaph's response.

"Wow, Lucy really did all that?" he said.

I took a step out from the shadows. "I did."

Asaph turned, his face wild with shock.

"Lucy!" Evie's eyes grew bright with joy. "I knew you'd come back!"

My heart swelled, seeing Evie's excitement. I walked toward her and reached for her hand. "And I knew you'd help Asaph learn the truth."

"I thought the Scribe Guards captured you," Asaph said once he finally picked his jaw off the ground. He sized me up, trying to decide if I was actually standing before him.

"*Captured* isn't the word I would use," I said coyly. "I let them take me."

Asaph rolled his eyes. "I'm sure. You love playing the part of some devious mastermind, but all I've seen is you scrambling through many mistakes. You would not willingly let the Scribe Guards take you."

I folded my arms, locking eyes with Asaph. "Tell me. What would happen if they got inside Taprin?"

Asaph let out a huff as he threw his arms up. "I get it. You turned yourself in to keep Taprin's secret. Still, that doesn't explain how you ended up here. How did you break free?"

"How do you think?" I asked, eager to see where Asaph stood. His usual defensiveness dripped away as he offered a half-hearted shrug.

I sighed. After listening to his conversation with Evie, I knew Asaph was opening up to new ideas. But seeing me again put him back on the defense. His despondent mood saturated the air, making me wonder if he was really ready to change.

"Since I'm not really here, it's easy to disappear." My response sounded like a riddle, and Asaph looked even more confused. I cleared my throat and tried again.

"I have access to the computer program that runs your world. This person," I said, tapping my chest, "is an avatar. The real me is sitting at a desk in a place called Scottsdale, Arizona. With a flip of the wrist, I can disappear. With a tap of a button, I can reappear someplace else. That's how I escaped."

"Prove it."

My smile widened, happy to see Asaph asking for evidence. "Sure thing, Ace."

I pulled off the VR headsets. My eyes landed on the computer screen in front of me. Asaph spun around. "What the hell?"

With a quick update to my avatar's code, I prepared to return —this time as Bianca. I slipped the goggles back on.

"What do you think?" Bianca's voice said. "The guards peed their pants a little when I vanished after arriving in New Freeda."

"Ah," Asaph said, more to himself than me, "that's why the officers left. They must be trying to find you."

"I knew it!" Evie said, her voice ripe with confidence. My eyes settled on her satisfied smirk as she waved a finger at me. "I knew it was you, Lucy."

"I wanted to tell you, but Asaph was eavesdropping on our conversation that first night, and I couldn't give myself away too soon." I vanished one more time and reappeared as Lucy.

"So you're like a god?" Asaph asked. "I thought that was Ian's role."

"Neither of us are gods." I shoved my hands in my pockets as if searching for the right words. "I mean, sure, Ian programmed the code that started this world and established certain rules—"

"You mean, like a god." Asaph smiled as he interrupted. "From what you and Evie are telling me, I'd literally be nothing without Ian. That makes him pretty god-like in my book."

I half-nodded, conceding to Asaph's point. "Okay, sure. Ian is the god of your world. But that world has taken on a life of its own, independent of him. Your cities, laws, and beliefs are all *your people's* creations." I paused, realizing that wasn't entirely fair. "Although I will admit Ian played a role in shaping those beliefs."

"Again, like a god." Asaph leaned closer to the bars.

"Does that mean he deserves your unyielding devotion? What kind of god demands his children to spend a lifetime worshiping him?"

Asaph ignored the question. "What about you? Where do you fit into all of this? Did you help create the code? Are you part-creator, too?"

I paused. "No, I didn't create the world. Ian invited me to join his experiment."

Thinking back to my first time inside *The Garden* triggered a dozen emotions. My insatiable desire to win TechEd had been the driving force initially. I only accepted Ian's invitation to prove myself and meet everyone's expectations. I had let others determine how to live my life, just like Asaph let Ian dictate his. Now that I knew better, I wanted Asaph to discover the freedom of choosing his own fate.

Asaph leaned in, his eyes sincere. "Why did Ian invite you? What did you have to offer?"

My imposter syndrome loomed over me, reminding me of

what I already knew. This world was Ian's masterpiece, and I was nothing more than a glorified tag-along.

I sighed. "My job was to interact and learn from the people. I walked among them and got a close-up view of their hopes, dreams, and fears."

"That's it?" Asaph said.

Blinking back tears, the tangled mess of my relationship with Ian resurfaced. I shook my head, finally admitting the truth. "Ian asked me to join because he loved me."

It was the first time I had said it out loud, but it was the pause after my words that said the most. Ian loved me, and I did not love him back—not the way he wanted.

Asaph stood silently, but his eyes told me he understood.

I folded my arms, shaking my head. "Ian never interacted with the people as I did, so he never fully believed they were real. It's hard to understand others from a distance, and Ian loved to keep his.

"The closer I got, the more I cared about everyone inside the program. When Ian realized I loved Evie and her people, he felt betrayed. His pain turned into rage. That anger infected this world, and Ian tried to fill the hole in his heart with your people's undying devotion."

A gust of wind whistled past the open window at the end of the hall. Asaph bit his lip, taking everything in before looking back at me. "So why are you *still* here? Why are you interfering now?"

I walked toward Evie's cell. "Because of her." Evie leaned against the bars, reaching her hand toward mine. My fingers clasped hers as a smile lifted my eyes. "Evie changed me with her courage and curiosity, and she stayed by my side even after Ian turned me into a demon."

Evie laughed. Her smile energized me.

"I'm here because I promised to help her," I said. "I don't intend to give up on that promise."

Asaph shook his head, slightly exasperated. "Then why did you pull her through the door? Evie wouldn't be in this mess—or me, for that matter—if you had just left things alone."

I grasped the bars of Asaph's cell, locking eyes with him. "Because I'm also here to help *you*. Evie would never sit back while others suffered. So why would I? Ian's influence has made a mess of things. I'm here to set things straight."

Asaph cleared his throat. "Well, you could start by snapping your fingers and breaking us free."

I pressed my lips together, shaking my head. "I can't do that."

"Are you kidding me?" Asaph scoffed. "You come, show off your powers, but as soon as someone else needs them, it's a no-go."

"That's not it." I sighed, sitting on the small wooden bench in the hallway. "It's one thing to edit and move my avatar, but Evie's coding—*your* coding—is so much more complex. All of you are elaborate, interconnected entities that can't just be reprogrammed without serious consequences. A million moments have molded your life. As I said, *you* are the real creator of your world. If I try to interfere, I could accidentally reset all your memories. Worse—I could delete you."

"So with all your knowledge and technology, you can't bust down this wall or hide me and Evie away?" Asaph plopped down on the ground.

"I didn't code this world, and I would hate to accidentally destroy something inside the program."

Asaph scoffed. "Some god you are."

"I already told you I'm not a god. Never was."

Asaph's eyes lit up. "But Ian is! You said he built this whole thing. Maybe you can convince him to fix things. It's been ages since anyone has heard from him. Tell him to talk to my dad and stop the Scribes. Surely you can give us that kind of miracle!"

My breath caught in my throat as my eyes looked away. "Ian is dead."

"What?" Asaph's voice cracked. He stood, shaking his head. "Wait—no. No, no, no. Hold on." Asaph squeezed his hands tight against the metal bars.

"Is that true?" Evie asked.

I nodded, swallowing hard. "Ian was visiting a cousin in Colorado. His car hit a patch of ice, sliding across a highway until he collided with a semi-truck. He's gone."

"When did this happen?" Asaph asked. "How long has he been gone?"

"It was about three months ago… in my time."

"Your time? What does that mean?" Asaph's eyes bounced back and forth, searching for answers.

I took a deep breath. "Ian could speed time up within the simulation. Those living inside wouldn't feel a difference. But in my world, time can pass in a blink of an eye. Ian often moved things forward to see how the civilization changed and grew."

Asaph's face contorted, piecing together timelines in his mind. "So, how long has Ian been dead in my world?"

I knew the answer would be difficult to hear. With a heavy sigh, I met Asaph's gaze. "Great has been gone for over two thousand years."

"But—but…" Asaph stuttered. "You mean, all those times I was praying—all those instances where I felt Great's warmth, His guiding light…"

"It was all you." I reached for Asaph's hands through the metal bars, eager to keep him grounded. "Don't you get it, Ace? It was *you*. Those bursts of inspiration, the guiding love, the small voice telling you what's right—it all comes from *you*."

As the weight of the revelation came crashing down, Asaph stumbled backward. He sat, contemplating the meaning of it all. "So it's my fault I'm stuck here."

"No, that's on me," I said. "The plan was always to get you jailed."

He stopped, raising his voice. "What kind of lousy plan is that?"

Jumping to my feet, I moved in closer. "Think about these last few days. Consider what you saw in Hadston and Taprin. Think about what you learned from Paige and Evie. Getting up close with the people and places you've been told to fear has prepared you for what comes next."

"And what is that?"

I smiled. "Breaking free."

Asaph threw his arms in the air. "That's what I've wanted this whole time! Dammit, you are exhausting."

With a small laugh, I grabbed Asaph's hand. "Here's the thing about prisons, Ace. The most dangerous ones are created in our minds. None of my so-called powers can free you from your thoughts. Don't let your beliefs hold you hostage. You must cultivate curiosity and stay open to new ideas."

Asaph's eyes softened as he nodded.

"Remember, it's only a prison if you make it one." I gently gestured toward the back corner of Asaph's cell. "This place couldn't keep me locked up, and I'm sure it won't keep you, either."

CHAPTER 22
FAMILIAR MELODIES

THE SECOND PORTAL—I remembered it as soon as Lucy gestured toward the back of my cell. She had told the Taprin City Council it was how she escaped that first night. Now I just hoped her story was true.

I ran toward the corner, guiding my fingers along the edge of the room. Pressing my palms against the solid rock, I moved down the wall, unsure of what to look for. My arm suddenly slipped through an invisible crack. I pulled my body back, keeping myself from falling through the space.

"Whoa," I said, watching my hand reappear before me. "How did you even find this?"

"Well..." Lucy's voice trailed off. "*Find* is probably the wrong word."

I turned. "Wait—are you suggesting you put this portal here? I thought you couldn't mess with the code!"

Lucy shook her head. "This was my only attempt. It was a tremendous risk copying Ian's original glitch, and I fully intend to fix it when this is all over."

"So I just walk through it? Is it safe?"

"Crawl is more like it. And yes, it's harmless. It will take you near the Ancient Altar."

"And then what? What's the plan after that?"

Lucy shook her head, letting out a heavy sigh. "This is where my plan ends, Ace. You'll have to come up with your own strategy after that."

"What? No!" My frustration spilled over. "You're saying you orchestrated this whole thing—being jailed, breaking free, bringing Evie back, Hadston, Taprin—and for what? What about Evie? What about telling the people the truth? I thought that was your plan!"

"It is," Lucy said. Her stoic confidence was unfazed by my outburst. "Remember what I said in the Place of Origin?"

I shook my head.

"You are the key, Asaph." Lucy's voice was calm and tender. "My plan has always been about *you*."

The inadequacy I felt was immediate. I choked back tears, my voice barely a whisper. "Why me?"

"Because actual change happens from within," Lucy said. "As I said, my powers cannot change minds. I can't force people to open their eyes. But—" she said, taking a step closer. "—*you* might encourage them to see things differently."

"Even if that's true, changing minds takes time."

Lucy nodded. "Absolutely."

"We don't have time," I said flatly. "Evie is going to be executed *in hours*, and unless you can snap your fingers and send her to safety, she's stuck. So what? Is she a casualty of this revolution of yours? Or am I supposed to fix that, too?"

"You've got this, Ace. I chose you for a reason."

I huffed, reluctant to go through the portal. No matter how eager I was to escape, leaving felt like signing a contract. My departure made me responsible for seeing things through to the end. What did the end even look like?

"It's okay, Asaph." Evie's reassuring voice broke the silence.

"No matter what happens, I know you've done your best." Her hand reached out from her cell.

Walking over, I grabbed it. "I wish I knew what to do. I want the answer."

Evie chuckled. "Sometimes, there isn't an answer—only questions. Faith isn't blinding following those claiming to know it all. It's about following the questions that lead to understanding. Certainty be damned."

Squeezing Evie's hand, I looked at Lucy. "Okay, I'm in."

Lucy smiled, placing her hand on ours. "I'll be watching from above."

"It's nice to know somebody is," I said. With a deep exhale, I moved toward the back of the cell. Crouching down on my knees, I gave Lucy one last nod before crawling through the portal. "Here goes nothing."

It was the strangest feeling. One moment I was in that dark, damp cell talking to Lucy and Evie, and then suddenly, I was under the night sky, covered by a canopy of trees. The Ancient Altar stood only thirty feet away. I couldn't believe this was the third time I had stood near the giant structure in three days. Even more challenging to comprehend was how differently I viewed the edifice this time. Once revered, now the altar carried the weight of a complicated history.

I strolled along the grassy field, making my way to the stairs. As my foot ascended the first step, something caught my eye. Reaching down, I grabbed what I thought was a scrap of paper, only to find a pamphlet loosely covered with dirt. My fingers traced its tattered edges as my eyes read the all too familiar title: *My Search for Answers.*

"How did this get here?" I looked around, half-expecting

Lucy to jump out of the bushes. The booklet must have fallen out of my bag the other day.

Holding the document in my hand, I wondered if the answers were really inside. After everything I'd learned in the last couple of hours—or days, I guess—was this pile of paper the missing piece? Had the truth been sitting in my nightstand drawer all this time?

I laughed, thinking how terrified I was of the pamphlet's pages just two days ago, and now it stood like a beacon of hope. Sitting on the altar stairs, I inhaled slowly and opened the book. To my surprise, it started with a letter:

Dear Brethren of the Quorum of the Scribes,

For years, I eagerly sat at the feet of your wisdom. The stories of Great's work filled my childhood with awe and wonder. But over the years, I have discovered more questions without adequate answers. What follows are my most pressing concerns about the world's current history, as verified by the Scribedom. I would be forever grateful for your response in helping me resolve these issues.

I flipped the page and continued reading:

Why would Great create this beautiful world, including an ocean full of fish to eat, only to forbid us from walking on its shores?

Why would a loving creator demand a father to sacrifice his son?

Why are women forced into loveless marriages and forever treated as men's servants?

Line by line, page after page, the pamphlet asked nearly a hundred questions. It pointed out contradictions, spoke of failing morality, and raised issues regarding the lack of transparency within the Scribes' laws and lifestyles. I read it all, drinking in the damning problems concerning the Scribe's work and Great's unfit authority over humanity.

But it wasn't until I got to the last page that I felt my heart drop into my gut.

I understand that life demands a level of faith. Some questions can't be answered. But until the Scribes commit to more transparent and equitable ways of working, you can expect the number of dissenters to grow.

Yours Respectfully,
Paige Stevens

I reread the name, unsure if I should laugh, cry, or applaud. Of course, Paige was the author. She always had her eyes open while everyone else walked with blinders. Still, I couldn't help but wonder when she had written the booklet. Had the Scribes ever seen it?

Then it hit me.

My mind replayed the moment the stranger dropped it at my feet before running away. That was Paige. She intended for me to find it—hoping I would share it with the Scribes.

I laughed, thinking back to what Evie said earlier: *Sometimes, there isn't an answer—only questions.*

But the right question was worth more than a million wrong answers, and Paige's hundred questions suddenly were priceless as they made space for new possibilities. It didn't matter if Great was real or not, dead or alive—His name had been used to control others and hoard power, and there was one simple way to take it all back.

Jumping to my feet, I bounded up the rest of the stairs. After three failed attempts in three days, I was finally going to the altar's top. But I was no longer interested in offering a gift to a faceless god. I was ready to make a promise to myself.

As I reached the peak, my breath caught in my chest. Still firmly positioned where I had left it nearly five years earlier was the violin I had offered on my sixteenth birthday. As a gift from my mother, the instrument gave me years of joy as I learned how to command its strings. Mom attended every lesson, swayed her head to the tune, and cheered me on with each new accomplishment. Giving up my violin was hard, but now that it was within reach again, I realized I had given up more than my music. I had given up my passions, my talents... me.

Gingerly, I picked the instrument up and inspected it. I couldn't believe it was still here. Brushing away years' worth of dirt and debris, I plucked one string. Searching for my bow, I found it under a pile of leaves. Surprised by the surge of emotions that tickled the back of my throat, I tucked the instrument under my chin and played.

The melody swirled around me, filling every nook of my soul. I leaned into the music, allowing my body to rise and fall with each crescendo. A tear danced down my cheek—a happy release after years of silence.

"I always loved your music," a voice spoke from behind.

I stopped and spun around. Paige stood, calm and radiant, as always. My mouth dropped. "What? How did you get here?"

Paige took a step closer, resting her hand on my cheek. Her eyes lingered on mine as a smile spread. "Lucy gave me a quick visit earlier. She said she had one last miracle for you."

I had so many questions, but they could wait. I wrapped my arms around Paige and squeezed her tight against me. She nestled her head under my chin, and I basked in the warmth of her body. Our breathing synchronized to the distant sound of waves crashing along an empty shore.

"I love you," I whispered, not wanting to ruin the moment but unable to keep it to myself.

Paige leaned back, her eyes dewy and sparkling. "I love you, too."

I wanted that to be it. It was our happy ending, our forever reunion. I was ready to do and give anything to be with Paige, insistent on giving her whatever life she wanted, no matter what I had to give up in the process.

But that was the problem—it would only be *our* happy ending. There were too many others suffering. There was still work to do.

My finger traced Paige's chin as my eyes locked on her. "I found something I think belongs to you."

Paige smiled. "I know." She reached behind, grabbing the pamphlet out of my back pocket. "I saw everything, A."

With a small chuckle, I shook my head. That's when the questions started spilling over. "When did you write this? When did you get here? *How* did you get here?"

Taking my hand, Paige sat down on the rocky surface of the altar's top. "Lucy stopped me after I left the party, just outside the banquet hall. She said you might need some support and showed me how to sneak into the Sanctum's basement—taking the same tunnel you used to escape the other night."

My eyes lit up. "Ah, so you came through the portal? Before me?"

"I've been here a while." Paige flipped through the pamphlet. "I'm glad you finally got around to reading this."

"I can't believe it was you this whole time. I'm sorry it took so long to read."

Paige smiled. "Well, as Lucy would say: It's all part of the plan."

"Yes. Speaking of plans, I still need one to help Evie."

"*We* need one," Paige said. "You're not doing this alone."

My heart was ready to burst. I leaned in and kissed her. My

finger caressed a strand of hair, tucking it behind her ear. "Thank you," I whispered.

"Don't mention it." Paige went in for another kiss.

I pulled back. "No, really—thank you... for *everything*. An hour ago, I felt like my world had turned upside down. It had shattered before my eyes. I was blind, scrambling in the dark."

Paige squeezed my hand.

"I've spent a lifetime fearing the shadows. I was certain the devil was waiting to destroy me. It turns out Lucy was guiding me back—to you." I paused, sinking into Paige's eyes. "You handed me a flashlight, and now I know the world isn't out to get me. In the light, my so-called enemies aren't that different from me. We're all just trying to make sense of this life we've been given."

"If anyone understands, A, it's me," Paige said quietly. "I know the fear of exploring the shadows. I also know the sweet relief of learning no demons are lurking within them."

"Too bad it took so much pain to see it. If only we had just looked in the first place, right?"

Paige chuckled as she leaned her head on my shoulder.

"Wait—that's it!" I jumped to my feet, rubbing the sides of my head to get an idea to blossom. "I was standing right there," I said, pointing below the altar. "After begging Lucy to tell me why she was here, she said, *I can't tell you, but I will show you.*"

"I'm not following," Paige said.

I led Paige down the stairs, nearly toppling over with urgency. "Think about it. What is the Scribes' most powerful weapon against the truth?"

Paige shrugged.

"Fear," I said. "Why didn't I read that pamphlet the minute I found it? Why did I refuse to visit Taprin? Because I was afraid. My whole life, I was told to fear anything and anyone outside the Scribedom. And I'm only here because someone pushed me to meet those fears head-on. I only learned the truth when Lucy forced me to *see*."

"Okay?" Paige said, still unclear.

"What time is it?" I looked up. A sliver of orange was growing along the horizon.

"I don't know, probably five or six in the morning," Paige said.

I stopped to calculate the time in my head. "Evie's execution is at noon." Pulling Paige along, I headed for the main entrance. "There's not much time. We gotta go."

Paige dug her heels into the ground, forcing me to a stop. "Wait. What's the plan?"

With a broad smile, I leaned over and kissed her cheek. "I'm going to make people see."

CHAPTER 23
LUCY'S POWER

A LONG ROW of sedans approached the Place of Origin's entrance. Evie's execution was an hour away. As I watched from my laptop, I was unsure how the events would unfold. My stomach tightened, wondering if I had made the right decision in trusting Asaph. Would he be able to save Evie? Could he persuade his people to see the truth? Or was I foolish for standing back when I had the world's powers at my fingertips?

When Ian and I first started working on *The Garden*, we debated about the culture we wanted to create. While I was eager to take the safest route, Ian thought he could program his way into a better life. His brilliance was unmatched, and his technology opened endless possibilities. So why did I fear him trying to make the perfect world?

Part of my hesitation was that Ian always acted alone—a habit of the perpetually isolated. He never asked anyone's permission to experiment because the rules didn't matter to him. As someone who lived by the expectations of others, it was hard for me to understand.

Ian manipulated time and space inside his program. He didn't just shape the world; he shaped the Simples' minds. In doing so, Ian turned the people's loyalty into a prison. His personal utopia was built from their bondage.

Sadly, even with his death, Ian's power didn't go away. Instead, it transferred to the Scribes, who claimed to speak on his behalf. They didn't need Ian's technology to manipulate the minds of those they led. The fear left in Ian's wake was enough to control them all.

And as the Scribes exited their cars that hazy morning, one thing was clear: They were eager to display the fullness of their power.

It was easy to think none of it was real. Sitting in the comfort of my suburban life, sipping coffee, and still in my pajamas—I could have convinced myself the events unfurling on my monitor were scenes from a movie. I watched the Scribes line up near the front gate, dressed in deep plum ceremonial robes with golden stoles draped around their shoulders. The yards of fabric swooshed with every heavy step they took.

I counted the men on my screen—only eleven. I realized High Scribe Zimran was missing just as another car approached. Zimran stepped out in a red satin robe and the same gold sash. His larger frame and blood-dyed frock made him stand out as the group's leader.

Unlike the people of New Freeda, I wasn't interested in these pious men. Their pretend authority did little to grab my attention. My only concern was confirming Evie was okay. I held my breath, waiting for her arrival.

When two armored trucks pulled up, my heart stopped. A few dozen guards leaped out, most falling into line a distance behind the Scribes. Two men moved toward the back of one truck. With swift and aggressive force, they yanked Evie out of the vehicle. Her arms were bound behind her back. She looked hungry and tired, but mostly, she looked resolved. Straightening herself as she planted her feet, her confidence outranked everyone else.

Seeing Evie reminded me how real this whole thing was.

My nerves began tingling. Only then did the temptation of my power creep into my mind. It would have been easy to change the code and intervene. And if anything could persuade me to come ripping through the skies with thunder and lightning, it was Evie. I wanted her safe. She needed to get home to her children. Knowing I had the tools to make it happen made me want to jump in and save the day.

But I also knew Evie would urge me to hold back. Ian had created this mess with his showy displays of power. The dominoes of his actions rippled over time, creating an incredible imbalance between the haves and have-nots. While I could swoop in and show my strength, where would that lead things? I would be no better than Ian, just another person to fear—or worse, worship. The people needed to regain their power, not transfer it to someone else.

So I stayed put. I had done my part. And honestly, I probably interfered too much already. It was in Asaph's hands now.

"Speaking of which, where is he?" I said to myself as I clicked through multiple camera angles on my computer.

When *The Garden* was just a tiny village, it was easy to monitor the entire program. But the world had grown exponentially since those early days. Rotating through the countless views could last a lifetime.

I stopped, thinking about the places Asaph was most likely to visit. He had talked with Paige before they left the Place of Origin earlier. I followed them into Hadston but lost their trail when I checked on Evie and the Scribes.

Moving through a dozen or more angles of Hadston, I finally caught a glimmer of Paige as she snuck into a tiny home on the outskirts of town. Fumbling around, I tapped furiously to find a better view. She had gathered with a group of people I didn't recognize, and Asaph stood at the front, speaking. I zoomed in and turned up the volume to ensure I didn't miss a thing.

· · ·

"I know I'm asking a lot," Asaph said. "And there are no guarantees. This plan could backfire. Things could go sideways. I can't promise your safety."

"Then why risk it?" asked a gruff old man in the back. His spindly fingers tapped the table as he stared at Asaph from across the room. "It took me twelve years to get back a fraction of the life them Scribes stole from me. Now you want me to risk their wrath with no assurance of success?"

A handful of others nodded in agreement. Paige stepped from behind Asaph, raising her voice over the growing murmurs, demanding the group's attention. "Imagine you could rewind time. Would you? Would you go back to your old life if given a chance? Could you do that now that you know what you know?"

"No way," a young twenty-something woman said. "I may be dirt poor and an outcast, but I would never go back. At least here, I'm free."

A few others mumbled in agreement.

Paige offered a knowing smile. "Now imagine if your family knew what you knew. Imagine if the world embraced new ideas instead of casting them out like lepers."

"I still don't understand," another man said. He stood, towering over everyone else in the room. "Won't the gates be guarded? There's no way we can sneak past the Scribe Guards. Evie's execution is a major event. It's being broadcast worldwide. Do you really expect us to just walk to the altar?"

The room burst with commotion as the group questioned the plan. I could see Asaph's face faltering. He leaned over to Paige, shaking his head. "They're right," he muttered. "They'll be guarding the entrance. How did I not think of that?"

It felt like my cue. I could fix this, right? They needed a way into the city, and I could provide it. But as I played out the scene,

I knew it wouldn't work. There were too many people. The consequence of a crowd witnessing my capabilities was dangerous. As much as I wanted to intervene, I told myself to stay put.

Paige jumped on a chair, waving her arms. "Listen up! Everyone—quiet!" The room fell into a silenced hush. "I get it. You're scared. We're all scared. But if anyone can find a solution, it's this group right here." Her eyes scanned the crowd as they exchanged glances.

Finally, a young girl, only twelve or thirteen, raised her hand. "There's another way in," she said timidly.

The gruff man in the back laughed.

"Shhhh," Paige hissed. "Let Lily-Mae talk." She reached for the girl's hand and pulled her to the front of the crowd.

"There's a crack near the Wall of Remembrance that I found last year when I arrived. It's a way off from the gathering spot, mostly covered by some bushes and shrubs. It's a tight fit, but I think most people here could squeeze through it."

"Wait, so you've snuck into the Place of Origin?" Asaph asked.

"Yes, sir," the girl said. She immediately tensed up, wondering if she was going to be punished. "I didn't mean to. I just wanted to pray like everyone else. But the crowds kept pushing me aside, so I prayed further away—hoping Great wouldn't mind. That's when I found the passageway. At first, I thought it was Great's way of blessing me." She chuckled. "Now I just think it's a fun secret hideaway."

"Then that's the plan," Asaph said, regaining his spirits. "For those willing, we'll head toward the Wall shortly."

Paige looked over at the crowd. "Do you all remember your role? If you want to back out, now is your chance. There will be no hard feelings. I know we're asking a lot. For those willing to take this chance, get ready. We leave in ten."

. . .

I watched as the group dispersed, and a swirl of emotions moved in. Asaph had put together a plan, just like I knew he would. My fears about Evie began to subside, and I breathed easier. A rush of pride washed over me, pleased that my hunch about Asaph was spot-on. If anyone could turn the tides, it was him.

But the satisfaction was short-lived. When it settled, I was left feeling anxious and sad. I tried to reconcile the feelings, unsure why I was suddenly despondent. After all, Asaph was working to save Evie. The truth was getting out to the people. I should be overjoyed.

So, why wasn't I?

After years of people-pleasing perfectionism, my embarrassing failure at Nationals was a turning point in my happiness. With my reputation stripped away, I found myself—the real me—among the rubble of rumors and scorns. The cares of others no longer sustained me as I learned to trust my inner voice.

Then Ian died, and my world muted into a dull nothing. There were so many unresolved issues between us, so many unanswered messages. I always believed we'd work things out. But no matter how hard I tried, Ian held onto his grudge, taking it to his grave. He never got his redemption story.

We never got a redemption story.

For months, everything felt hopeless—until Bianca. Slipping into Bianca's character over the last few weeks filled me with surprising purpose. Her determined, willful spirit gave me hope that I still had some fight inside me. Even more, it made me believe I could save Ian's world even now that he was gone. The weeks of planning and then working to show Asaph the underbelly of his indoctrinated life made me feel alive for the first time in months.

But now that I had handed Asaph the reins, I was suddenly empty-handed.

I was just Lucy again—more alone than ever.

Worse, for the first time, I found myself tempted by the power that started this whole mess. With a few taps, I could reinsert myself into the program and never feel invisible again. I could get the people to love me. I could make them see me.

Suddenly, I understood some of Ian's pain. The loneliness was heavier than I imagined, and the appeal of simulating the love missing in your life was tangible. When the ability to code the world of your dreams is within reach, only a fool sets it aside.

Except, my dream included the very people I would hurt if I went down that path. Unlike Ian, I knew these people—their hopes, dreams, and fears. I couldn't insert myself without taking something away from them. And no temptation was big enough to do that.

So I kept my distance. I used every ounce of strength to push my power aside for the ones I loved. My hope remained tied to Asaph and Paige, and I carefully monitored them as they finalized their plan.

Maybe I was alone, but I vowed not to lose myself.

Through it all, I wanted to think Ian was somehow learning from all of this. Sometimes I imagined him watching from above just like he used to observe me inside *The Garden*. Does Ian know his people are fighting for what's right? Even if they were ultimately fighting against him, those leading the revolution were part of his legacy. Asaph would be nothing without Ian.

I guess that is its own kind of redemption story.

MESSAGE TO IAN GIBSON

TUE, MAY 16

For a long time, I didn't understand why you permeated the Simples world the way you did. I think maybe now I do.

I'm not saying what you did was right, just that I know what loneliness can make a person do.

I guess this is my way of saying I miss you.

CHAPTER 24
BY THEIR FRUITS

"This way," Lily-Mae said as she led us through the crowded streets of Hadston.

The day's event magnetized people toward the Wall of Remembrance, where Evie's execution was scheduled to be broadcast. The air was thick with prayerful songs and chatter from bystanders. Moving through the congestion was difficult, with so many people clamoring for a spot at the Wall.

Gripping Paige's hand, I pulled her close, shielding her from the throng of people as we followed Lily-Mae. I glanced back at the group trailing behind me, counting heads to ensure we still had all twenty-nine people. "We've lost someone."

Paige kept her eyes straight ahead. "Gary Wright backed out at the last minute."

The news rattled me, but I shook it off. Gary had been the most vocal about the risks; we were better off without him. Besides, we still had enough people to carry out the plan. My feet picked up their pace. "What's the time?"

Paige glanced at her watch. "11:43"

"Shoot. We don't have much time." I looked over my

shoulder at a thin, redheaded woman. "Sarah! Tell the others to hurry."

"It's no use," Sarah said as she squeezed between two large bodies. "There are too many people. We can't move any faster."

Lily-Mae continued to maneuver through the crowds. Her petite body had no problem weaving in between tight spaces. Forcing myself to be bolder, I pushed past a clump of onlookers, dragging Paige behind me.

"How much longer?" I asked as I caught up.

"Almost there," Lily-Mae said, slightly out of breath. "Wait!" The young girl suddenly stopped, and I nearly bull-dozed into her. She pointed toward a line of shrubs. "It's just behind that bush."

Following her finger, I couldn't make out any break in the wall. "Are you sure?"

"Positive." Lily-Mae glanced behind me and then back at the wall. "How will we get through without being seen by all these people?"

I scanned the area. "Everyone is moving toward the city center. I doubt anybody will care what we're doing. Let's get closer to the wall. A few can stay behind to cover us."

With less than fifteen minutes, there wasn't time for other ideas. I hurried toward the bush, pulling our people toward the spot.

"Stand here," I said, picking out the largest bodies to form a wall around us.

"Aren't we going in?" a man named Gabe said.

"I need you to stand watch and ensure nobody follows us. Okay?" I signaled for Lily-Mae to move through the crack, still uncertain it was large enough to let a person through. Sure enough, once her body crouched down, I could see where a piece of the wall had crumbled, making a small but passable doorway.

As soon as Lily-Mae made it to the other side, I began

directing others to follow. "Keep close to the ground and try to stay hidden," I whispered as each person passed.

Too rushed to acknowledge my rising anxiety, I couldn't ignore the overwhelming gratitude I felt as I met each pair of eyes. These people were practically strangers, but they entrusted me to lead them. Once Paige made it to the other side, it was finally my turn. Nodding to the seven men who stayed behind—their bodies acting like shields, I crawled through the crack.

Relieved the space opened into a thick patch of trees, I carefully made my way to the front of the group. The weighty thud of a kettle drum sunk into the earth. I could feel the rhythmic pulse under my feet as it synchronized with the beat of my heart. One by one, we moved closer to the grassy patch on the other side of the forest. Huddled with twenty-two other people, Paige and I silently waited for our moment to act.

The altar was in plain sight, but something seemed different about the view. Taking in the scene, I realized all the former offerings had been cleaned up. The grass was no longer littered with jewels and golden trinkets. I wondered what the Scribes did with all the precious things that were supposed to be gifts for Great. Maybe they didn't want the world to see their wealth. Their lack of transparency was another sign of their guilt.

Dad climbed the stairs, his red robe kissing the ground as if floating to the top. Evie sat, bound and gagged, with her legs dangling off the side of the grand structure. Once Dad reached her, a satisfied smirk turned his lips heavenward. But I recognized the anger in his eyes. Bianca and I had escaped, and our absence had Dad seething.

The other Scribes formed a semi-circle around the tower in the grassy field below. Scribe Walters, the most junior quorum member, stood next to the large drum as he struck it with massive blows: *Thump, thump, thump.* The acceleration of the beats signaled my already racing heart to move faster.

A few Scribe Guards stood further back with cameras and

equipment, ready to broadcast the event. I found it odd there was no other security detail nearby, mainly because the Scribes had lost not one—but *two* prisoners in the last twelve hours. It was safe to assume more guards were hiding nearby. I just hoped they hadn't already made our position.

Dad raised his arms over his head as he nodded to the group below. Scribe Walters gave the drum one final whack, allowing the reverberation to echo through the field. Even in the drum's silence, my heart beat against my chest as sweat beaded across my brow. It was almost time.

"My fellow citizens, I send my blessings." Dad's booming voice had no trouble reaching everyone below. "I come before you with sorrow in my soul. There is much to fear in these troubled times. Wickedness is rising as the devil has sunk her teeth into the hearts of men. Too many believers have given into their useless doubts, adding numbers to the dissenters."

Paige pressed her hand against my back, instinctively steadying me as my breath grew erratic. "You okay?" she whispered.

I nodded as my throat tightened. From the corner of my eye, I took inventory of our group. Men and women of all ages congregated behind the trees. Plenty seemed nervous, but none looked quite as agitated as I felt.

"Still," Dad continued with brash confidence, "despite all the follies of the world, there is reason to rejoice. In His infinite wisdom, Great has provided a way for us to prove our devotion."

"Bullshit," I muttered.

"Amen," Paige said.

With a sweeping gesture toward Evie, Dad grew more severe. "As prophesied, Evie has returned. She was the first to defy Great and partner with the devil, reminding us of the evil capable of infecting our hearts."

Evie remained unflinching in her resolve. I envied her surety. Her gentle fortitude guided me through the darkness last night

—an impressive feat, considering she was dealing with her own terrifying future. With all the chaos in life, maybe the secret to finding peace was leaning into the unknown.

I closed my eyes, steadying my breath. My thoughts rained down, drenching me in the countless ways this plan could backfire. I had no idea how everything would unfold, but as I thought of Evie, I tried to embrace the uncertainty. With a leap of faith, I decided to bet on myself. And that single decision did more to calm my frayed nerves than any prayer I had ever muttered.

Dad reached into the inner pocket of his robe, pulling out a small knife and raising it high above his head. "And now, in the name of Great, our one and only creator, we offer this woman's life as a token of our devotion—"

I pulled all the air from my lungs and yelled as I lunged forward. "Stop!" My feet sprinted toward the group of Scribes. "This is not the way!"

The camera panned my direction while my gaze lasered in on Dad. His eyes grew wide before narrowing in on me. "Asaph! What is the meaning of this?"

"Please, stop!" I reached the bottom of the altar, catching my breath as Paige and the others followed behind.

Scribe Lloyd pulled a whistle from around his neck. The high pitch screeched against my ear. "Guards! Seize them!"

A group of soldiers sprinting toward us appeared from the opposite side of the forest. I watched James as he zeroed in on me. Thankfully, our little group had counted on the guards' presence, and everyone stuck to the plan. Raising our hands, we peacefully let them bind us. James grabbed my arms, forcing them behind my back.

"Don't even think of breaking free," he whispered.

My eyes met his, and I could see the fear behind them. He tried to mask it with a furrowed brow and stern lips, but hidden behind his scowl was a shadow of a doubt and a pang of regret.

Dad dropped the knife and hurried down the stairs. Through gritted teeth, he leaned in toward me. "What is the meaning of this, Asaph!"

"I have a message from Great," I shouted, taking my chance to speak before being silenced.

The Scribes sneered and rolled their eyes.

"You?" Scribe Lloyd said. "A message from Great? He only speaks to Scribes, a title you will never possess after what you did." The satisfaction on his face drew the corners of his mouth up into a disturbing smile.

I met his gaze, calmly standing my ground. "And why don't you tell the world what I did?"

Scribe Lloyd scoffed. "Gladly." He grabbed my arm and turned toward the camera. "Behold history's youngest Junior Scribe: Asaph Zimran. Many believed he'd eventually follow in his father's footsteps and become the High Scribe someday. He had so much promise, but no more! Yesterday we stripped him of his title after discovering he broke the dissenter Bianca from jail and accompanied her to the depraved city of Taprin."

"A grave sin, indeed," I said. "And tell me, do the Scribes hold themselves to the same moral standards they use to punish others?"

Scribe Lloyd's face pinched inward. "Of course."

I looked over at Lily-Mae. With a nod, I signaled her to speak.

"Uncle George," Lily-Mae yelled.

The color in Scribe Lloyd's face drained at the sound. Uneasy, he glanced toward the girl before yelling at the guard who held her. "Silence her!"

Lily-Mae lifted her knee and stomped on the soldier's foot, who recoiled in pain. She ran toward the camera, defiant and determined.

"Scribe Lloyd is my uncle," Lily-Mae said. "For years, he abused me. When I finally told my parents, the Scribes banished me to Hadston. My great sin was standing up to my abuser!"

The other Scribes exchanged concerned looks.

Scribe Lloyd's eyes filled with rage. "Lies! Guards, grab her. Now!"

As a handful of officers chased after her, an older man named Fred spoke out. "I'm Fred Robles. I refused Scribe Dalton's request for tithes. My wife was sick—she needed that money. But Dalton kicked us to the curb and helped himself to my house. My great sin was trying to save my wife's life!"

"I'm Katy Flores, and I was exiled to Hadston after requesting admission to the men's university. My great sin was a desire for an equal education!"

"I'm Jay King, and I was exiled because Scribe Nickles wanted to marry my wife!"

"I'm Shayla Gonzales, and I was exiled because my husband publicly expressed doubts about the Scribedom!"

One by one, the group of dissenters spoke their statement with powerful precision, painting a disturbing picture of the many ways the Scribedom had failed them.

The Guards scrambled to stop the protestors, but each time they got one, another declared their own injustice. Some accusations were so vile my head spun imagining the pain inflicted. The weight of their crushing stories was almost too much to bear, but there was strength in speaking the truth. Connected by their grief, the people were determined to ensure these odious crimes never happened to anyone else.

The crowd grew unruly. Fighting to keep the people under control, some Guards began yelling back at the protestors. Others stepped aside, unsure who to believe or what to do. Whenever a Scribe was accused, they hollered their objections. The noise from all of it made it impossible to think straight.

"Enough!" Dad's voice cut the congregation's uproar. He pushed his weight to the front of the group, eying each person as he passed. Despite his calm, calculating demeanor—I knew Dad well enough to tell he was floundering.

A smile inched across my face as I realized we had done it. We had thrown a rock into the Scribe's machine, spewing seeds of doubt far and wide. The guilt sweeping across their faces as they frantically tried to deny the accusations only verified the stories. I hoped the world would finally see the Scribes for who they really were.

Dad approached me, his face inches away from mine. I could see him wrestling for the right words, but before he could speak, a loud thump echoed through the air.

We all looked up, unsure of what had caused the noise. *Thump.* It grew louder. *THUMP.* A flock of birds ripped from the trees. With one more pounding thud and a deafening crash, a chorus of shouts grew like a tsunami.

"What's happening?" Paige asked, squeezing my arm.

I had no clue, but it was clear whatever it was—it was getting closer.

CHAPTER 25
NO ANSWERS

I FELT a spark of relief when I saw Gabe sprinting toward us. The other men we had left guarding the wall followed him, and I hoped they were coming to help somehow. But the respite died fast. The men waved their arms, gesturing toward the city wall. I couldn't hear them over the roar moving in from behind. But it didn't take long to realize what was happening as dozens of angry eyes peeked through the forest.

A mob was coming.

I won't lie. A part of me enjoyed seeing the most powerful men huddled together in fear of their unknown future. After wrestling with my inner demons, the payback was delightful. Or at least it would have been had I not been freaking out myself. My hope hung on a balance, and I wanted to know if the people were coming in support or defiance.

As their screams unified into a rallying battle cry, I had my answer.

"Down with the Scribes! Down with the Scribes!"

It was hard to estimate the size of the crowd, but at least a hundred people sprinted through the forest. It was more than enough to overpower the Scribes and their guards. Stuck in the middle of it all, I pushed Paige away. "Get out of here! You can't be here."

"No way," Paige said, holding her ground. "We need to fix this."

"How?" I could barely hear myself over the noise.

An elbow knocked me over, and for a second, I thought the crowd would trample me to death. A firm grip around my arm pulled me to my feet. James pushed one rebel back as he pulled Paige and me to the outer edge of the mob. "It's not safe here, man. You guys need to leave!"

"No," I snapped back. "We need to stop this before someone gets hurt."

James nodded. Things continued to escalate as we helplessly stood and watched. Knowing we needed to stop the crowd and actually doing it were two very different things. Even the Scribe Guards, with all their training, seemed threatened by the angry horde.

A few feet away, Scribe Lloyd's wiry voice rang above the chanting. "Stop! Don't touch me!"

Two hefty men were wrestling Scribe Lloyd to the ground. One grabbed the shiny whistle from his neck and tossed it aside. The glimmer of metal caught my eye, and I lunged forward to grab it.

I tapped James on the shoulder. "Protect Paige. I'll be back."

Weaving through the throngs of people, I reached the altar and ran up the stairs. By some miracle, nobody followed, giving me hope that the mob wasn't looking to harm me. I prayed the whistle would be loud enough to get the people's attention below. But as I reached the top, I saw Evie, still bound and gagged. With my promise to Paige fresh in my mind, I knew this was my chance to save her.

I untied Evie as I whispered in her ear. "You need to get out of here. Nobody is watching the portal right now. Sneak behind the altar and go."

"Let me help you," Evie said. "Or come with me. It's safer than staying here."

I hoisted Evie to her feet. "No, I need to save my people, and you need to get back to your sons." Guarding Evie as I guided her down the stairs, she squeezed my hand when we reached the bottom.

"Thank you! I'll never forget what you did," she whispered before darting behind the altar and sprinting away.

My eyes stayed with her through the foliage until she disappeared from view. I scanned the crowd, ensuring nobody followed, and then ran back to the top of the altar. From there, I could see the scene below getting crazier by the minute. With no other options, I pressed my lips against the cold metal of Scribe Lloyd's whistle, blowing as hard as I could. The sound hit everyone's ears with perfect precision.

"Everybody, STOP!"

And to my surprise—and utter relief—they did.

Scribe Walters was on the ground sobbing while Scribe Johnson tended to an open gash on his forehead. The angry crowd heaved a collective sigh, waiting for me to justify this forced truce. Two Scribes had ropes dangling around their necks, makeshift nooses that made me realize how determined the mob was.

But one man was missing. I scanned the crowd, searching for the blood-red robe that should have made Dad easy to find. Only after I turned around did I see him standing behind me.

He raised his arms above his head, moving his lips as if silently praying.

"What are you doing?" I asked. "Is this your way of helping?"

Dad opened his eyes and gazed down at the crowd. "Behold, the fulfillment of prophecy!"

"What are you talking about?" I yelled.

Dad took a solemn step forward. His voice was strong and confident. "After two thousand years of silence, Great has finally returned to offer his wisdom." He bowed his head with practiced humility as the crowd murmured in disbelief. A hushed gasp rippled through the crowd.

My feet were cemented to the ground. I still wasn't sure what was happening, and my bewilderment only grew when Dad yelled to the officers.

"Guards! Seize the Scribes. Now!"

Confusion morphed into chaos. The Scribe Guards exchanged fearful looks, unsure if they should follow the order. After all, one wrong step could get them kicked out of the Scribedom's good graces. But High Scribe Zimran had spoken, and in the end, James was the first to follow his command.

"You heard him!" James said. "Grab them."

The Scribes protested, refusing to believe their leader had demanded their capture. A couple of men tried to run away, but the heaviness of their robes was no match for the speed of the soldiers. Within a minute, the Quorum had been herded like cattle. The dissenters cheered as the once-holy men succumbed to their fate.

Paige stood off to the side, her expression as confused as I felt. I rushed down the stairs. "Are you okay?" I asked, hugging her tightly.

"What's going on? What is he doing?"

I pulled back, looking into her eyes. As the color from Paige's face drained, I turned to see Dad's blood-red robe trailing behind him as he approached me. Every eye followed his calculated steps. My heart rate spiked as I tried to swallow. Dad clasped my shoulders, and I didn't know if he would hug or stab me. I pulled back, prepared for his fist, but was surprised when his jowls shook with a hearty laugh.

"Well done, son!" Dad said, patting my back. "You passed the test!"

I looked around, waiting for the punchline of the joke. "What are you talking about?"

Dad faced the camera, always performing with perfect aplomb. "Great has shown me everything. You have earned His favor, son."

Paige shot me a concerned look. Terrified, I shrugged.

Dad didn't waste a moment of the undivided attention suddenly bestowed on him. "Great told me about the corruption that has infected the once holy Quorum of Scribes." He eyed Scribe Lloyd, shaking his head with a disappointed *tsk-tsk*. "Needless to say, it crushed me. I couldn't fathom it. As a simple man, I always believed the best in my brethren, so I did not suspect any foul play."

Paige scoffed. Her eyes met mine, and I could see her concern increasing. She muttered under her breath. "A, you're not buying this, right?"

I didn't know.

Dad raised his arm with a flourish. "Great told me about the mob that would take their justified revenge."

The crowd cheered.

"And most importantly, Great told me he had prepared a way to rectify the situation." Dad turned to face me. "To my utter amazement and joy, Great used my son to bring the truth to light." He reached for my hand, lifting my arm with his. "Behold your future High Scribe."

My eyes nearly bulged out of their sockets. "What—are you serious?"

"Of course," Dad said. "You've always looked to Great for answers and proven your heart is pure."

My mouth went dry as my pulse accelerated. Surely, my dad was lying, right? It was so obvious, and yet...

What if it was true?

"But, I... I'm just..." My mind couldn't keep up with the churning storm inside. Light-headed and shaky, I glanced back at Paige.

"Stick to the plan," she whispered.

Dad directed my attention to the camera. "Great demands a change in the Scribedom. The riches of the world easily persuade the hearts of men. Great has commanded me to dissolve the Quorum to keep corruption away. From now on, only one will speak for Great: The High Scribe. When my service ends, I will happily turn the mantle over to my son, Asaph."

After letting his words linger with importance, he turned to me. "Well? What do you say?"

I pushed down the fear that had gathered in my throat. The memory of my prayer during the banquet resurfaced. Hadn't I felt Great's presence? Didn't He tell my heart He was using me to bring honor back into the Scribedom? But that thought was quickly challenged by Lucy's story. Supposedly, Great was dead. If that were true, He couldn't speak to my father any more than He could me.

Someone was lying, but I didn't know who.

My eyes bounced from Dad to Paige to the mob, who now stood with bated breath. The silence was deafening, but it didn't last long. A voice from the crowd punctured the air.

"Don't believe him, son!" someone cried.

"He speaks the truth!" another said.

"Great would never let his High Scribe deceive us!"

"It's all lies!"

Suddenly the people were in a flurry of debate—split between those who believed Dad's story and those still fuming in their righteous indignation. Even if I could think through the constant shouting, my own mind was split on the matter.

With a squeeze of my shoulders, Dad smiled. "It all comes down to you, son. You have the power to make things right. Great wants you by my side. Will you accept the call? Or will you let the devil destroy your soul?"

I closed my eyes, trying to silence the voices in my head. A lifetime of belief collided with the information I had learned in the last few days. The debate between Dad's and Lucy's stories raged on. There was no way to stop the countless questions from firing inside my brain. I desperately tried to sift through it all, trying to find the one thing I desired: Certainty.

Did Great speak to Dad? Was this a test? Or was Great dead and all of this another Scribe lie? There was no way to know for sure. All I could do was dig deep and choose for myself.

"Well? What is it?" Dad hovered over me.

Wiping my sweaty hands along my pants, I felt Paige's pamphlet sticking out from my back pocket. That's when it hit me.

All I ever wanted was to know Great's will—to have the answers. Yet the Scribes, who claimed to know it all, proved certainty was a breeding ground for ignorance.

Instead of answers, I had a multitude of questions. But as Paige taught me, maybe that's all I needed. The lack of answers was its own kind of explanation.

Lengthening my spine, I met my dad's gaze. "What does Great sound like?"

Dad balked. "What? What does that have to do with anything?"

"Describe His voice," I said, leaning in.

Shaking his head, Dad stumbled for an answer. "It's, uh… low and mighty."

"What does He look like?"

"Asaph, please—"

"He spoke to you, right? Does He have brown hair or blond?"

Dad cleared his throat. "Brown."

"And why now, Dad?" I took a step closer.

Dad stepped back. "What do you mean?"

"Why now? Why did Great finally decide to talk *now*? Why didn't He answer the other countless prayers over the past two thousand years? Why did He ignore the millions of people struggling to meet their basic needs, pleading for relief?"

"Son, I think you're missing—"

"Why did Great forbid us from going on the shores of that mighty ocean? Why don't women get a say in who they marry? Why is it okay to kill non-believers for sins far less heinous than murder? And why did Great allow the Scribes to get away with so many horrific acts before stepping in?"

I could feel my energy increasing with every pointed question. For the first time, I no longer felt overshadowed by Dad's stature.

"Asaph, stop! You know it's not for us to question Great's will!" Dad tried to regain the upper hand, pushing his weight forward. His jowls sunk as he shot an intimidating scowl.

"You're right," I said. "We can't understand Great's will. So maybe you can tell me about *your* will." My hand pointed to Paige. "Why did you send Paige away? Why did you exile her mother? And why the hell did you hide it from me?"

Dad stood knee-deep in the accusation.

The last shred of my allegiance slipped through the cracks of my clenched fist. At that moment, I didn't care if Great was alive or not. By His fruits, I knew who He was. Maybe Great was waiting to snap His fingers and destroy me. It didn't matter. All I knew, with absolute certainty, was that I would rather die standing up for my values than live an eternity betraying them.

Dead or alive—Great was not worthy of my devotion, and neither were His Scribes.

"Well?" I said.

Dad scanned the faces of the people waiting for a response. James caught my attention. His eyes were desperate for an answer. Nobody knew what to do, and the silence grew heavy with anticipation as everyone tried to plan their next move.

"What do you want me to do, son?" Dad finally asked. The thunder from his voice had diminished into a dull whimper. "Are you asking me to defy Great?"

The group's collective stare reminded me the world was

listening. With a deep breath, I took a step forward and made my case.

"For too long, we have lived in fear." I swallowed hard and lifted my chest. "For too long, we've let a shitty god excuse our shitty actions."

With a wave of my arm, I motioned to the people. "My whole life, I justified the circumstances of those I thought were beneath me—wrongly assuming they deserved the punishments handed down by those in power. No more! You deserve better!" A lump in my throat caught my voice. "*We* must do better."

"Do you believe in Great?" Someone yelled from the crowd.

My eyes landed on James, recognizing his voice immediately. The desperation in his eyes had grown stark. His conflicted face was familiar, and I imagined him struggling with the same demons that had haunted me for too long.

"Tell me," he said as he repeated the question. "Do you still believe in Great?"

"Does it matter?" I asked.

"It does to me." James choked back the emotion rising in his throat.

I contemplated my words. Whatever budding beliefs I felt growing within were still too new to understand fully. I had to be careful not to trample them with unearned confidence.

"Do I believe He created this world? Sure. Do I believe He is worthy of my devotion? No," I finally admitted. "The problem is we've all created a different version of Great in our minds."

"What do you mean?" Lily-Mae asked as she walked to the front of the group.

"Whether real or not, Great has been absent for thousands of years. So we each created a version of Him that best suits our needs. How else can there be so many interpretations of His word? The people of Hadston imagine a very different god than those of New Freeda. The god of my world blessed me with prosperity and told me I was special. I spoke of His compassion but turned a blind eye to the multitudes in need." My eyes met Dad's. "Others focused on His power and punishments."

I looked back at James. "Great is a manifestation of our own hopes, dreams, and fears because it's easier to trust an imagined authority than take responsibility for ourselves. Sometimes we use Great to give us hope, other times to justify our bad behavior."

"Blasphemy!" Scribe Johnson yelled, still tending to his wound. A handful of others murmured in agreement.

"Is it?" I asked. "What power does Great have that we haven't created ourselves? Think about it. Nobody has seen Great in two thousand years. Has that stopped us from building massive temples or enacting arbitrary laws in His name? We can choose how we treat others. We have the ability to find purpose and meaning. It's up to us to decide what kind of world we want to create."

"But I saw Great!" Dad said, still defending his story. "I am his chosen leader."

"Then what's the answer?" I asked. "What is His solution for the gross imbalance of influence and wealth? Why does He insist on us wasting our lives worshiping Him? Why does He only talk to the *one* guy who benefits from all that power?"

Dad opened his mouth. No words came.

A small voice squeaked above the crowd. "Down with the Scribes! Down with the Scribes!" It didn't take long for the people to reunite with the chant. I could sense their pain bubbling back into a rage. I quickly blew the whistle again.

"No! This is not the way."

"But the Scribes must pay for their lies!" someone yelled.

"And they will. But not under mob rule. If we want a better, more equitable world, we must start now—*with them.*"

Dad leaned in, his voice barely a whisper. "What will you do with me, son?"

"That's not for me to decide. But no matter what happens to you, I'll hold on to hope."

Dad's shoulders slumped with a heaviness I had never seen. "Hope for what?"

"Hope that you can learn from your mistakes," I said, touching his shoulder. "I hope you'll work to be a better man than you are today."

It was the first time Dad had ever looked small to me. Whether he was ashamed of his actions or just sorry to see his reign end, I didn't know. But finally, I wasn't afraid of him.

"And what about you?" Dad asked. "What will you do now?"

I thought it over, taking a deep breath. "The same thing. I will learn from the pain and lean into the struggle—hoping I can be a better man, too."

Turning to the crowd, I raised my voice. "We're free to choose how we live. We can make our lives whatever we want. It won't be easy. We will make mistakes. But it will be worth it—of that, I'm certain."

A NOTE ON MY 21ST BIRTHDAY

There is no darkness where you shine a light. It's amazing how simple that idea is.

For too long, I avoided the shadows, insisting an enemy must be hiding within. But only a curious mind, willing to face the unknown, can see the world as it really is.

When I finally found the courage to explore the world—including the dark corners of my mind—I found a mirror reflecting the parts of me I craved to understand. The only demon hoping to destroy me was the fear inside myself.

- Asaph Zimran

CHAPTER 26
A NEW PATH

ONE YEAR LATER.

I pulled the bow across the violin's strings. My chest lifted and fell with the swell of the sound, savoring the hum as the last note lingered in the air. The silence that followed marked the moment with a meaningful stillness, giving the music a chance to settle into my bones.

"Wow," Lily-Mae said, her eyes and mouth wide. She pulled her instrument from under her chin. "I'll never be as good as you."

"Give it time," I said with a smile. "And lots of practice."

Standing up, I arched my back, opening the space in my ribs as I stretched my arms above my head. I put my violin back in its case and snapped it shut.

"That's it for this week's lesson. Spend some time practicing those double notes in your recital piece. You're just about there!"

Lily-Mae nodded as she gathered her things. "Will do, Mr. Asaph." She followed me to the entry of my small home, tossing her bag over her shoulder.

As I opened the door, my heart jumped to find James standing on the porch.

"James!"

"Hey," James said carefully. "I hope it's okay that I'm here."

"Of course! Come in, come in." I ushered him into the house and turned to Lily-Mae. "Great job this week. I'll see you next Monday, right?"

"Yes, thanks again!" Lily-Mae snuck past James and marched toward her home.

"Cute kid," James said. "I heard you were teaching music. You doing that full-time?"

"No, just on Mondays. I enjoy working with the students, but I'm at the shore most days, working on the expansion project."

James's expression fell flat. "Right," he said, stuffing his hands in his jacket pocket. "I forgot the forbidden beach is open for business. Still feels weird."

"It's open, but not necessarily for business," I said with a chuckle, trying to keep the mood light. "We've got teams of scientists working on cataloging the fauna and wildlife. Some parts are open for visitors and fishermen, and with that comes new restaurants and services, but we're working hard to preserve the area's natural beauty."

James nodded, his eyes drifting downward.

I rocked back on my heels, searching for something to say. It had been months since we had last talked, and a lot had changed. After the events at the altar, not everyone was happy with how things unfolded, James included.

The Scribedom was dissolved, and we organized the first democratic vote to establish new leadership over the former Scribe territories. The Sanctum, Scribe mansion, and other large Scribe estates were slowly being renovated and transformed into universities, libraries, and public housing. Large-scale efforts to revitalize the more rundown cities and neighborhoods outside New Freeda were ongoing.

Most people were thrilled with the progress, but there was some pushback. High officials in the Scribedom feared losing the many privileges they had enjoyed under Scribe rule. More surprising was the resistance from a small but vocal minority of average citizens. Even with all the injustices of the Scribedom publicized, some people refused to believe the corruption was real. They saw the changes as the devil's work, afraid the End of Days was still near.

People like my father used that fear to their advantage. While many Scribes were sentenced to prison after standing trial for their crimes, Dad managed to escape punishment. He had masterfully used his colleagues, staining their hands with the blood of his intentions while ensuring his remained clean. There wasn't enough evidence of substantial infractions, so Dad was released.

Still, my father suffered the consequences of his actions in other ways. Mom left him and led the charge to make divorce legal in New Freeda. Dad moved to the outskirts of Eastview, still committed to his story that he alone spoke for Great. Despite being stripped of any governing power, Dad had a small but loyal band of followers who clung to his every word. He lived off the monetary offerings of those who refused to abandon the old ways.

And then there was James.

James had been disgusted to learn about the filthy underworking of the Scribedom. He led the charges against Scribes Lloyd and Dalton and was relieved when the Scribe Guards disbanded.

But through it all, James clung to Great. He longed for the surety of following His commands and hated anything that challenged them. Even after sharing my experiences, James wasn't convinced Lucy was the ally she claimed to be. He refused to believe Great was dead or unworthy of devotion. Even after admitting the Scribedom had become corrupt, James still considered the Ancient Scrolls sacred.

We tried putting our differences aside and worked toward the common good, but I could tell James wasn't happy with the changes he saw in me. My relationship with Paige, my mother's growing independence, and opening the beach—they all attacked his beliefs, making it difficult for us to come together. James wanted a black-and-white world, and I was now a million shades of gray.

"So, what brings you to town?" I asked, offering him a seat in the living room. The last I had heard, James had moved to Middleton, joining a congregation of Reformed Believers who shared his views.

"You." James sighed as he took a seat. He seemed to be summoning all his courage. "I wanted to apologize."

"Apologize? For what?"

"For shutting you down."

I shook my head. "I don't understand."

James pulled a pamphlet out of his pocket. "Remember when you tried to show me this?" He handed the booklet to me. My fingers traced the title, *My Search for Answers.*

Paige's words had been the final piece of a long, complicated puzzle. After that chaotic day at the Altar, I made copies of her pamphlet, sharing it with as many people as possible. It was a powerful tool in helping change the tides.

"Of course, I remember this," I said with a smile. "The book with a hundred unanswered questions that somehow answered mine."

With a slight nod, James smiled. "Yeah, well, I finally read it."

My eyes lit up. "Really?"

"Yeah. At first, I just scanned it. I was only interested in reading the parts about the Scribes. You know how I feel about them."

I laughed. "Not your favorite group of people, if I recall."

James chuckled. "To put it lightly. But I finally forced myself to read the parts about Great, too. Something you said to me just wouldn't leave my mind."

"What's that?"

"If something is true, it can't be destroyed by investigating it," James said. "If it's not true, it should be destroyed."

"So?" I asked, eager to hear more. "What do you think?"

"I think I'm ready to live according to my values instead of some ancient scripture. I'm ready to be the creator of my life." James looked down, his knee bouncing with nerves. "And I'm hoping we can be friends again."

I jumped, pulling James to his feet. "I don't know what you're talking about. We never stopped being friends."

James laughed and hugged me. We chatted for over an hour, updating each other on work, relationships, and everything in between. When he got up to leave, I felt lighter. My friend was back in my life. It was a sweet reunion I didn't expect.

"I didn't mean to talk your ear off," James said as he got up to leave. "But it was good to see you, man. Here's to more fun in our future."

We said our goodbyes, and I waved from the front porch as he left. Moments later, Paige drove into the driveway. My heart fluttered, and I bounded down the stairs to meet her. I swung the car door open even before the engine had turned off.

"How did it go?" I asked.

Paige looked over her shoulder. "Was that James leaving? What did he want?"

"I'll tell you all about it later. Good things are happening," I said, my energy increasing every moment. I pulled her from the car. "But first, I want to hear about your day. Tell me. How did it go?"

A huge smile spread across Paige's face. "The city council finalized the arrangements. The vote was unanimous."

It was the news we had been waiting for, and now that it had finally come, I couldn't contain my excitement. I gave Paige an enormous hug, spinning her around. "Amazing news! I knew you'd make it happen, Madam President."

Paige settled into the embrace. The smell of her shampoo hit my nose, and I squeezed her tighter. She pulled back, meeting my gaze, her smile still as wide as her face. "It's taken a lot longer than we hoped, but Taprin is finally ready to open their borders now that we can offer them the resources to expand their town."

After establishing democracy in New Freeda and the surrounding cities, a wave of women eagerly took their chance to lead the people. Mom was excited to join the city council, finally getting her chance to put her ideas to work. But it was Paige who earned the highest office, overseeing the collaborative efforts of all city governments. Her clarity of vision and unyielding compassion were finally put to good use.

I took Paige's briefcase and led her into the house. Setting her things down, I turned the kettle on and grabbed a couple of mugs from the cupboard. "This is fantastic. Do you know what this means? Once we implement the new irrigation system and expand Taprin's borders, we can reform Hadston!"

"Hadston is already unrecognizable," Paige said, sitting at the small table in the kitchen. "The revitalization efforts have gone beyond what anyone could imagine. Poverty rates are down 60%. Employment is at record highs."

"And the faint smell of urine is gone," I said. "That's a bonus."

Paige laughed. "The city looks so much better! And now that Taprin will accept more refugees, improvements will only speed up."

I poured hot water into the mugs and dropped a tea bag in each. Handing one to Paige, I couldn't help but stand in awe of the woman before me. Empathetic, confident, and intelligent, I was overwhelmed that she had chosen to stay with me. "Paige, it's amazing. You're amazing. Congratulations on making it happen."

"Thank you," Paige said with a slight blush. She lifted the mug and nodded. "And thank you for this. The day ended with good news, but getting there was a slog. I need this little pick-me-up more than ever."

I sat down with my cup in hand, gently blowing on the steam. My knee bounced with anticipation. I opened my mouth to speak but stopped, glancing out the window.

"What's on your mind?" Paige asked.

With a heavy exhale, I shook my head. "Oh, nothing."

We both knew it was a lie. Paige could always read my emotions, even when we were teenagers. She tilted her head, waiting for me to get to the point.

I exhaled slowly, putting the mug down as I leaned in closer. "I was just wondering if the committee had made any other decisions."

"Mmmm...." Paige said, nodding slowly. "About visiting Evie?"

Leaning back, I folded my arms. I felt terrible bringing the matter up again, but I couldn't help it. There were so many unanswered questions—so much regret.

"I'm sorry to keep pulling on that thread," I said. "I just hate wondering if she's okay. After everything she endured, I still don't know if she actually made it through the portal safely."

Evie had left as quickly as she came. She went from the ultimate threat to a trusted confidant to gone in hours. I was relieved she escaped unharmed, and I tried telling myself I had fulfilled my promise. Evie made it home safely. All was well. But without any real closure, I couldn't help but wonder if she got the happy ending she deserved.

Paige reached over and rested her hand on mine. "You had your hands full with a mob, remember? Evie would have died if you hadn't released her. You shouldn't feel bad."

"I know. It's just—" I sighed. "I want to see her. And not just to check in but to thank her. I barely knew the woman, but she pulled me out when I was drowning. Her steadiness helped save me."

Paige squeezed my hand, her eyes filled with kindness. "It was your decision to keep the portal off-limits, remember? With the world in such a delicate transition, you said it was too risky for Evie's people to leave it open."

I took a slow sip of tea. The liquid warmed me as it ran down my throat. "You're right, and I still stand by that decision." I took another sip, and a smile crept along my face. "But sometimes I miss my Scribe privileges."

Paige rolled her eyes and smiled. "You had your chance," she said, sipping from her mug. "The people were begging you to be High Scribe, and you refused."

"The world didn't need another Zimran telling them what to do—or any Scribe, for that matter. I stand by my decision to close the portal and am even more confident in my resolve to dismantle the Scribedom."

Paige took another sip. "A, you're the best man I know, and while I respect your decision to let others lead, I still can't imagine anyone more worthy of the job."

"I can, and I'm looking at her." I locked onto Paige's steel blue eyes. "Your brilliance, clarity, and courage make you indispensable. The people are lucky to have you, and so am I."

"Well, I don't think the people realize just how much you continue to guide the path," Paige said with a small laugh as she tapped the side of her mug. "Every day, the council asks for your advice. I sometimes wonder if I should just take you to work with me."

"Nah. I enjoy dividing my time between music lessons and the expansion project."

Paige smiled. "Well, it's paid off. Opening the shores has

boosted the economy in ways we couldn't imagine. More jobs, food, land—your work has increased it all."

I winked. "Not sure I'd spend so many weekends away tending to it all without my partner in crime."

Standing up, Paige leaned over and kissed my cheek. "It's crazy when you think about it. Practically everything you do now really was a crime before." With one last sip of her tea, she walked to the sink to rinse her cup. "Oh, I almost forgot."

"What's that?" I asked, watching a bird land in a tree outside the window.

"The committee *did* make a decision." Paige spun around as a mischievous grin crept across her face. "You're free to go as long as you take an Official Member with you."

My heart pounded against my chest as I jumped to my feet. "What? Really?" I ran, swooping Paige up in my arms.

Paige laughed. "Really. And if it's okay with you, I was hoping to be the one to accompany you."

I squeezed her tight, wanting nothing more than to hold on to her forever. "Obviously. Yes, yes! When can we go?"

"I've got nothing going on Friday. What do you say?"

Putting Paige down, I leaned in for a kiss. I took her hands and laughed. It was crazy how much could change in a year. My life was simpler and less extravagant, but I was happier in ways I couldn't quite explain. The old fears that used to dictate my every decision had long subsided as Paige and I built a life together based on our mutual values. I was no longer tortured by the anxiety of slipping off the path or inadvertently offending a god waiting to punish me.

I still strived to do my best to be a worthy partner, friend, and teacher. But I no longer was a slave to the certainty I once craved. Questions, curiosity, and even failure were familiar friends. Sometimes, straying from the path was the only way to forge a better one.

"I wonder what my younger self would think of me now," I

said as we walked toward the living room. "A year ago, I was terrified of anything outside my little world. And now I'm itching to go through the Doorway of Death and say *thank you* to a woman I was told would drag me to hell. Life really is crazy."

Paige giggled. "Crazy and wonderful."

CHAPTER 27
LUCY'S FINAL LESSON

WITH A HEAVY SIGH, I logged out of *The Garden* and closed my laptop. With Paige and Asaph leading the way, things were heading in the right direction. An age of enlightenment and equality was rolling in, and now that Taprin was finally opening its borders, things would only get better.

It was a thought that made me incredibly proud but also a little sad. After finishing my first year at Stanford, where a deluge of new problems, people, and ideas had submerged me—I was eager to jump back into *The Garden* and reconnect with the people I loved so dearly.

But college had forced me to think more critically. No matter how much I loved seeing the inner workings of a civilization finding its way—I couldn't help but feel the invasion of privacy was problematic.

If I genuinely believe the people inside *The Garden* were real, shouldn't they have the same rights as me? Did I have the right to view their lives without their consent?

My instincts told me it was time to disconnect, but the thought of walking away gutted me. I was like a parent struggling to let their grown children leave home. For so long, I felt responsible for the Simples' safety. Now that the people had proven they could keep their world turning without me, it seemed only fair to cut the cord. But unlike my parents, who dropped me off in California with tears in their eyes, I never got my chance to say goodbye.

Light from the Gibson's house across the street flickered through my bedroom window, reminding me of another goodbye I never got to say.

What would I tell Ian if he were alive? I wanted to believe he could change—that I could have redeemed him somehow. Ian had caused so much pain, but I knew it was only a reflection of his own suffering. Maybe he would have made things right if given a chance.

But sometimes, there are no second chances.

It was a fact that haunted me since the day I learned about Ian's death. The thought also made me want to take every opportunity to do the right thing. The urge to act led me to create Bianca and meet Asaph. It kept me committed to making Ian's world better.

Now that my part was done, could I really just leave them alone?

Deep in thought, my eyes landed on my notebook from senior year. I pulled the spiral-bound pad from the bookshelf and scanned the notes I had meticulously kept while working on *The Garden*.

I turned to the last page, reading the final entry dated a week after Nationals:

The Garden forced me into the shadows—away from the people and rules that used to define me. And now, I know the truth. You must go inward to find yourself. There is no other way. You have to face your darkness before you can bring the light.

In the end, there is only me.

My hard-earned epiphany suddenly mocked me.

There *was* only me, and I hated it.

I hated that I always kept Asaph and Evie at arm's length. I believed it was safer to have a computer screen between us. They needed to take care of themselves, I told myself. I was convinced the distance was necessary to ensure I didn't interfere too much.

But you know who else kept his distance? Ian.

Ian never walked among his people or listened to their hopes and fears. He didn't consider their feelings or point of view. The unnatural separation between creator and creation made it easy to see the Simples as nothing more than lines of code, easily manipulated at will. Ian missed the spark that made his people real and, in doing so, lost his own humanity.

A steely determination anchored my heart as one single desire rose to the surface: I wanted to see Evie again. And Asaph. And Paige. I wanted to believe I didn't need a world-saving mission to justify my presence in their lives. Because, unlike Ian, my end hadn't yet come, and I was determined to say goodbye while I still had the chance.

Sitting tall, I opened my laptop and logged back into *The Garden*. Checking the local time inside Asaph's world, I quickly calculated and used the time dial to speed things up to Friday— the day Asaph and Paige planned to visit Evie. Reaching for my headset, I typed a few commands and slid on the goggles.

As I entered the program, the black arch came into view, and my heart raced with anticipation. The simple glitch had become a pivotal part of the world's history. I always wondered why Ian had never fixed it. He could have easily patched the code when Evie first discovered the invisible crack. But he didn't seal it up even after she took a third of the Simples through the doorway.

Instead, Ian marked the error with a foreboding structure making me wonder if there was a reason behind it all.

Whether it was laziness or a hidden agenda that kept Ian from mending his mistake, I was grateful for the glitch. The invisible doorway had served the people in so many ways, and today I would finally walk through it.

A gentle breeze whistled through the trees as I approached the arch. Otherwise, the world was quiet. The Place of Origin was still off-limits to the general public while the new government decided what to do with the abandoned city. Knowing Asaph and Paige would arrive shortly, I basked in the solitude while I waited.

Evie's hometown had transformed so much over the centuries, but the memory of its beginning was fresh in my mind. The overgrown field with scattered ruins had been a lively village with curious people figuring themselves out. The endless possibility of those first days had energized me, and I tried recapturing that feeling as I walked the grounds.

I stood under the arch, admiring its craftsmanship. The polished rock looked like black glass with intricate details carved into it. My fingers traced the inside of the dome, feeling the cold obsidian underneath. I followed the curve until I saw a small inscription at the bottom.

"Lucy?" a voice said, interrupting my thoughts.

I looked up to see Asaph and Paige walking toward me.

Asaph's eyes and smile widened as he dropped his bag and ran. He picked me up, wrapping me tightly in his arms. "Lucy! What are you doing here?"

I laughed as he put me down. "Hey, Ace! Good to see you."

Paige ran to meet us, gently pushing Asaph aside as she gave me a less intense but still warm embrace. "I didn't think we'd see you again!"

"Seriously, what are you doing here?" Asaph asked. "It's been so long! So much has changed."

"I know," I said, hinting at the sky above. "You guys have done amazing work."

Asaph smiled. "So?"

"I wanted to see you one last time." My throat tightened at the words.

"Last time?" Paige's pupils bounced between Asaph and me. "Are you dying?"

"No!" I said, eager to ease their nerves. "No, I'm fine. It's just that you guys don't need me anymore. But I never got to say *goodbye*."

"What are you talking about?" Asaph said. "Who says we don't need you?"

I scoffed. "I do! You guys have things under control. I've intervened enough. My job is done."

Paige cocked her head, smiling. "You don't have to perform a task to deserve our attention, you know. Friends don't need a reason to visit."

She said it like it was the most obvious thing in the world, making me realize just how much I subconsciously believed I had to earn my relationships. A surge of joy filled my body, and I pulled both of them in for a hug. The three of us stood quiet, silently acknowledging the moment.

"Thank you," I whispered. Pulling back, I remembered the inscription I had been inspecting just before they arrived. "Hey, have you guys seen this before?" I pointed toward the bottom of the arch.

Asaph leaned in, examining the line of characters. "I've seen pictures of it. Nobody knows what it means. If it's a message, it's not in any language I know."

"And he knows a lot," Paige said, nudging Asaph.

I turned, trying to see the letters from a different angle. The characters were English, but the words were gibberish:

HBSSFU GMPZE OFWFS TPPE B DIBODF.

Still, something about the pattern was annoyingly familiar, but I couldn't quite place it. "Who constructed the arch?" I asked. "Did the Scribes build it?"

"No," Asaph said. "Great did—or, Ian, I guess. At least, that's what the records suggest."

I nodded, my eyes still stuck on the symbols when the answer finally hit me. "Holy crap! I know what it is!" I jumped to my feet, barely able to contain my energy. "This is the coded language we made in fourth grade!"

Asaph leaned in for a closer look. "What do you mean?"

"What does it say?" Paige asked.

The memory crystallized just thinking about it. "Ian and I had spent all afternoon trying to make a secret language for the two of us," I said with a chuckle. "We wanted a way to share secrets in class. B is A, C is B. You just move down the alphabet one time for each letter. We were only nine, so it's not the most sophisticated cipher, but it did the job."

Crouching low, I used my finger in the dirt to work out the translation. Once I deciphered it, I stood, scratching my head. "It says: *Garret Floyd never stood a chance.*"

The world around me shifted as soon as the words left my lips. My pulse quickened as my body steadied itself. I reached for Paige, ensuring she didn't fall, but as my hand grabbed her wrist, I found her suspended like a statue.

It wasn't just Paige who stood petrified. Everything froze—everything except me.

I had experienced this phenomenon before. The eerie stale air of a world on hold was a familiar feature of Ian's time dial. There were no chirping birds, no gentle breeze, and no scent of the nearby evergreens. Life around me had literally paused. I just didn't know why.

"I knew you'd come back, Luce."

The voice stopped my heart. I turned around, my body shaking in disbelief.

"Ian?" I could barely speak the words.

It was him. Tall and lanky, Ian pushed back his shaggy blonde curls as his long frame shifted from one foot to the other the way he did when he was nervous.

"I'm glad you remembered our secret code," Ian said, his lips curling upward. "The fact that you found your way back into my program and discovered this final clue proves you're smarter than you think."

"How is this—you're not—this can't be—" I couldn't think straight as I tripped over my words. I sidestepped a frozen Asaph to get a better look. Ian's pale blue eyes stayed focused straight ahead as if seeing past me.

"In case you're worried, no, I'm not really here," Ian said. "I know, I know—you're heartbroken it's just a recording, but you have to admit, it's a pretty cool way to get a message to someone, right?"

It was exquisite and awful all at once. Ian's all-too-familiar sarcasm made the irony of his words that much more painful. I *was* heartbroken. It was only a recording, a shadow of his former self. More than anything, I wanted Ian to be standing in front of me. But at the same time, this unearthed message felt like a miraculous gift I didn't want to end.

Ian laughed. "I'm just glad you said the code phrase out loud; otherwise, this whole idea would flop."

I giggled, pushing back tears. *Garrett Floyd didn't stand a chance.*

Garret was the bully who threatened Ian the first day I met him. Standing up to Garret ignited our friendship, tethering Ian to me for many years. It seemed only fitting his name should reconnect us one last time.

Ian sighed, his face softening. "Listen, Luce. I'm going to make this short. If you're watching this, it can only mean one thing: You've found your way back into *The Garden.*

"I don't know how you gained access, but I never stopped

believing you would. You're too entangled with the Simples to leave them alone and too smart not to hack your way back in. So, I'm guessing you're here to save them—from me."

Ian rocked back on his heels, taking a moment to organize his thoughts. When he looked up, his eyes locked onto mine. "I know you, Luce. You don't let bullies win."

A tear streamed down my cheek as I shook my head. I couldn't believe what I was hearing. Despite his many faults, Ian had always been perceptive. The fact that he embedded this message, knowing I would someday find it was incredible.

Ian continued. "So if you made it to the portal, it means I've probably taken things too far, and I'm sorry. I've always viewed the Simples as a scientific experiment. I wanted to know what it takes to gain someone's unyielding devotion. How do you get someone to love you?" Ian paused, shaking his head. "But we both know it's not really love."

He sighed. "I don't want to hear how I went down the wrong path or made mistakes. I've heard it all before. I know I let you down. We didn't see eye to eye on many things, but for better or worse, you're the nagging voice in my head telling me I can be better. I'm just not great at listening. You know that."

I chuckled, wiping away another tear.

"So, I'm going to bow out," Ian said. "The moment this recording ends my avatar will be permanently deleted. You've proven you've got the smarts and heart to take charge. This world is yours, Luce. I know you'll do the right thing."

I choked back my emotions, knowing Ian's message had come too late. He was forced from the world before being given a chance to leave on his own accord. But the fact that he had inserted this failsafe convinced me Ian had died with at least a spark of humanity still inside. And that flame was enough to keep me going.

"No matter what was said or done, this world was always

meant for you." Ian's voice caught in his throat. "Because there are pieces of you in everything I do."

I inched closer to the avatar before me. My eyes locked onto my friend, wishing the real Ian was somehow listening. I wrapped my arms around his body. Tears ran down my cheek as I whispered in his ears, "There are pieces of *you* in everything *I* do, too."

His arms wrapped around me, most likely due to his sophisticated programming skills. But I imagined it was really Ian holding me tight, giving me one last moment with my oldest friend. A second later, my arms collided with my body as the avatar disappeared.

And just like that, Ian was gone. Like before, there was no official goodbye, no warning. But there was a willingness to let go.

Now, maybe I could, too.

A moment later, my senses were inundated by a world coming back to life. The rush of wind carried the chirps of birds and floral scents. Paige and Asaph reanimated, still crouching down by the archway.

"Who is Garrett Floyd?" Asaph asked. His eyes widened as he saw the empty space where I had been standing before the world paused. Jumping to his feet, he scanned the horizon, finding me several yards away. "How did you get over there?"

I smiled, considering what to tell them. "Don't worry about it," I said.

Maybe I'd explain everything one day, but for now, I wanted to savor Ian's final message, keeping it just for myself.

Asaph eyed Paige. She shrugged her shoulders. "Everything okay?"

"It will be," I said, walking back toward them. "I want to see Evie." My voice was quiet but firm.

"Sure," Asaph said. "That's where I'm headed. Wait. Have

you not seen Evie this whole time? Weren't you guys close? Can't you just pop yourself into her world?"

I bit my lip, thinking about all the time that had passed. "I promised I would stay away."

"Why?" Paige asked.

Taking a deep breath, I exhaled loudly. "Because I was afraid I'd turn into Ian. I didn't want to impose on their world or influence them."

Asaph and Paige exchanged glances.

"I think it's clear you work from very different values," Asaph said.

"And who's to say your influence wouldn't be good?" Paige added.

I smiled. "Do you think Evie will be mad if I break my promise?"

Asaph grabbed my hand, giving it a hardy squeeze before letting go. "Not even a little. I'm sure she'll be as excited to see you as we are." He smiled at Paige before meeting my eyes again. "Besides, it's your world. You can do whatever you want."

My mind replayed Ian's message. *This world is yours, Luce.*

I shook my head. "No, it's not my world. It belongs to all of you."

My reunion with Evie and her boys was beautiful. I soaked in her radiant energy as she reintroduced me to her community. She was relieved to see Asaph in good health and loved hearing about the changes that had occurred since that chaotic day at the altar. But despite her upbeat spirits, I could tell their people were struggling to survive.

Thankfully, it didn't take much to persuade them to join Asaph in the modern world, especially now that the threat of Ian —and his Scribes—was gone. After some negotiations, the governing councils granted Evie's people land rights for The Place of Origin. Within a few months, Fredenia was reestablished and on its way to becoming fully settled.

Evie continued to grow as a leader, standing next to Paige as they worked to build a better world. Asaph led in a different, more subtle way. Energized by a newfound curiosity, he took any opportunity to meet and talk with people from all over. Every person offered a new way to see the world, and Asaph couldn't get enough.

Meanwhile, I restricted my access to *The Garden*, making watching the people from above impossible. They deserved their privacy as much as their freedom, and I was happy to give up my god-like powers.

Still, I didn't stay away entirely. I logged in and visited my friends as often as possible. Up close, it was easy to work from my values. I got to know the people and see the world through their eyes. I didn't have to decide anyone's fate or fix every problem. There was no crushing anxiety telling me to prove my worth. I didn't need to be anything other than myself, and for my friends, that was enough.

It turns out I was never alone.

SCROLLS OF PROPHECY DISCUSSION QUESTIONS

The following questions can be used for book club discussions, personal reflection, or writing prompts.

1. Bianca said the best kind of revolution starts from within the system of oppression. Can you think of any examples that support this idea? Is it possible to overcome oppression from the outside? Why or why not?

2. Asaph desperately wants to follow the laws of the Scribedom. For much of the story, he only trusts his instincts when he believes those promptings are coming from Great. How do you think Asaph felt when he learned those impressions were his own ideas all along? How could a realization of that magnitude be both terrifying and comforting?

3. Bianca said history is more story-telling than record-keeping. Do you agree or disagree? Can you think of any personal or cultural examples where shaping a historical narrative had a long-lasting impact on you or the world?

4. Asaph grew up with many luxuries because of his father's role within the Scribedom. He was told his prosperity was a direct result of his faithfulness. How can this kind of mentality influence someone's life for better or worse? What are some unintended consequences of prosperity theology?

5. Bianca often told Asaph he had no idea who she was or what she was trying to do. Once you learned Bianca's secret, did it change how you viewed her? Were you more or less understanding of her actions? Why or why not?

6. Lucy's complicated relationship with Ian continued even after he kicked her out of *The Garden*. She recognized both the pain he had caused and the pain he had been carrying. Do you think she betrayed the Simples by trying to mend her friendship with Ian? Does everyone deserve a second chance?

7. Paige said, "Maybe we need to stop questioning the supposed sins of every fallen believer. Instead, it's time to question whoever is silencing their voices." Have you ever felt silenced? Do those in power silence people in today's world? How can we elevate such voices, and what would result from it?

8. When Asaph found out his world was a simulation, he had a very different reaction than when Evie learned the truth. He said, "Knowing Lucy fought to keep us alive made me think there was value to all of it." How would you respond if you discovered your world was a simulated reality?

9. Lucy said fear transformed Ian from a hopeful creator to an oppressive dictator. What fears infiltrate society today? How can we help reduce those fears to make the world safer and more equitable?

10. Asaph had to renegotiate his entire identity as his beliefs changed. Have you ever experienced a crisis of faith? What are some of the challenges of dramatically shifting your worldview? Is it worth the pain to learn the truth? Why or why not?

11. Lucy learned to let go of the expectations of others but continued to hold herself to impossible standards as she tried to fix Ian's world. What realization did she have as this story ended? How can we help our teens find the balance between doing their best and understanding their innate worth as human beings worthy of love and connection?

ACKNOWLEDGMENTS

A big thanks to my incredible family for cheering me on throughout this project. Tom, you always provide such great feedback and encourage me to keep chugging along when stuck in the messy middle. I'm grateful to my beta-readers, who help me refine the story through their insight and enthusiasm. A specific shout out to Mark, Dawn, Katie G, Katie H, and Lincoln for going the extra mile in helping me refine the story and being enthusiastic cheerleaders.

As always, thank you, my fantastic reader. Your time invested in this journey means the world to me. I hope you had as much fun as I did. If so, please take a moment to post a review and tell a friend.

ABOUT THE AUTHOR

With an MFA in Modern Dance, Robin Strong is a former university professor turned freelance editor and author. As a TEDx speaker and creativity junkie, she is excited to share this sequel to her debut novel, *Gods of the Garden*. When she's not playing with words, Robin is usually hanging with her family in Indiana, dancing in the kitchen, or walking the dog.

**Be the first to learn about Robin's new releases
and receive exclusive content when
you subscribe at robinstrongbooks.com.**

Instagram: @robinstrongbooks
Goodreads: goodreads.com/RobinStrong